DELAYED PENALTY

An Aviators Hockey Novel

SOPHIA HENRY

Krasivo Creative

Delayed Penalty
Copyright © 2015 by Sophia Henry
All rights reserved
Republished with changes 2021 by Krasivo Creative
ISBN: 978-1-949786-46-0

This book is a work of fiction. Names, places, characters, and incidents either are products of the author's imagination or are used fictitiously. Any resemblance to actual events, locales, or persons, living or dead, is entirely coincidental. Any trademarks, service marks, product names, or named features are assumed to be the property of their respective owners, and are used only for reference.
No part of this book may be reproduced in any form or by electronic or mechanical means including information storage and retrieval systems, without the express written permission of the author. The only exception is by a reviewer who may quote short excerpts in a review.

Cover design: Amanda Shepard, Shepard Originals
Editing by: Angel Nyx

*To all the Motherless Daughters out there,
especially Chuck, the one I love the most.*

CONNECT* with *Sophia:
www.sophiahenry.com

*PATREON
INSTAGRAM
AMAZON
BOOKBUB*

Chapter One

AUDEN

When you're twenty years old, there's nothing music and a drink can't cure.

At least that was my best friend's response when I told her I'd been cut from Central State's women's soccer team this morning.

The overzealous stylings of two drunk chicks bellowing "It's Raining Men" wafts through the air, and I've just received my vodka soda from the bartender.

So why does it still feel like someone scratched my heart out with a serrated shovel?

Maybe "It's Raining Men" isn't the right song?

Or maybe my friend's remedy lacked one vital ingredient.

Like five minutes locked in a bathroom stall with the crazy-haired hottie approaching me.

His head is buzzed short on the sides, leaving a thick patch of dark locks, gelled into a neat pompadour in front. Sort of like a 1920s gangster, except less slicked, more height.

Every muscle in Crazy Hair's body ripples under his clothing as he walks. He has to be over six feet tall, with a broad chest and massive arms stretching the seams of his long-sleeved black Henley. His smooth, pale skin is a contrast to the thick dark eyebrows resting above his jump-in-and-drown-in-me blue eyes.

From the scar on his left cheek to the smug smirk of his lips, he looks exactly my type: dangerous, confident, and totally lickable.

I flip my long blond hair behind my shoulder and glance to my left, pretending Crazy Hair's advance has no effect on me.

In reality, I'm checking to make sure he isn't about to pass me up on the way to some beautiful bombshell I hadn't noticed standing in the vicinity.

Like when you see someone wave, so you wave back. Then you realize they weren't waving at you but the person behind you. Then you try to play off your lame wave like you were batting away mosquitoes—which aren't there because it's December in Canada.

Just trying to avoid an awkward situation like that.

Crazy Hair continues to close in, before stopping just inches away.

I open my mouth to ream him out for stepping too far into my personal space, but the sweet scent of clove cigarettes floods warmth through me like a sip of steaming hot chocolate on a January morning in the Upper Peninsula.

"You work at post office?" he asks in a thick Slavic accent.

"Um, no." I take a swig of my drink. Though I'm unsure where he's going with that line, he's hot enough for me to stick around.

The left corner of his mouth curves into that sexy little smirk. "Because I see you check out my package."

Carbonation stings my nose as I snort and choke trying to hold in my laugh. Without time to turn my head, I spray vodka, soda, and saliva across the front of Crazy Hair's shirt.

Awesome.

"Weak!" I hear from somewhere behind me.

I turn to see who yelled, still coughing as I notice a group of guys and girls at the high-top table behind me. Shaggy blond hair bounces against one guy's forehead as he snickers. The dude next to him holds his fist in front of his mouth in a horrible attempt to hide his laughter. A brunette in a tight red sweater doesn't look amused. At all.

Crazy Hair throws the guys not one—but both—middle fingers.

"That girl's a fucking smoke show. Why'd he use a shitty line like that?" the blond one asks.

Smoke show? I bite down hard on my lip to fight back a smile. The last time I'd heard that phrase was in high school from my hockey-playing best friend, who'd informed me that "smoke show" was player lingo for "hot girl."

Unsure of how to recover any semblance of cool after spitting my drink across Crazy Hair's muscular chest, I spin around and shuffle back to the table my friends occupied in front of the karaoke stage.

It feels weird to drink in public, though we've been to Canada on multiple occasions. As lifelong residents of Detroit, Michigan, we think of Windsor—the Canadian city connected to Detroit by a bridge and a tunnel—as the next town over, rather than a foreign country. Nineteen is the legal drinking age in Windsor, so it makes sense that underage Americans like us cross the border for some legit cocktails.

My butt barely brushes my seat when I hear my name, and my name alone, called over the speakers. I lift my eyes to the outdated popcorn ceiling, as if the voice is resonating from the heavens beyond, rather than the karaoke host.

"Why is he calling my name?" I ask Kristen.

"I picked you a song," she responds, then tips her beer back.

"You picked *us* a song, you mean?" Emphasis on the us, because I've never sung alone in my life—not counting the shower and car, of course.

"Nope. Just you." Kristen places both hands on my back and pushes me toward the stage. "You need to sing it out. Keeping shit bottled up never works."

I wouldn't have a problem singing it out if I were singing with other people, but just me? Haven't I been embarrassed enough today?

My short-lived "smoke show" happiness vanishes, and the embarrassment of making a fool of myself in front of Crazy Hair returns. I try to reverse, but Kristen's trampoline-like hands propel me back toward the stage.

Climbing onto the stage, I snatch the microphone out of the host's hand. I almost feel bad about taking my anger out on him until I see the lyrics to "Proud Mary" light up in white against the teleprompter's blue screen.

What the hell? I exhale and lift my eyes to Kristen.

"Girl power!" She salutes me with her glass.

Is "Proud Mary" a girl-power song? I thought it was about a boat.

She's trying to lift my spirits, but belting out an anthem is the last thing on my mind when I don't feel so powerful right now. On the contrary, I feel like I could jump off the Proud Mary.

"Do you have 'Good Feeling'?" I ask the karaoke host. He's around my age, with big brown eyes that match his neat, trimmed beard and shoulder-length hair.

"Flo Rida?" he asks, as disapproving wrinkles form on his smooth forehead.

"Oh, no," I say, shaking my head. "The Violent Femmes."

A smile spreads across his lips, and he nods. "Give me a second."

While waiting for my song, I take in the scenery at Mickey O'Callaghan's Irish Pub. The space itself is cozy; small and narrow with red and beige brick walls and mahogany overkill. The dark wood is everywhere—the long bar, the wainscoting, the narrow beams on the ceiling, even the tables and chairs.

Mickey's Friday-night karaoke must be the hot-spot because bodies occupy every seat, and the bar is two people deep all the way across.

Instead of looking toward the table Crazy Hair threw double birds to earlier, I watch the karaoke host fiddle with his machine. After a minute, the screen glows with the lyrics to my request.

My cheeks burn when my voice cracks delivering the first few notes. I keep my eyes glued to the teleprompter, even though I know the words by heart. After the first few lines, I get my vocals on track, and there's some clapping, which surprises me.

Halfway through the song, I lift my eyes to see people on their feet—people other than the friends I had come with—although my friends are on their feet as well. By the time I finish the song, the crowd is hooting and whistling. Someone yells for me to sing again, but I just smile as I refasten the microphone to the stand.

"You were amazing, Aud!" Kristen squeezes me when I get back to the table.

"I didn't know you could sing like that." Lacy raises her hand for a high five.

"I didn't either," I admit, skimming my palm against hers, sure I'd zap her with the electricity tingling through my limbs. Being on stage felt like overtime in a soccer match: exhilarating and exciting.

"Hey," someone says, tapping my shoulder. I spin around to see the karaoke host.

"Greg." He thrusts his hand at me.

"Auden," I say, taking his outstretched palm. "Thanks for switching songs."

"Tina Turner didn't seem like your thing."

Greg might have a cute face hiding under his beard, but he's still not my type. Too monotone. Even the plaid flannel hanging off his lean frame is brown. His style screams Eddie-Vedder-nineties-grunge rather than today's hipster cool.

"Oh, I can rock some Tina. Just wasn't feeling 'Proud Mary' without my backup singers." I point to Kristen and Lacy.

Greg laughs. "Need a drink?"

"I already have—" I search the table for my drink, spotting it in Lacy's boyfriend's hand. "Actually, I do."

Ignoring Kristen's megawatt smile, I follow Greg to the bar. She better not have set him on me to boost my spirits. She knows he isn't my type.

Douche bags like Crazy Hair and the guys he'd flipped off got my motor running. Douche bags and I are on the same wavelength. Neither of us want more than what the other could offer.

Greg moves to the side so I can order. "Vodka soda with three limes, please."

"And a Steam Whistle." Greg points to a beer I don't recognize in the stand-up cooler behind the bar. The bartender nods and extracts a bottle.

"You've got a killer voice," Greg says.

"Well, there're no Tina Turner–type vocals in that song." I blow off his compliment.

"No, but it's hard to sing that softly and keep your key." His mouth curves into a wide, kind smile. "You from around here?"

"Detroit," I say, nodding. "But I go to Central State."

"Are you kidding?"

I shake my head and pick up the drink the bartender placed in front of me.

"So do I. That's crazy." Greg holds up a few bills, waiting until the bartender sees the money before setting it on the bar. "My roommates and I have a band. We're looking for a singer right now."

"You're in a band? That's awesome," I say, focused on mashing the limes in my drink. I raise my glass to him. "Thank you, by the way."

"No problem." He picks at the label on his beer. "Any interest?"

"In what?" I ask, looking at Greg over the top of my cup.

"Singing for our band." He doesn't even blink.

"You're joking, right?" I laugh. Asking me to sing in his band after hearing one karaoke song was hilarious. I've never taken voice lessons, and as far as I can tell, I don't have any significant talent.

"Why would I joke?" He doesn't seem to understand my laughter at all.

"I just sang in public alone for the first time and you're asking me if I want to be in a band?" Being the center of attention for five minutes in a karaoke bar is one thing; standing on stage in front of people expecting a show is a different beast.

"That explains your lack of stage presence," Greg says, running his fingers over his beard, looking more English professor than rocker.

"Quite the charmer, aren't you, G-man?" I take a drink. I know I don't have stage presence. Hell, I could barely make eye contact with anyone.

"Stage presence can be learned," he says. "You have a great voice and a hot look."

Once I realize he's not kidding, I'm speechless.

Greg continues peeling the label off his beer bottle as he waits for me to speak. "It's nothing crazy. We just play bars in Bridgeland, well, mostly at Wreckage." He chuckles.

"Yeah, I don't think so, but thanks for asking." I force a half smile.

"Come on," he pleads. "Just try out. If you like it, great."

"I don't think I could even learn to be comfortable on stage."

"I can get you over your stage fright." Greg's voice is molasses, thick and smooth; a contrast to his grunge-hipster vibe. The lights flickering above give his previously plain eyes a sexy sparkle as he waits for my answer.

Why do I have to be a sucker for sparkles? "Okay, sure." My head bobs in reluctant consent. "The worst that could happen is I fail miserably, right?"

"I don't know. You might surprise me." Greg winks. He searches the bar before grabbing a pen lying on an abandoned credit card receipt. Then he flips over a coaster advertising some brewing company's winter ale and begins scribbling. "Here's my number. Call me next week for an audition."

"This is crazy." I take the coaster from him.

"What do you have to lose?" His eyes are solid and intense as he stares at me.

Nothing. I'd long since lost it all. But he doesn't know that.

Without another word, he walks away, leaving me alone at the bar, perplexed by the interaction.

"What did Eddie Vedder's son have to say?" Kristen asks, nodding toward Greg, who's resumed his place behind the karaoke machine.

Of course, Kristen would think of a similar description for his look. It's one of the many reasons we'd been calling each other our 'other half" since the first day of freshman year when we were assigned to the same dorm room.

"He wants me to try out for his band," I say, flashing her the coaster. "Which is stupid."

"No, it isn't." She snatches my hand and squeezes. "You're really good."

I shake my head. Right now, I'm high from my time on stage and the applause and compliments I'd received, but as soon as I get home and start over-analyzing the unexpected conclusion to my soccer career again, the euphoria will abandon me. Just like my team had.

Just like everyone does.

"You're a popular lady tonight. The Mohawked hottie stared at you the entire time you talked to karaoke guy."

I follow Kristen's gaze to the table where Crazy Hair and his friends are sitting. Though the group seems to be leaving, downing their drinks and grabbing their coats, Crazy Hair stands still, his penetrating eyes on me.

I have a feeling he's the type of guy who would say anything to get me to take him home, and then slink away without a word the next morning. Though drinking has usually been involved when that had happened, I can't even blame the alcohol. I fall for guys like him because I need the attention. I need to feel like someone wants me. I need to pretend that someone might be able to love me.

The way my parents should have loved me.

It's an impossible void to fill.

Crazy Hair slides one of the muscular arms I'd admired earlier around the shoulders of the girl in the tight red sweater. She has big everything; big hair, big boobs, big smile.

Still holding my gaze, he says something against her ear, which makes her throw her head back in a laugh revealing big white teeth. Grazing his hand down her back, he allows her to go first as they follow the rest of the group toward the door.

Which reminds me of another definition of smoke show: to dominate, crush, or otherwise humiliate the opposition.

Mission accomplished.

Douche.

Chapter Two
AUDEN

"I hope you don't think you're going to sit on your butt your whole break," my grandfather says, punctuating his sentence with a quick snap of his newspaper. He'd done it to lift a falling corner, but he may as well have cracked an invisible whip.

"Come on, *Dedushka*," I say, stopping my arm midair and lifting my tired eyes from the milk dripping off my spoon to his customary stern face. "I just got home yesterday."

"And you start your job today." His steel blue eyes catch mine before returning to the paper.

"Funny. I don't remember interviewing." I smirk, then shovel the spoonful of soggy cereal into my mouth.

"Oh, how I've missed your smart mouth, Auden," he deadpans without looking up.

Though I'll only be home for a month, living with my grandparents again will be rough. After my first taste of freedom living in the dorms during freshman year, going back to Hawk-eye Land will be a challenge.

All my life I wished I'd had a sibling, but the yearning was never so prominent as when I came home from school.

It's been fourteen years since my mom died. Fourteen years of being the only person my grandparents had to worry about. While I appreciate the motive behind their undivided attention, I've always wanted someone who understood my rants about their constant hovering. Someone to talk with and share silly inside jokes.

Since my well-being is my grandparents' first priority, they're always on my case. It would've been nice to have a sibling to pick up some of the slack. I never want to sound ungrateful for what they've done for me, but sometimes I need a break.

"What kind of job is it?" I ask, keeping any smart-mouth comments to myself. Don't feel like ticking him off today.

"Translating." Grandpa folds the newspaper into a rectangle and sets it next to his 'Not only perfect, but Russian, too' coffee mug.

My grandfather, Viktor Berezin, is a retired Russian language professor at a state university outside of Detroit. He's taken on various translating jobs for friends and coworkers his whole life, and has set me up with small projects since my junior year of high school.

The work was never difficult; translating documents or contracts from Russian into English or vice versa. It's great money for a teenager, since it pays better than babysitting or a part-time retail job.

"Documents again?" I ask.

"No. It's for a person. He needs a translator to speak with the media for his job. You will help him."

"He speaks with the media for his job? Is he super-high profile?"

"In some circles, I suppose." Grandpa shrugs.

"You trust me to be someone's PR person? I have a pretty smart mouth, you know," I joke, shoveling more cereal into my mouth.

"I'm counting on it, *Audushka*."

"Is he an actor? A model?" I push my empty cereal bowl to the side. "Wait! Is he some kind of dignitary?"

"I think I'd handle the dignitary if he were one." Grandpa takes a sip of his coffee. "He's a hockey player."

"A hockey player," I repeat. "For the Red Wings?"

Excitement bubbles in my stomach. I've been a Detroit Red Wings fan since before I could speak. Being a translator for a Russian player on my favorite team in the history of the universe would complete my life.

"Not *that* high profile." Grandpa laughs. "He plays for the Aviators."

A minor-league player? The bubbles in my stomach fizzle and pop, and my tense, excited shoulders drop.

"Where am I meeting him?"

"You will meet *Zhenya* at Robinson Arena at noon."

Zhenya is the Russian term of endearment for the name Evgeny. Evgeny Orlenko is one of Grandpa's lifelong friends. Personally, I think of *Zhenya* as an uncle, since he and Grandpa are as close as brothers.

Professionally, he's a sports agent who represents a number of Russian hockey players. According to recent documents I'd translated, he's peppered his clientele list with a few basketball players as well.

"Hey, Gram," I greet my grandmother. She walks into the tiny kitchen with the electric lighted mirror she swears by.

For someone who doesn't approve of her kids or grandkids being vain, Gram is pretty concerned with her looks. She never wears foundation or mascara, but her cheeks are always powdered and her lips never without lipstick in public. Though her fair skin is wrinkled with soft lines, it doesn't take away from the beauty of her features. Her hair stays perpetually blonde—thanks to the magic of hair dye—but it works because the color compliments her blue-gray eyes and high cheekbones. She'd be beautiful even if she let her hair go gray. I can only hope I got some of those graceful-aging genes.

"What time did you get home last night?" she asks, setting the mirror on the table and flipping it to the ultra-magnifying side before stooping to plug it in.

"Around one-thirty, I guess."

"I can tell. You're puffy." She reaches over to pat my cheek before turning to inspect her own face in the mirror.

Thanks, I think, though I don't dare say it out loud. My grandparents and I have a better relationship since I'd left for college than we ever had when I was growing up. Don't want to mess up a good thing.

"Where are you off to?"

"It's my week to clean the church," Gram answers as she slicks a rose shade across her lips. Then she pats the skin under her eyes with her fingers and turns the mirror's light off.

"Do you need any help?"

"Pat and Emma will be there, but thank you for asking."

My breath of relief is almost audible. I haven't been back to church since I left for college three years ago. Just thinking about the place makes me itchy.

I slide out of my seat, tap my inseams together with a flourish, and straighten my arms at my sides.

"Are you going to tell me my client's name or is this a super-secret mission, Sir?" I ask in a military monotone.

My grandpa shakes his head, picks up the newspaper, and straightens it out. "I don't know it. I just told *Zhenya* you'd be happy to do it."

"Super-secret. Got it. I won't let you down, Sir." I salute him. Still staring straight ahead, I wait to be excused.

Grandpa lowers the paper. "Is there something else?"

"May I be excused? I have to shower and dress for the mission."

"You are a ridiculous girl, *Audushka*." He dismisses me with a shake of his head.

"Auden, you're only home for a month. Please try not to drive your grandfather crazy," my grandma says.

With a salute to both of them, I ignore her warning because driving my grandpa crazy isn't something I have to worry about. I'd accomplished that years ago.

I thought my grandfather would continue to reward my almost-native knowledge of reading, writing, and speaking Russian by giving me tedious translating projects my whole life. I never expected him to allow me to work directly with a client, let alone a client in the public eye. Maybe he has more faith in me than I realized.

*****

I arrive at Robinson Arena fifteen minutes early to prove I'm taking my first translating assignment with an actual human to heart. There's no doubt *Zhenya* will report my professionalism, or lack thereof, to Grandpa. My mission, other than translating, is to keep my grandfather's stellar reputation intact.

I spot him waiting for me at the top of the stairs, outside the main entrance to the arena.

"*Audushka!*" He leans in to kiss my cheeks, as is Russian custom, but he stops himself and offers me his leather-gloved hand instead. I shake it firmly. "We'll keep this professional, yes? It's good to see you again."

"Good to see you, too," I respond as a smile creeps across my face.

Zhenya wastes no time getting to business, greeting me with the Russian-inspired diminutive of my name and continuing the conversation in his native language. I throw my grandpa a mental fist-bump for teaching me Russian so well I could've been born and raised in Moscow.

"Your destiny awaits," he says with a wink, holding a heavy blue door open. "Tell me how you got *Vitya* to give you this assignment. I thought he'd have you translating contracts until you were a little old lady."

Since *Zhenya* is the only person who calls Grandpa by his diminutive, *Vitya*, I have to think for a minute. My grandma, being of Irish descent, doesn't use diminutives—or any nicknames. She's only ever called Grandpa by two names: Viktor or Horse's Ass.

"I have no clue. I thought the same thing, except I always throw in some cats. Little old cat lady translating Pushkin and Tolstoy until her arthritic hand falls off."

Zhenya's deep laugh echoes through the empty concourse as we enter the arena. When the heavy door slams shut, the frigid air hits my exposed skin, sending an involuntary ripple from my fingertips to my toes.

"You will be spending quite a bit of time here, so you may want to dress for warmth," he says.

I nod. Wearing a black skirt suit for a job at an ice arena hadn't been the smartest decision, but it's the only suit I own, so I didn't have another option. Maybe my grandparents would take pity on me and spot me some cash for appropriate work attire.

I follow *Zhenya* through the arena's concourse and down a few long hallways into the dank, fluorescent-lit basement.

Stan Martin, Michigan furniture store guru and owner of the Aviators, is in the process of building a brand-new arena downtown, but it won't open until next fall. Until then, the Aviators call Robinson Arena home. A state-of-the-art arena in its heyday, Robinson has become a massive eyesore over its thirty-five-year existence. And I've only ever observed it from the exterior.

The basement gives deteriorating a whole new meaning. The floors, walls, and ceilings show their age as numerous cracks and chips mar the painted concrete surfaces. The Aviators logo, a wheel with propellers, sparkles in comparison, having been painted onto the walls within the last two years. The logo guides us down the hall like we're jets lurching forward on a runway waiting for our turn to take off.

Just when I think I'd get lost in the maze of dull white walls, we turn right into a hallway covered in light wood paneling and historic team photographs hiding the grubby concrete.

Massive, teal double doors with the Aviators logo welcome us at the end of the hallway. Above the logo is a sign: Authorized Personnel Only.

Before we enter the locker room, a ripple of pride rushes through me. I feel like a true professional.

And then I watch *Zhenya* try to pull open the door. It barely budges, so he grabs the long, thin handle with both hands and tugs it with all his might. If I have to do that every day, I'll yank my arms out of their sockets.

Undeterred, I take a deep, optimistic breath before following him into the locker room, where the stench of sweaty hockey gear immediately assaults my senses.

Now I understand why my grandfather gave me this assignment. Well played, *Dedushka*. Well played.

Instead of focusing on the smell, I take in the surroundings of my new "office." Tall, open oak lockers span three walls of the compact room. The space might not be that small, but it seems that way with all the large bodies crammed into it.

Large men's bodies.

Large men's bodies in various states of undress.

Fully clothed men—and women—with cameras, microphones, and handheld recording devices fill the room, as well. The media.

Keep your eyes up. I can't be caught staring at the men with towels wrapped inches below muscular abs. Abs that must have taken more than eight minutes a day to chisel out.

Zhenya weaves his way through the swarm of people to the back wall of the locker room. He stops behind a group of reporters and taps a short cameraman on the shoulder. I can't see the player who's being swarmed by the media, but judging from the Russian nameplate attached to the locker, it's my client.

Varenkov.

"Excuse me." *Zhenya* interrupts the stream of questions being directed at the guy I still can't see. "Aleksandr is done with questions for today. Thank you."

I rise up on my toes, craning my neck to get a glimpse of my client before the crowd dissipates. No such luck, until the two men in front of me who'd been blocking my vision excuse themselves and inch past.

"Couldn't resist my package?" a voice asks in Russian.

I jerk my head up and lock eyes with Crazy Hair from the karaoke bar.

And he's half naked.

Chapter Three
ALEKSANDR

Looking up and seeing the smoke show from O'Callahan's rocked me, but I can tell by her wide, blue eyes and hanging jaw that realizing I'd be her client surprised her even more. Her gaze travels down my body—taking in every inch. I guess I understand her appreciation since I'm sitting at my locker wearing nothing but the lower half of my uniform—skates and all.

"Aleksandr, this is Auden Berezin. She will be your translator."

"I don't need a translator," I say, leaning down to unlace one of my skates and pull it off. I start on the other one, giving myself a few seconds to compose myself. The last thing I want is for either of them to know how much her presence affects me.

My translator bites her lip, which makes my dick swell under my pants. Thank god for thick padding.

"You must talk with the media at some point, *Sasha*. They're riding my ass to get better answers from you than 'was good game.'"

I laugh at *Zhenya's* impression of me, then grab my skates and stand up.

"You have your teeth in, but you haven't even showered yet?" he asks.

"I wanted to look good for pictures." I wink at Auden.

She shifts from one foot to the other without taking her gaze from my chest. As her eyes follow the perspiration traveling over my pecs creating a happy trail all the way into my hockey pants she bites her lip.

Since checking me out has her all hot and bothered, I decided to add to the discomfort. "Sometimes I talk in the shower. Will she translate for me in there?"

Her cheeks turn bright pink and her eyes dart to mine, then to my tattoos—black Cyrillic script inked down both sides. Suddenly, as if realizes the direction her gaze is headed, she drops her eyes to study the gray, rubber flooring below our feet.

"Aleks—" *Zhenya* sighs, rubbing his forehead.

"*Zhenya*," I say. "You know I'm kidding, yes?" I shove my skates onto the shelf below my nameplate and walk away without waiting for an answer.

Without looking back, I shuffle to the gym, still laughing at the interesting range of reactions from my translator.

Surprise. Annoyance. Interest. Attraction. Definitely attraction. And back to annoyance—maybe even anger.

When I get to the gym, which is a small room near the showers, I finish undressing until I'm only in the compression leggings I wear under my pads. Then I swing my leg over a bike and press a few buttons on the screen to start my ride.

"Dude!" Landon Taylor, my best friend and roommate, yells while whipping my side with a towel.

"Ow, motherfucker! Why you do this?" I ask, rubbing the skin.

"Why is that hottie from O'Callahan's here?" he asks.

"She is translator."

All heads turn toward me—even a few that were still in the locker room stopped to peer into the gym.

"*She's* your translator?" Our captain, Luke Daniels, asks from the doorway. "The girl who sent you down in flames last night?"

My jaw tightens and I tap the screen a few times to increase the incline and speed of the bike.

"That is—what is it? Karma? Murphy's Law?" he searches for the right phenomenon.

"Luck?" Landon asks.

"It's definitely luck if you get to stare at that ass for the rest of the year," Viktor Kravtsov says, as he rubs deodorant over his pits.

"It's only for a month," I say in Russian. He's a first generation Russian American, but he's native in both English and Russian.

"Why would they get you a translator for a month?" he asks.

"Speak English," Nikolai Antonov reminds us, nodding to all the nosy-ass men waiting to hear more about Auden.

It's not like I was really trying. I'd used the shittiest line I possibly could hoping it would make her laugh.

A move that worked and totally backfired at the same time since she did laugh—and covered my shirt with her drink. Unfortunately, she wasn't impressed.

It almost feels like I never left home with all the Russians we have on our team. Antonov and Kravtsov are cousins—and I'm pretty sure they're both mafia, but I'll never ask. Antonov has to be, because his father is Kirill Antonov, who—technically—is one of the owners of the Russian Dining Room, a world-famous restaurant in New York City. But that's just a front. Legend is, he came over from Moscow years ago to run North American operations when his uncle was murdered.

So, I've heard.

Everything I "know" is through the grapevine. When it comes to the Russian mafia, I live by the "don't ask don't tell" mentality. As long as they aren't trying to extort me for money, I keep my eyes closed and mouth shut.

And *Kolya*, as we Russians call Nick, is a really chill guy—off the ice. When he laces up his skates it's like he transforms into a different person. He loves to mix it up and chirp like no other, but he's got great hands and a killer slap shot from the point, so coach lets him get his tussles in.

Personally, I like having the muscle out there. After all these years, some North American hockey purists still think Russians are pussies.

But I guess that's what people say when they're jealous.

"She is here for one month," I repeat in English.

"Why would they get you a translator for only one month?" Landon asks. He's one of the only guys on the team who knows that I'm pretty good with my English. I mean, I still have issues, but it's better than I let on.

"Because I am leader on this team. Coach say I need to talk to media more."

It's true, ever since I got made an Alternate Captain, my responsibilities shifted. Not only am I a leader on the ice, but I need to be one in the community as well. I'm not opposed to the responsibility, I just don't feel comfortable with the media yet. I hate having my words twisted or people not understanding what I mean. And I absolutely hate having personal articles written about me.

No one needs to know my background—or how my parents died. I'm not looking for pity or praise.

Which is why I refuse to have any social media. My teammates think I'm like an old man. But I don't see the point in putting your entire life out there for all to see. What I do off the ice is my business.

Which brings me back to my beautiful new translator whom I plan on having so much fun with over the next few weeks.

And most of that fun will happen outside of this stank-ass locker room.

Chapter Four
AUDEN

When Aleksandr walks away without so much as a look back, I wonder what my grandpa has gotten me into.

Zhenya clears his throat and says, "Well, that was Aleksandr Varenkov, your client. He's a talented player and a good man. But he can be a little—"

"Douchey?" I offer in English.

I shouldn't have said it, considering Grandpa's professional reputation is in my hands. Then again, Evgeny Orlenko and Grandpa are friends first, so maybe he'll give me a pass. Besides, my grandfather knows what kind of mouth I have, and he sent me for the job anyway.

Zhenya laughs before continuing in Russian. "Wild was the word I was looking for, but your adjective may not be that far off."

"Don't worry. I've got it."

"Are you sure?" He inspects me through thick black-rimmed glasses that are too small for his puffy face.

"As a college student with an active social life, I've learned how to handle arrogant douche bags." Only this time, I'm being paid to handle one.

"I shouldn't be having this conversation about one of my clients," *Zhenya* says, his lips quirking up, then back into a tight line. At least he's trying to keep a straight face. "You're like a breath of fresh air, *Audushka*. I hope you stay that way even with his off-ice antics."

Off-ice antics? What the hell does that mean and why would I have to deal with them?

"Will I have to hang out with him outside of the arena? I thought I was here to translate for media interviews after games and some practices."

"Aleksandr speaks very little English. He'll need your assistance in all aspects of his career; interviews, community service. At least, until he gets acclimated. *Vitya* said you were here for the month, is that correct?"

"Yep. All of winter break."

"You'll be putting in a lot of hours."

"I'm a hard worker. And I need the cash. Got cut from the soccer team, and I have to replace the scholarship money I lost." I'm running my mouth again. Maybe I do need to tone it down.

"Well, I'm sorry to hear that. The being-cut part." He clears his throat. "Here's my card. I wrote my cell number on the back. If you have any trouble or if Aleksandr makes you uncomfortable in any way, please give me a call."

"Thanks." I scan the card wondering if I should try to memorize his number now, since I'm not sure how stable this client sounds.

After Orlenko leaves the locker room, I realize I didn't ask him what I should do next, and he didn't give me instructions as to where I should wait while Aleksandr showered. Since I'm not part of the media, I'm extremely aware of being the intruder standing in a room of half-naked men. A shower shouldn't take very long, so I dig my e-reader out of my messenger bag and sit down on the stool that Aleksandr just vacated.

"Ewww." I jump up and skim my palm against my damp backside. Hadn't even thought about any runaway sweat that might've dripped from Aleksandr's lean, hard body onto the seat.

Stop. Just stop thinking about the shiny, wet flesh covering his impeccably carved frame.

Since I don't see a cleaner choice within reach, I pinch the funky-smelling towel Aleksandr shoved into his locker with my thumb and index finger and remove it with caution. Then I bat at any remaining sweat drops, though I'm sure my skirt absorbed most of the moisture.

I've always been under the impression that guys shower fast, but Aleksandr takes forever. According to the clock on my tablet, it's been forty-five minutes since he left. I can't help but scan the room a few times, catching odd looks from some of the guys. I ignore their questioning eyes and keep my head down.

When Aleksandr finally comes out, an hour and a half later, the locker room has cleared significantly.

"Couldn't find your lipstick?" I ask.

"Excuse me?" Aleksandr readjusts the strap of the messenger bag slung over his shoulder. He looks like something straight out of a high-fashion magazine, in a gray, high-neck military-style peacoat, a crisp, white button-down, and dark blue jeans.

Though I'd asked my original question in Russian, I clarify with my next sentence. "You took so long. I thought you were putting on your face."

"Funny," he says without a smile. "I always ride the bike after the game." He reaches over me and shoves something onto the shelf above my head. "What are you doing?"

"Reading." I hold up my e-reader as proof.

"At my stall?"

"Well, neither you nor Mr. Orlenko told me where to go, so I waited for you. Right here, where you both left me."

This time Aleksandr laughs. "I'm glad *Zhenya* got me a devoted translator."

"So, what now? Looks like all the media is gone. Should I come back tomorrow?"

"No. Now, we get to know each other."

"Do we have to?" I know all I need to about the jerk who left me sitting in this smelly locker room for over an hour while he "rode the bike" and showered. How am I supposed to know he worked out after games?

Aleksandr cocks his head, the skin around his eyes wrinkling like he can't believe I'd said no. He must be used to women falling all over him. Well, I've met a hundred like him, and though he's by far the best looking, I'll never give him the satisfaction of letting him know he affects me.

"Yes, we have to." He turns, taking long strides toward the door. I follow, since there's only one way out of the locker room. I can bolt when we get to the arena doors.

Aleksandr doesn't speak as we navigate our way down the concrete hallways. He pushes open the same doors I'd come through earlier and starts descending the stairs. I continue to follow him.

"Do you park out here, too?" I ask. I thought players would have a secret parking lot, or at least gated. Sure, most of them made a decent wage, but some of the guys have NHL contracts, and the paycheck that accompanies it.

"I'm walking you to your car," Aleksandr says without turning to look at me.

"Oh, well, thanks," I stammer. An arrogant douche bag who walks women to their cars in the middle of the day. Never met one of those, but I can roll with it.

Since he doesn't know where I parked, I hurry to match his long strides, which is a bit difficult in my skirt. Once we arrive at my old black Taurus, he stands by the passenger side with his hand on the dull, silver handle. He shakes it up and down a few times as he stares at me.

"What are you doing?" I ask.

"Waiting for you to unlock the door so I can get in."

I press the button on my key fob twice, and the doors unlock. "Do you need me to drive you to your car?"

"No. I need you to drive me home." He sets his bag on the floor before sliding into the passenger seat.

I pause before getting in, counting to ten in my head. The nerve of this guy. Leaving me at his locker. Making me drive him home.

"I wasn't aware chauffeur was part of the job," I say, slamming my door shut.

"Your eyebrows are almost one." Aleksandr points to my forehead.

I rub the skin above my nose. Couldn't be. I had them waxed last week.

"You were so mad, they were like one line." He wiggles his index finger in front of my eyes.

"I'm not mad," I snap. I know I don't have a unibrow. And why would I care if I did? I'm not trying to impress him. I only have one month, and this assignment will be over. "Where to?" I ask as I turn the key in the ignition and the radio comes on.

"The Coney Island on Seven Mile and Mack." He sits up straighter, digging into the inside front pocket of his coat and pulling out his cell phone. As he leans over to turn down the volume on my radio with one hand, he swipes his thumb over the front of his phone.

"You live at the Coney Island on Seven Mile and Mack?"

Aleksandr catches my eyes, shaking his head as if my question had been serious. "I'm hungry."

I'm a bit perturbed that I'm not taking him straight home, but if the man has to eat, I'm glad he chose Coney Island. It's my favorite place.

As I cruise Mack Avenue toward our destination, Aleksandr makes a phone call. While I'm not trying to eavesdrop, I hear most of the conversation. He's telling the person on the other end about last night's game, where he'd had two assists, but "Couldn't get the fucking rubber between the motherfucking pipes." When I hear "Not as annoying as the last bunny," I crank the volume on the radio. He looks at me with one raised eyebrow.

"Sorry," I whisper but don't turn the radio down. I'm actually not trying to be rude. Cranking the volume for an Arctic Monkeys song is mandatory.

Once we arrive at Coney Island, my annoyance grows as I circle around the block, unable to find a parking spot on the street in front of the restaurant or in the dedicated lot around back.

"Park there." Aleksandr reaches across me, his arm brushing against my chest as he points out the driver's side window.

Ignoring the unnerving contact, I slam on the brakes and the car screeches to a halt. When I look out the window, the only parking spot I see is between two other cars.

"Yeah, right. I can't parallel park," I say glancing over my shoulder to see if anyone is coming up behind me before I pull back into traffic.

"Stop!" he commands. I stomp on the brake pedal again, sending us both jerking forward.

"I'll do it." Aleksandr throws his door open and walks around to my side. I don't move, keeping my hands on the wheel, foot on the brake.

"Are you kidding me? Get back in the car," I plead.

"Move over," he orders, scooting into the driver's seat. I have no choice but to throw the gear into park and climb over the console to the passenger side.

Aleksandr reaches underneath the seat, fumbling with the lever that slides it back. Then, he maneuvers my car into the tight space between a Sebring and a Tahoe. Welcome to Detroit: Home of the Big Three auto manufacturers. Despite being put off by his tactics, I'm impressed with his skills. I haven't parallel parked since my driving test.

Aleksandr jumps out of the car and comes around to my side to open the door.

"Thanks," I say as I climb out.

"Didn't want to park in the next city. I'm starving." Aleksandr slams the door.

I grab his arm, forcing him to look at me. "Is this how it's gonna be for a month? Pissy with me because I didn't fall for your stupid-ass pickup line at the bar?"

"Don't flatter yourself, sweetheart," Aleksandr says in perfect, but heavily-accented, English. "I could have a different woman every night of the week."

I release his arm as if it's covered in thorns, looking around to see if anyone else heard the stream of English coming out of his mouth. "Excuse me?"

"I said, don't flatter—"

"You speak English?" My squeaky pitch sounds accusatory rather than questioning.

"I do. And you are the only person who knows that."

"Why?"

He walks away as if that's the end of the conversation. I hurry after him, pulling open the heavy glass door he hadn't bothered to hold for me. Guess he lost his manners when he got pissed off.

Chapter Five
ALEKSANDR

Auden scans the restaurant as she slides into the tattered, green vinyl booth across from me. Instead of wallpaper or paint, mirrored tiles cover the wall behind the booths.

Neither of us pick up a menu. She raises an eyebrow. "No menu?"

"Menu? Who needs a menu here?"

She chuckles.

The art of ordering a Coney Dog is well known to Detroiters—one (or two or five) with everything, says it all. Everything means chili, mustard, and onions—the makeup of the classic Coney.

The first time I went to Lafayette Coney Island, the restaurant close to my condo downtown, I asked for a menu. Not only did my teammates laugh at me, the guy behind the counter gave me a dirty look before searching around dramatically. When he finally found one, he pretended to blow the dust off. I still haven't lived that one down with the boys.

"I take it you've been here before?" she asks, pulling a napkin from the holder and wiping the already clean surface.

"It's my favorite." I answer, sliding out of the booth. "When our server stops at our booth, can you order me three with everything and a side of fries? I'll be right back."

"Okaaay."

I walk to the back of the restaurant, down the hallway toward the bathrooms and out the back door. As soon as I get outside, I light up a cigarette. I'm trying to quit, but when I get anxious, the scent of cloves calms me.

When I get back to the booth, Auden leans over the table and inhales the air around me.

"Did you just sniff me?"

"I like the smell of cloves." She shrugs and drops back against the booth. "Reminds me of my grandma."

"That's exactly what every man wants a woman to say after inhaling him." I wink.

She fumbles with her necklace, then glances at me quickly and drops it.

Her nervousness comes from excitement, but she's too stubborn to flirt. It's cute.

"Tell me about you," I ask.

"What you see is what you get. Blond-haired, blue-eyed Russian translator to the stars."

"Start with the Russian-translator part. How did that happen?" I lean forward, momentarily swept out to sea by the tiny matching ocean-colored irises she mentioned.

She meets my gaze, squinty slightly as she holds it. It's like she's looking inside me rather than at me, which is unsettling. It feels like she can see into my soul.

"Auden?" I ask, waving a hand in front of her face.

"What?" She blinks a few times as if come back to reality. "Sorry. What was the question?"

Though, she'd been doing her best to play it off, now I know she's completely enthralled. Maybe I'm projecting.

"You left me." I raise my hand to my temple then sweep it across the air as if saluting goodbye to my brain.

"I do that sometimes," she stammers, spinning her index finger around one of her ears. "Always turning."

"How," I begin, saying each word slowly. "Did you. Become. A Russian translator?"

"My grandpa has been teaching me since I was a kid. He was born just outside of Moscow, but moved here when he was a few years old. Growing up, they spoke both Russian and English in their home. He taught Russian Language and Literature classes at Michigan University for, like, forty years," she explains. "Being a translator is a side job, hobby-type thing for him. But it keeps him busy in retirement. I help him translate documents sometimes. This is the first time he's assigned me to a client. Hey!" She waves her hand in front of her cleavage, then points to her face. "Eyes up here."

"I was looking at your necklace," I say, raising my eyes to hers and flashing her a sexy smirk. It's not a lie—though, her boobs happen to be in the same vicinity and I *did* sneak a peek.

Her hand moves to her neck, where she fingers the gold charm hanging from a delicate chain. It's a beautiful owl with two tiny amber stones for eyes.

I can't help when my gaze drops to her boobs again, since she's holding the charm right in front of them. She must notice because she scowls and changes the subject.

"Speaking of languages, if you know English, why am I here?"

I push back against the booth and stretch my arms above my head. "The media wants us to give interviews on the bench. They want us to mic-up during the game. Then we curse or chirp, and they blast us in the papers or on TV. What do they expect to hear in the middle of a game?"

"Yeah." She nods. "When Frank started standing between the benches, it became my least favorite thing in the history of hockey broadcasting."

"Ugh! Yeah," I groan. "How are we supposed to think politically correct when we're in the heat of battle?"

François LaRue, a former hockey coach who now works as a TV analyst, broadcasts from between the two teams' benches during hockey games.

And it annoys the shit out of me.

Broadcasting itself is fine—slightly irritating—but fine. It's when he grabs players during the game to talk to him that really aggravates me. The last thing I want to do is lose concentration or miss something coach or my teammates are calling because I get snagged for a mid-period interview.

Don't get me wrong, I'm all about giving fans the ultimate experience, but being on the ice is my job. Players and coaches are paid to worry about—and play—the game. We're always available for questions after. And yet, we have to do stupid shit to make the networks happy. To get the ratings up.

Not that I have to worry about it right now, since it's not a thing in the AHL. Since the NHL is the ultimate goal, I need to be prepared for circumstances that will take me out of the zone, and figure out how to get back in.

When Auden genuinely smiles, her bottom lip dips ever so slightly on the left side, like a kink in a hose. It doesn't dip when she flashes her teasing smirk. That no-holds-barred dip-lip smile is a million times hotter.

I'm just about to slip up and tell her she has a great smile, but I catch myself. Too soon. I'm just happy I got her to grin. It's much better than the daggers she's been shooting me.

"I get it," she says in English. "But you need to suck it up because talking to the media is part of your job."

"Russian," I correct. "Always use Russian between the two of us."

"*Okay.*" She nods to confirm my request. "Tell me more about hockey. How'd you get so good?"

"How do you know I'm good?" I ask.

"I Googled you while I waited for you to shower," she admits, tucking a piece of hair behind her ear. "You're one of the Aviators' best players. Spill your secrets."

Without sounding too arrogant, it's a true statement. But that's why the Monarchs, their NHL affiliate, drafted me.

"Years of practice." I reach over my shoulder and knock three times on top of our booth's wooden frame. "I joined the Scarlet Army youth program when I was six. Since then it's been all hockey all the time. That was an intense program. Very strict. Very disciplined."

When our waitress interrupts our conversation by sliding plates in front of us, I'm slightly thankful for the interruption. Talking with Auden is comfortable and easy. I want to get to know her better—and when that happens I usually end up spilling too much about myself.

The glorious aroma of the Coney dogs and fries on the table transitions my brain from one sensory stupor to another.

Chili drips out the back of the bun when Auden lifts her Coney to her mouth. Her eyes dart to me quickly, as if she expects me to be looking at our waitress. But I can't take my eyes off my translator.

"Can I get you anything else?" the woman asks.

"*Nyet*," I answer, my eyes planted on Auden.

"No, thanks," Auden answers in English. "That's a hard-core schedule," she says, before taking a bite.

"Very," I agree.

She sets it back on her plate and wipes her mouth as she chews. "Do you have any family here?"

"No, everybody's back in Russia. Aunts and uncles, cousins. Gribov and I have been playing together for awhile, so that's helpful. And some of the older guys let me hang with their families if I'm feeling homesick."

"If you ever want to hang out with an old Russian guy, come on over to my house." She throws it out absently, but I see her eyes widen as if she's done something wrong.

"First, I smell like your grandmother, now you want to set me up with your grandfather. You flatter me." I put a hand to my heart dramatically. My phone buzzes in my pocket, so I reach in and grab it. It's a text from Landon Taylor, my teammate—and roommate.

Landon: Dude, where are you?

"Excuse me," I say, holding up a finger to Auden before typing back quickly.

Me: I'm eating.
Landon: Who?
Me: Fuck off.

Landon: Well, smack her ass and say goodbye. Because I'm locked out.
Me: Go to your parent's house.

Landon is a Detroiter—born and raised. With the exception of juniors, he's never really lived outside of the city. His parent's house is only about ten minutes from our condo.

Landon: I've got a girl coming over.
Me: Go to the bar.

We live in the Westin-Book Cadillac, a historic building in Detroit that was renovated into hotel rooms and condos in the recent rejuvenation of Detroit. There's a bar and a restaurant right in the building.

Landon: She's not 21.

I roll my eyes. They'd still let her sit there, but I don't want to get into it over text. He hasn't had a girl over in months so he probably wants to get pretty for her beforehand.

Me: Let me scarf this coney. I'll be there as soon as I can.

"Was that the 'help me' text?" Auden asks as I shove my phone back into my pocket.
"The what?" I shovel a still steaming handful of fries into my mouth.
"The text you tell a friend to send so you have an excuse to leave."
I laugh. "Now why would I need that when we were having such an amazing time?"
Banter is so easy between us and there's obvious attraction. Too bad she'd never give me the time of day.
"It's always time to wrap it up when a girl starts trying to set you up with her grandfather." She grins.
We finish our lunches in record time, which is fine with me,

because once you start eating a Coney, you have to finish fast. Cold chili dogs don't taste good.

Though I'm reluctant to leave, I can't keep Landon stranded on the doorstep with a girl on her way.

As we stand, I snatch the bill off the table. When Auden opens her purse, I clasp my hand over hers. She pulls away fast, and her head snaps up as if I'd slapped her.

"I got it."

When I first moved here, I was surprised the first time a woman tried to pay. I still don't understand where Americans got the idea women should ever pay for anything when they're on a date.

Are men that rude? Or is it some feminist thing? Maybe a mix of both?

In my country, there would be no second date if I ever asked a woman to pay—or even split—the bill. Some of the guys tell me I'm old fashioned—or too "Alpha"—whatever the hell that means. But for me, it's manners.

A man should always take care of his girl. Even if she's independent and able to take care of herself.

Not that Auden's my girl.

Not yet anyway.

I drop a five on the table and walk to the cash register. As the woman at the counter rings me up, I grab two red-and-white mints from the bowl on the counter, handing Auden one and untwisting the wrapper on the other before popping it into my mouth.

When we step outside, Auden pretzels her arms across her chest, bracing herself from the brisk air whipping around us. Instinctively, I sweep my arm across her back, and cradle her to my side as we hurry to her car.

It's totally inappropriate, and she's probably seething inside, but she's so cold she's shaking, so she doesn't say anything.

As we scramble into the car to escape the chill, she hands me her keys. I chuckle to myself, finding her fear of parking fucking hilarious —and endearing. I enjoy being relied on for something.

Before turning the key, I pause as the car accident that killed my parents flashes though my head—just like it does every time I start a car. Some kind of PTSD thing I haven't been able to shake.

When the engine purrs to life, I switch on the heat and sit quietly, checking my mirrors and rubbing my hands together, contemplating the situation.

She either digs me or she's nervous around guys because she's obviously trying to keep her guard up. Maybe she's just trying to keep our relationship professional and I unnerved her. I want to kiss her so badly to see if it's the first scenario, but that would be totally inappropriate and a bit caveman-like. Instead, I let the rush of frigid air from the vents blast my face, hoping it helps me clear my head.

Out of the blue, Auden laughs and I twist my head. "What?"

"You can't get out of this spot, can you?"

"You think I'm waiting because I can't move the car?" I ask, with amusement.

She shrugs. "Why else would you be waiting?"

Now's my chance. And this time, there's no one around to see if she sends me down in flames—again.

I lean in, place a hand on each of her cheeks, and pull her face toward mine.

"Dude, get off!" She pushes me back, avoiding the lip collision. "I'm not one of your bunnies."

Ding! Ding! Ding!

She totally digs me. I definitely didn't choose the correct way to find out, but her first reaction was to talk about bunnies—which means she's jealous.

"You aren't a bunny. I don't buy bunnies dinner." I smirk. "Breakfast maybe."

Her eyebrows veer together and she balls her fists at her side as if resisting the urge to smack me. "That's the other reason nothing's going to happen. You're an ass."

"I'm joking, Auden."

"Yeah, right. I'm on to you, Varenkov."

"I wish," I mumble before checking the mirrors for traffic, flicking on the turn signal, and pulling onto the road.

"Where do you live?" she asks, ignoring my comment.

"Landon and I share a condo in the Westin Book Cadillac."

"Excuse me?" Her voice drips with annoyance.

"The Westin Book Cadillac," I repeat.

"You live downtown—where we just came from—in the building around the corner from the best Coney Island in the city, yet I drove us all the way up here for lunch?"

"I go to Lafayette most of the time, but I knew it would be busy now. This is the next best place." I shrug, ignoring the smoke coming out of her ears.

Though she's boiling, she must realize I have a point—a very good point. With as much of a Coney snob I am, I could be a native Detroiter.

She takes a deep breath and lets it out audibly. "Fine."

Did I win that?

I think I won. But I don't know what made her stand down, so I'm not going to rub it in.

We drive in silence, which allows me time to observe the streets without having to worry if the next thing I say or do will piss her off.

When I was drafted by the Charlotte Monarchs in the NHL Entry draft, I was ecstatic. It's a top-notch organization in a beautiful state. I knew I'd probably be assigned to Detroit first, and I was fine with it because it's one of the best hockey cities in the country.

Only, I wasn't prepared for the state of the city.

According to locals, it's been deteriorating since before I was born. But those same people are so proud to live here. It's an eerie hometown appreciation an outsider can't quite understand. People want others to know they're from Detroit—in particular—and Michigan—in general. You can barely pass a person who isn't wearing some logo that represents the state.

And the cars! Every fucking car has a sticker of a sport team, a university, or the lakes. The pride runs deeper here than anywhere I've ever been—even Mother Russia.

I can only speak from a visitor's perspective, someone who doesn't have a long-term tie to the city, but with the exception of the revitalization going on downtown, the rest of the city is a heart-wrenching eyesore.

Driving Mack Avenue toward downtown, the view barely changes. Businesses that probably once thrived have been razed to piles of rubble. The few churches or liquor stores still standing have large areas of paint chipping off the sides, or they've been sprayed with gang graffiti. The buildings that aren't completely gone are boarded up, hollowed-out shells of their former glory. Broken doors and windows allow an unobstructed view of the inside, where remains lay singed from burned-out fires.

Maybe that's a candid description of the city itself: a once-blazing fire that burned out long ago.

I hope to see the day where the majority of the city has been revitalized, not just certain downtown areas. But change has to start somewhere, which is why Landon and I chose to live in the heart of the city.

Most of the guys on the team live in nicer neighborhoods in the surrounding Metro Detroit area, but Landon has been in the city his entire life. His family owns a store in Eastern Market and his parents live close to that. Despite so many families fleeing to the suburbs, they stayed and rolled with the changes—good and bad.

There's something special about being part of the change.

Jesus, I sound like a hipster. Speaking of...

I tear my eyes away from the unmanaged weeds growing up from the jagged sidewalk and blurt, "Are you and that grunge guy from the bar an item?"

"Um, no." Auden glares at me.

I can't tell if she's offended because I asked about her personal life or because I think she would be with a guy like that.

"You and your friends sat at that table up front—right near him." I meet her eyes, trying to gauge her reaction. "Why did you talk to him so long?"

"He wants me to sing in his band." A laugh escapes as she studies her French-manicured fingernails. "Which is ridiculous."

"You have a great voice. You should do it."

She ignores my compliment and unsolicited advice. "I'm not seeing anyone right now. Not that it's any of your business."

"Just checking out the competition."

"You have no competition because you aren't in the running. We have to work together. We can't be involved. Simple as that."

Maybe that's true, but that can't be her only reason for rejecting me.

"Nothing is ever simple, Auden."

Chapter Six
AUDEN

Judging by the I-just-scored gleam in Aleksandr's eyes yesterday, he thinks he's going to wear me down. Part of me expected to see the familiar flashes of red across his face from the light behind the goal at Robinson Arena that blinks and spins after someone scores in a hockey game.

Aleksandr doesn't realize who he's hitting on, because no matter how attracted we are to each other, I'll never give him a chance.

An entirely different flashing red light runs through my mind when I look at him.

The kind that's accompanied by a deafening buzz alerting people to evacuate in an emergency. The way my stomach bubbles with excitement every time I'm around him is reason enough for my emotions to make an emergency evacuation.

Having been abandoned by both parents before age seven, the last person I need to get involved with is a professional athlete whose job requires him to leave.

And yet, here I am—completely and utterly infatuated with him.

But that's nothing new for me. I've always had massive crushes on fictional characters and unattainable men. I have a million book boyfriends and I lust after one too many musicians.

It's better for my heart knowing I have zero chance from day one.

That's how I'm brushing off the tingles coursing under my skin at the mere thought of Aleksandr Varenkov. It's just a little crush—a silly infatuation with an untouchable man.

The only problem is that this isn't an untouchable man on a TV screen or over the radio waves. This is a man with whom I have to interact almost every day.

A man who just flicked the puck into the opposing team's goal and is being mobbed by his teammates against the glass in front of me.

A man who, as he breaks free from the group, pounds on the glass, points his thick glove at me, and flashes me a radiant, though semi-toothless, smile.

Aleksandr is an untouchable man I want to touch so badly.

But I'm not interested in a one-night stand with someone I work with. Those are saved for people you never see again.

I'm convinced *Zhenya* can see my shaking hands and hear my racing heart, so I straighten up and watch Aleksandr skate to the bench as I would any other player on the ice. Though I try to keep an aloof appearance, I know the flush of heat spreading across my pale cheeks gives me away.

Call it paranoia, but every time *Zhenya* looks my way I squirm in my seat, feeling scrutinized by his judging eyes. Of course, I pay close attention to Aleksandr. As his translator, I have to be ready for the question-and-answer session with the media afterward.

Technically, the job requires me to translate Aleksandr's words, and that's it. But I'm going the extra mile, digging into this assignment to get it right. At least, that's how I justify keeping my eyes on him.

Who wouldn't want to watch his deft body sail across the ice and label it "research?"

"Do you go to all of Aleksandr's games?" I ask *Zhenya*, diverting my eyes from Aleksandr's limber leg climbing over the boards.

"No. I need to talk to him about some community projects after he showers. Then I'm back on the road. I have a client in Vancouver to touch base with." He pats his chest a few times before pulling his cell phone out of the inside pocket of his navy-blue suit jacket.

Come on, Zhenya, don't talk about him showering, I think.

As a lifelong hockey-player appreciator, my brief encounter with a semi-dressed Aleksandr already had my below-the-belly-button areas buzzing like bees on speed. Thinking about him showering could push me over the edge—or into his arms.

I glance at Aleksandr, who's sitting on the bench talking to the guy on his left. His shoulders rise and fall and sweat trickles down his nose. He leans over and bangs his gloved hand against the boards. Just watching him makes my breathing increase and my stomach tighten.

If simply watching him sit on a bench and breathe makes my heart rate soar—I'm in way over my head.

Out of all the types of Russian men that Grandpa could have assigned me to, why did it have to be a hockey player—my kryptonite? I need to remember to keep the emphasis on the *player* part. He's a young, hot athlete—which is definitely *not* boyfriend material.

Despite my prayers to no one in particular, time flies by so fast that it feels like someone is tapping my personal hourglass. When the scoreboard clock glows with orange zeros, it shows the Aviators won 5–2. Aleksandr scored two more goals in the game, acknowledging me after each.

The entire game, my brain was torn between wanting to hide under the stiff blue stadium seat and blowing him kisses. Thankfully, I kept my composure and ignored him.

After the game, I head down to the locker room, happy to have *Zhenya* there for moral support. He wouldn't flirt relentlessly with his agent there.

When we reach Aleksandr, my knees almost buckle. He's stripped off his jersey, pads, and the blue shirt he wears underneath. He's also removed his hockey pants, socks and skates, and the pads from the lower half of his body. He sits at his locker in nothing but sweat-soaked, black compression shorts clinging to his thick thighs.

Is he trying to get a rise out of me? Gauging how much sex-charged flirtation I can take?

However, when I stop in front of him and catch his eyes, all I see is exhaustion.

I shake my head, annoyed by the stupid thought. He just finished a game. Of course, he's going to take off his sweaty, smelly gear. I have to stop the obsessive thoughts and focus on the job I'm here to do: Translate for a hot, Russian hockey god.

"*Zhenya*. Auden." He nods at each of us before wiping his face with a thin, white towel.

"Great game, *Sasha*. I need to talk to you about community service before I leave for the airport. I'll check back in an hour." *Zhenya* stops to shake hands with the guy standing at the locker to Aleksandr's right, whom I recognize as Landon Taylor, one of the Aviators defensemen, before leaving the locker room.

"You ready for this?" Aleksandr asks, nodding his head toward the reporters flooding the locker room.

"Yep." I throw my shoulders back and take my place next to him.

When six reporters fire off questions at once, my eyes dart from face to face, unsure of whose question I should translate first. Aleksandr nudges my arm, then points to a short, stocky white-haired man with circular wire-framed glasses. I exhale a breath of relief, thankful that my client is in a helpful—rather than snarky—mood.

"You had three goals tonight. Did you feel like you had to take control to make something happen out there?"

I translate and wait for Aleksandr to respond.

"Those glasses should have gone to the grave with that guy from the Beatles," he says in Russian, biceps flexing as he squeezes both ends of the towel hanging around his neck.

With my gaze locked on his arms, I start translating his words without thinking, then suddenly stop, stunned into silence as I process what he'd said.

How could he do that to me?

I press my lips together, racking my brain for something generic and cliché; AKA: PR acceptable.

"Everyone is doing what they can to help the team win. You want to do well because you want the team to do well," I say, recovering well. Very well.

Aleksandr moves a hand to his mouth and coughs into his fist.

The bastard is hiding a laugh. It makes me want to kick him—in the junk.

Instead, I point to the next reporter myself, trying to establish some sort of control. I can only identify people by their heads, since I can't see their bodies in the crowd. This guy has a brown comb-over and floppy ears. I focus on the question, preparing myself in case my jackass client doesn't know when to stop his little game.

"You seemed a bit frustrated with Penner's goal in the second. Looked like you wanted the ref to make a call."

"You have the nicest ass I have ever seen in my life," Aleksandr responds to my translated question, his gaze on a body part much lower than my eyes.

I glare at him before responding to the reporter. "It was a nice goal. The ref was right there. If there was a call, he would've made it."

I've never been so relieved I'd paid attention to the hockey game and was well-versed in the sport.

An older blonde woman with way too many buttons undone on her blouse to be interviewing in a locker room full of men raises her hand. I point to her.

"How did you feel about having Gribov switched to your line?" she asks.

Instead of translating, I say, "Answer the fucking question or I will kick you in the balls. Then you'll have no way to fuck *her* or anyone else tonight."

When I look up, I catch his Russian line mate, Pavel Gribov, watching me. The scowl and shake of his sweaty head give me all the validation I need. But I'm sure he was in on these stupid shenanigans, so I ignore him.

Aleksandr chuckles. "We have a lot of chemistry. We played together in Russia, so it was just about getting that groove back. We get along great and have confidence in each other."

I translate word for word.

The questions go on for another twenty minutes, and Aleksandr doesn't pull another translation trick on me.

When the reporters move on to another player, he stands up, pulls the towel from around his neck, and throws it into a bin on his way toward the showers.

"Excuse me," I call out in Russian. He's not getting away that easily. I won't start this assignment letting him believe I'm a pushover.

Aleksandr turns around. Despite my anger, it takes every ounce of willpower to not be derailed by his godly physique. Instead, I use the fact that I'll never have that body to fuel my anger.

"That was ridiculous." I step toward him, narrowing the space between our bodies to a few inches, and rise to my tippy-toes. He has me by almost a foot, but my extra height gives me a feeling of power.

"I was just giving you a hard time. It was a joke." He rolls his eyes, which incenses me.

"Don't you realize that I can make you look like a total ass? I could've told all those reporters that you felt you had to take control because this team couldn't win in a beer league without you."

"That would've been shitty."

"What you just did to me was shitty. And it was sexual harassment. I know that you don't care because you're Mr."—I have no clue how to say douche bag in Russian, so I switch to English—"Douche bag. King of all Douches." Back to Russian. "You can't treat me like that." I jab his chest with my index finger. "You might be better off declining interviews until you have enough English skills to get by. I'm not sure I want this job anymore."

The locker room, which had been buzzing when we'd started our conversation, is silent. Not because everyone had cleared out, either. On the contrary, players who had already left returned to listen to us go at it.

I almost feel bad about calling Aleksandr out in front of his teammates, but we've been arguing in Russian, so most of them have no idea what we're saying.

Aleksandr circles his hand around my wrist and lowers my arm to my side.

"See this?" He drops my hand to grab a chunk of hair from the top of his head. "My first day here, the veteran guys got me with clippers. Shaved off hair on both sides. It was a joke. A prank. Hockey players do that to rookies. I got this haircut to prove I can roll with it. You're gonna quit over a stupid joke?" He shakes his head, letting out a faint chuckle. "Go ahead."

Aleksandr turns around and stomps to the showers like an oversized toddler.

I swing my messenger bag over my shoulder and stalk toward the locker-room door. Absolutely humiliated.

"Hey." Landon, one of Aleksandr's teammates, touches my arm to stop my beeline. "You okay?"

I nod, but a ridiculous, revealing tear escapes. I let it roll rather than draw any more attention to myself by wiping my cheek.

"Dude can be a jerk at first, but he's not a bad guy."

I nod. "Tell the jerk I'll see him on Thursday after the game."

* * * * *

After dinner the next night, I follow Gram upstairs to her bedroom, sprawling across her floral quilt while she flicks on the television.

"Why am I such a loser?" I ask, staring at the white tiles covering the ceiling of her attic room.

"What happened?" she asks, though her eyes don't leave the screen.

She's used to my emotional melodrama. If I weren't so afraid of being the center of attention, I think I could have been a theatre major.

"Aleksandr humiliated me on my first day. He played this stupid prank where he said nonsensical things in Russian and made me figure out answers on the fly. I'm not a professional hockey translator. I didn't know what to say."

"Did you come up with something?"

"Well, yeah. I didn't want to be the idiot he was trying to make me out to be. So, of course I confronted him, because it was a super shitty thing to do."

She looks down at the remote, then points it at the screen.

"I blew up and he blew up. I don't think he's ever going to speak to me again." I keep staring at the ceiling as if it holds hidden answers.

Gram stops flipping through the channels. "Sounds like you're making a mountain out of a molehill, Auden. He did something jerky. You told him you didn't like it. Move on."

Move on. Move on? Where was the protective I'm-going-to-sic-your-grandfather-on-that-jackass talk I wanted to hear right now?

"Do you think I can tell *Zhenya* I'm sick for Thursday's game? Grandpa can handle it, right?" I ask, completely aware that my grandfather would never cover for me. I throw in a fake cough and rub my neck. "I think I feel a sore throat coming on."

"Gargle with warm salt water and get into bed." Gram continues zipping through channels, not even fazed. Evidently, raising three of her own kids before getting stuck with me made her heartless.

"You know, Gram, it's okay to allow me to skip work one time in my life to avoid extreme embarrassment." I roll onto my side and rest my head on the back of my hand.

"You know, Auden," Gram mocks me, "it's better to face your problems head-on. Avoiding the situation just causes more anxiety. I'll bet you're worrying about nothing."

It's not like I have a choice. She's the one who passed on the anxiety trait. She worries about everything.

* * * * *

On Thursday night, I listen to the radio broadcast in my car until the third period. When there are only a few minutes left, I scramble out and make my way into the arena. I studied generic interview answers earlier so I'd be prepared for anything the reporters asked, in case Aleksandr pulled another stupid translating prank.

Once inside, I make the familiar trek to the dungeon, walking slowly so I arrive at the same time as the media. Making small talk with Aleksandr isn't high on my list of things to do.

Maybe my grandma was right. Maybe I should let it go. Maybe I was making too big of a deal of it. I just can't believe he would embarrass me on my first night translating. I knew he was a cocky jerk, but didn't realize he was evil.

Peering through the crowd of bodies in front of the lockers, I notice Aleksandr and Landon laughing with the beat writer from the Detroit Times. I slide my fingers through my meticulously straightened hair, then smooth the front of my black sheath dress. Though the sleek dress hugs the curves of my hips and backside, it's completely professional.

I threw a hot pink cardigan over it because it's sleeveless, which isn't ideal in the freezing arena. The bold color gives me the confidence I need before facing whatever Aleksandr has in store for me tonight.

Landon must spot me first because he swats Aleksandr's shoulder and nods my way. When his gaze follows Landon's prompt, his smile vanishes, his eyes widen, and his mouth falls open. He shifts in his seat as I approach.

Excusing myself as I slide past the group of reporters, I make my way to Aleksandr's locker. Once I'm standing in front on him, I bend over slowly and set my messenger bag on the floor.

Hopefully, he's getting an eyeful of the ass he enjoys looking at so much because the only times he's going to see it are when I'm standing here and when I'm walking away.

Revenge is sweet.

The media session goes smoothly, with Aleksandr answering every question, and even joking around with the reporters. When we finish, I grab my bag from the floor, smoothing my skirt over my butt when I stand back up, and follow the mob of reporters toward the doors.

"So what? You aren't going to speak to me?" Aleksandr touches my arm just as the locker-room door swings shut in front of me. Damn.

I turn to face him. "No need to talk. All I need to do is translate."

His eyes find mine and when he speaks, his voice is soft. "I'm sorry, *Audushka*."

"It's Auden." I refuse to let my guard down again. I'd trusted him with a piece of myself and gotten humiliated. He doesn't get another chance.

"Don't be like that. I said I was sorry. What else do you want?"

"I just want to do my job and go home."

"You're ridiculous, *Auden*." Aleksandr pounds the locker-room door with his fist, and I flinch. He spins around and trudges to the showers. If we were in a cartoon, steam would be pouring from his ears.

"He's not interested," an unfamiliar Russian voice says.

Startled, I turn to see Aviators forward, Pavel Gribov, standing so close I can smell the grape sports drink on his breath. I back away. "Excuse me?"

He slithers into my space, towering over me as he leans close. His face gleams, slimy with sweat, and there's a black void where his two front teeth should be.

"He has no interest in you. But if you want to tease someone's cock, I've got one right here." He grabs his crotch, jiggling the front of his gray boxer briefs at me.

I tighten my hold on my messenger bag, shuddering as I elbow my way past him. The interaction with him reminds me of an old saying I'd modified.

When the going gets tough—get going.

Chapter Seven

AUDEN

"When's your audition?" Kristen asks, plopping onto the couch next to me.

Kristen and Lacy came over to hang out at my grandparents' house, which I appreciated because I still feel like a child around my grandparents, despite my age. Having my college friends around creates a sense of normalcy and keeps my head in a relatively mature place.

"Sorry?" I ask.

Page fifty-three of my book should be ingrained in my memory, considering the amount of time I stared at it. But instead of reading, I've been analyzing Aleksandr's aggravating shenanigans. The more I obsessed about it, the more irritated I become. If the intense, emotional, pissed-off frenzy going on in my head could manifest itself physically, I'd be covered in hives.

"When's the singing audition with the hipster from Canada? I thought for sure you'd tell us so we could help you pick out something to wear," Kristen explains as she leans toward me to tuck her lower leg under her butt.

"And a song," Lacy adds, wandering into the living room with a plate piled with apple slices and graham crackers. Gram must be at work in the kitchen. It's been her trademark snack to make for my friends since I was in elementary school. Throw in some hot chocolate, and we're in second grade again.

So much for feeling like an adult.

"Oh, um, yeah. I haven't called him." I remove the beer coaster on which Greg had written his number from my book.

"I can't believe you haven't called him yet." Kristen snatches it out of my hand. "I'm doing it."

"KK, don't," I plead, reaching for the coaster.

"What can it hurt?" she asks, grabbing her cell phone off the side table. "It's only a tryout."

I shrug and look down at my book. What would it hurt? After being cut from the soccer team and humiliated by my client, I'm one kick in the gut away from shaving my head and going on a deranged Twitter rant. I should start taking drugs, so I'd have something to blame it all on.

"If you don't want me to call, I won't," Kristen says. She holds the coaster in one hand and her cell phone in the other.

I take a deep breath and swivel my head between Kristen and Lacy. They'll be disappointed in me if I don't do it, and, more important, I'll be disappointed in myself. An unfamiliar, narcissistic gnawing feeling plagues me, telling me I need to be good at something again. I hate feeling like a disappointment.

I close my eyes and let out my breath. "Do whatever you want."

"You sure?" Kristen asks.

"Just do it before I change my mind." I cover my face with my hands, refusing to watch as Kristen dials the numbers scrawled on the coaster.

"May I speak to Greg, please?" Kristen asks, sounding confident and professional. "I'm calling on behalf of Auden Berezin. Who am I? Um, I'm her manager." She covers her mouth to conceal her laugh.

I kick her shin with my bare foot. Lacy throws an apple slice at her.

"When can she meet you?" Kristen pauses, waving for us to shut up then putting her finger in her free ear. "Tonight is perfect. Yes. Sure. She'll be there. Thanks, Greg. Nice speaking with you."

Kristen presses the screen and drops her phone onto the couch. "That's how it's done, ladies."

"Tonight? Did you say tonight?" I ask.

"Well, if you would have called sooner, you might have had more time to prepare," she scolds.

"So you're her manager?" Lacy asks. "Does that mean you get a cut of what she makes?"

"Whoa." I hold my hands out in front of me. "Let's see if I get the job before we talk about who gets cuts of what. It might pay in beer for all we know."

"Almost as good as cash," Kristen says. Then she clasps her hands together. "What are you gonna wear?"

"What are you going to sing?" Lacy asks.

I fall back onto the couch. "I don't know. I need to start getting ready now."

"Your audition isn't until eight. Eight o'clock at his place," Kristen tells me.

I turn my head to look at her. "Are you kidding me?"

"No, that's what he said," Kristen answers, feigning innocence.

"Please throw another apple at her," I tell Lacy.

She holds the fruit, poised to fire. "On your command."

Eight o'clock tonight at Greg's place. The thought hits me with a flood of nerves. "I was hoping it would be more of an afternoon audition in a garage."

"Singing for a hot man after dark." Lacy bites into the un-thrown apple slice. "Lucky girl."

"He wasn't hot," I say.

"That's because you love Crazy Hair," Kristen teases.

"Speaking of him," I begin. "Turns out he's the client that Viktor got me a job with."

"No!" Kristen and Lacy say in unison.

"Yeah. So that was awkward."

"Spill," Kristen commands, tapping my arm. "Tell us everything!"

"The jackass played a prank on me on my first night translating. Saying a ton of stuff I couldn't tell reporters. I had to make up answers on the spot. It was super embarrassing." I pull a pillow to my chest and hug it.

"Why would he do that?" Lacy asks.

"He said it's what hockey players do. Prank the rookies." Just thinking about it gets me all worked up. Again.

"What did he say?" Kristen asks.

"He made fun of a reporter's glasses and said I had a nice ass."

"And you're mad, why?" She twists her face in confusion.

"Come on, KK. It was my first night on the job. He was trying to make me mess up and look like an idiot."

When Kristen starts to open her mouth, I lean over and put my palm over it.

"Stop. Even if I do find it in my heart to forgive him, I cannot date him. He is my client. In a professional job," I say.

When my best friend licks my hand, I recoil and wipe it against my jeans. "You're disgusting."

"I think you're making too big a deal of it," she says. "I'm not saying it wasn't a jerk-off thing to do. I'm just saying it could've been way worse."

Perfect time for a subject change. "Greg told me I didn't have stage presence."

Kristen scrunches up her face and sticks her tongue out at me, but I ignore the immaturity. "How do I get that?"

"I know! I know," Lacy exclaims. "You've gotta have a sexy outfit and a sexy song. *And* you have to sing it sexy."

"Keyword—sexy," Kristen teases.

Lacy continues, undeterred. "You have to make him want to get in your pants before the song is through. But don't let him," she warns. "He's sort of like your boss, isn't he?"

"Okay." I sit up and roll my head from shoulder to shoulder like I'm about to check into the biggest game of my life. "Ultimate sexiness and no getting in my pants. Got it. Anything else?"

Lacy bursts out laughing. "You should wear those leather pants you have. You really do have a great ass."

I guess Aleksandr was right.

"I think black, smoky eyes with a red lip, very rock and roll," Kristen adds. "Maybe a nude lip. Red might be a bit much with the eyes."

"No! She should definitely go with red lipstick. A matte rather than a gloss. We want to make an impact," Lacy agreed. "It's not a date. It's an audition for rock chick."

I stop listening, since it's clear my opinion won't be factored into the equation. Let these girls figure out my look. I need to come up with a song and that "stage presence."

I love music and can name a song that corresponds to every significant event in my life. So why isn't one popping out at me? Maybe because I don't know what an audition song is supposed to be. I don't know what songs work best with my voice. When I sing, it's whatever I'm thinking about or listening to at the time.

My friends and I discuss the outfit possibilities for over an hour before we can't stand it any longer and start experimenting. After trying on what feels like a hundred different clothing ensembles, from jeans and a vintage Rolling Stones T-shirt to a skintight black dress, I finally decide on one.

As the clock ticks closer to eight p.m., Kristen and Lacy work feverishly, straightening my hair and applying makeup. They want to get done with enough time to spare for a dress rehearsal.

When I step in front of the full-length mirror hanging on the back of my closet door, I don't recognize myself. My hair falls in soft, blond waves down my back, glistening with shine serum. Kristen did an amazing job on my thick, black-rimmed eye makeup and the deep, red lip stain she and Lacy decided on, but I'm stunned by the outfit I chose.

My boobs are the focal point of my costume, having been maneuvered, taped, and squeezed into a black corset top. I have a sinking feeling they'll pop out if I hit too high a note. A pair of black leather pants I bought last year when I dressed up as Gene Simmons from KISS for Halloween sit low on my hips, while red patent heels complete the ensemble.

You look like a streetwalker, Gram's voice echoes in my head. That had been her comment on the one occasion during high school when I'd worn black mascara and coated my lips in sheer pink gloss instead of my normal Lunar Lime Lip Smackers.

"I can't wear this." I shake my head and begin unbuttoning the pants.

Lacy slaps my hand. "You look hot. Leave it alone. Here." She thrusts a bottle of vodka at me. "Stop worrying and loosen those hips."

"Hope this helps me figure out how I'm going to get out of the house in this outfit." I salute my friends before squeezing my eyes shut and taking a tiny swig. "No chaser?" I squeak, handing the bottle back to Lacy.

"Buck up, Auden. Act like a lead singer." Lacy lifts the vodka to her lips, then passes it to Kristen.

In an effort to calm my nerves, I count sheep as I scroll through the music library on my laptop. Kristen and Lacy are my friends; they wouldn't let me bomb my first audition.

"Thanks for coming," Greg greets me, holding the door open until I walk through. I follow him down a flight of stairs.

"This place is amazing." A complete music studio takes up the entire basement. I immediately feel better about auditioning at Greg's house. It's not as sketchy a situation as I'd imagined.

"Yeah, my dad's a musician, so he lets us practice here when I'm home from school." Greg shrugs. "That's Josh." He points to a tall, skinny guy with spiky black hair sitting behind a full drum kit.

"I'm Aaron." A short guy leaning against the far wall raises his hand. I hope he's starting dreads, because his light brown hair clumps in various spots, like he's twisted it that way to get them started. "'Sup, beautiful?"

"It's Auden," I correct him in a sharp tone. I want them to treat me as an equal, not a piece of meat.

"Alrighty then." Greg slips a guitar strap over his neck. "What do you need us to play?"

"Do you guys know Social Distortion? 'Making Believe'?" I ask, looking from Greg to Josh to Aaron.

Josh's blank face and Aaron's scowl tell me they don't. Great, I've pissed them off in the first two minutes.

"How the fuck are we supposed to know that?" Aaron asks. He

turns to Greg. "I thought you said she was singing the Violent Femmes."

"She can sing whatever she wants." Greg glares at Aaron.

I try not to let the guitarist's glower throw me off. This is all in good fun, just me stepping out of the tiny box I'd sealed myself in when I'd chosen soccer above all other interests.

"Sorry." I tuck hair behind my ears. "I know it's a random song."

I hoped the comment helped mellow the situation. Instead, it's met with more blank stares and more scowling. So far, the audition is going exactly as I'd imagined.

Crash-and-Burn Berezin at my best.

Since I've never auditioned before, I have a difficult time keeping my pitch singing a cappella while remembering to have some sort of stage presence. As I get lost in the song, I go with the moves that come to me, hoping that nodding my head and rapping my hand against my thigh with the beat impresses them.

When I finish, I look up through the thick, fake eyelashes Lacy glued to my lash line. None of the guys speak. Josh moves to the edge of his stool and crosses his arms over his chest. Greg and Aaron stand off to the side, assessing my performance, I assume. Nerves pulse through me as the silence persists.

"That was fucking wicked!" Josh yells, jumping off his stool. "Where did you say you found her? Karaoke at O'Callahan's?"

I chuckle to myself as I fasten the microphone back into the stand and let them talk like I'm not even in the room.

"Sing another," Aaron demands, challenging me without looking up. He's still standing as far away as possible.

"Sure," I say, pausing a moment before breaking into "I'll Stand by You." It's one of my favorite songs, plus it's a believable ballad to accompany my rocker-chic facade.

Greg joins in first, strumming along with my lyrics. After a minute Josh jumps in, too. Pulling the microphone from the stand, I approach Aaron, like a cheetah stalking her annoyed prey. I touch his shoulder, but he shrugs me off. When I start serenading him using ridiculous, exaggerated hand and arm movements, his lips curve into a smile.

"You're mental," he says.

I don't even attempt to deny it.

"All right, we've heard enough," Greg says flipping a switch that cuts off the microphone. I walk back to the stand grinning. Humor can break almost anyone down.

"So, what did you think?" I ask.

"You've got a great voice. You're obviously hot," Greg says quickly, before turning to his bandmates. "We're considering you."

"Are you considering many others?" I ask. I don't want to get my hopes up, but I'm interested to find out if I have competition.

"We got nothing," Josh says. Though it sounded more like "Me mot mutten" because he's flicking a lighter at the cigarette dangling out of the corner of his mouth.

"Dude! You can't smoke in here," Greg tells him. Josh rolls his eyes, but lowers the lighter.

"I appreciate you guys letting me audition." I start toward the stairs, but then stop and turn around before my foot hits the first step. "So, um, when should I expect to hear from you?"

"When you come back on Wednesday for rehearsal," Greg says.

"Seriously?" I ask.

"After our old singer left, we ran ads in the Central State Post and on the campus radio station. A few people tried out, but no one with pipes like yours. I still can't believe you've never sung before." Greg shakes his head as if in disbelief.

"Awesome. Thanks. Oh, I have a job, so is it okay if I check my schedule and let you know when I can be back?"

"Are you kidding me?" Aaron asks. "You know this takes time and dedication, right?"

Geez, I thought I'd won that dude over.

"I swear, I'm not trying to be a jerk," I explain quickly. "I just got cut from the soccer team and I have to have a job because I lost my scholarship."

"Damn. That's harsh." Josh grabs a black hoodie off the chair next to me.

"Yeah, well—" Aaron's eyes lose some of their fighting flare. "See you later, Auden."

"I'll walk you out," Josh says.

I climb the steps two at a time, push the door open, and hold it for Josh, who's on my heels.

"Holy shit. I'm in a band," I say, unable to contain my excitement.

"Welcome to the jungle." Josh cups a hand around his cigarette and flicks his lighter multiple times to unfavorable results. The blustery winds won't let up, so I stand in front of him to shield the next gust.

"You're a kick-ass girl." He turns his head and blows the smoke away from me.

"Gotta take care of my boys." I wink and skip to my car.

Very rock and roll.

Soccer. A band. It's all the same to me. And it feels damn good to be part of a team again.

Chapter Eight
AUDEN

"Soccer. Kerby Field. I'll pick you up in ten minutes," Drew Bertucci orders when I answer the phone the following morning.

"It's out of your way. I'll just drive over there," I hold the phone to my ear with my shoulder, crawling to shut my bedroom door.

"I'm going through Auden withdrawals," he whines.

"Okay. I'll be ready."

Drew is one of my oldest friends, having known each other since second grade. One of my favorite childhood memories is when we rode our bikes to the sports store three blocks from my house to buy hockey cards when one of us would come into some birthday or holiday cash. Our friendship survived even after I'd made a fool of myself in eighth grade by writing him a note asking if he wanted to be more than friends.

The lesson: Don't write down your feelings about a guy. And if you do, don't ever share them with him. Unless, of course, your heart is made of rubber and you can bounce back from the embarrassing backlash unscathed.

I trade my pj's for a Liverpool F.C. T-shirt and soccer shorts, then pull on black warm-ups over that. After shoving my cleats and shin guards into my duffel bag, I throw it over my shoulder and wander into the living room to wait for Drew.

Grandpa is lounging in his recliner when I drop my bag and park myself into the chair across from him.

"What are you doing with that?" Grandpa asks, eyeing my soccer duffel.

Evidently, when you're cut from a team, you can never play that sport again.

"I'm heading over to Kerby to play with some kids from high school."

"What kids?"

"Drew and the hockey guys," I answer, knowing my answer would end Grandpa's interrogation. Drew is on the approved-friends list because our families have known each other so long. Drew's parents went to high school with my mom.

When I hear the three quick honks signaling his arrival, I grab my gear and run out the door, calling goodbye to Grandpa over my shoulder.

"Hey, Drewseph!" I say, sliding into the passenger seat of his faded red SUV. Drew comes from a large Italian family where it seems like everyone is a Joseph—except him.

"What's up, Aud?" he asks, alternating looks over his shoulder and in his mirrors as he backs out of the driveway.

"Not much." I shrug. "Just working. Viktor set me up with a job for the month."

"Translating the Communist Manifesto?"

I laugh. He knows all about my previous projects. "No. He let me work with a real person this time. I'm a translator for a hockey player."

"Really? Who?"

Drew, a former hockey player himself, choose to focus on his studies when he didn't get a scholarship to play at a big state school. He said he'd rather give up hockey to go where they had a Landscape Design program than attend a small school that didn't have his major just to keep playing.

"Aleksandr Varenkov from the Aviators." I kick an empty water bottle rolling back and forth on the floor.

"No way." Drew glances at me.

"Way," I reply, happy to be around a friend I'd known so long we have inside jokes.

When we were in seventh grade, we had a movie marathon. Since neither of us could drive, we had to choose movies from his dad's collection. We'd picked Wayne's World, Tommy Boy, and Billy Madison. Absolute classics. People still quoting them today is totally understandable.

"I heard he's—" Drew begins.

"Douchey?" I supply.

He snorts. "Exactly."

"He's not so bad. I've learned how to rein him in."

"I bet. He's got a reputation with the ladies."

"Oh my gosh, Drew! That's not what I was talking about." I smack his thigh. "I meant, Viktor will kick his arrogant Russian ass if he steps out of line."

As I say it, I realize, I never told my grandfather about Aleksandr's prank. Deep down, I don't want him to take me off the job.

"Okay, good. I didn't want to hear that you were one of his conquests."

"He knows I'm not a bunny."

"You're a hot girl hanging around hockey players. To them you're a bunny."

Frowning, I give Drew a sidelong glance. "I'm hanging around with hockey players for *my job*," I emphasize. "It's not like I'm going to bars with them."

"Don't get involved with him, Auden."

The big-brother role, which I've appreciated every other time he's played it, annoys me now. Where does he get off trying to interfere in my dating life? I hold back my anger, as I always do with my friends. I don't have very many, so there's no reason to rock the boat with the close ones I do have.

"You don't have to worry about that. I called him out in the locker room in front of his team. It was in Russian, but I think he got the point."

"Good. I've heard he's a total dick afterward."

"Oh! This isn't about protecting me at all, is it? It's really about you trying to hook up with Varenkov's leftovers? No wonder you're mad," I joke, pinching at his bicep in an attempt to ease the tension between us.

"I am looking out for you." He shrugs off my hand and my comment.

"Thanks, Drewseph. I appreciate your concern," I say, hoping he understands I'm being sincere.

A few silent minutes later, Drew whips his Explorer into a parking spot at Kerby Field.

Instead of following Drew toward the group of guys warming up near one of the soccer goals, I scout out an empty patch of grass on the sideline near the white chalk line and sit down. The dry, brittle blades prickle my calves when I tug off my warm-up pants. Though the ground is hard and frozen, the grass's earthy scent is so ingrained in me, the memory of the smell alone brings me close to tears.

Being cut from Central State's soccer team hadn't only been a hit on my college finances, it majorly bruised my entire sense of self. Soccer, the one thing I excelled at and never gave up on, had been taken away from me.

Coach Tamber's words still echo in my head: *There's no easy way to put this, Berezin, but we're gonna have to cut you. We've got some talented upcoming freshmen, and we need to make room. Now, I'm not saying you shouldn't try to walk-on next year. I just can't hold your spot.*

Or my scholarship. Or my pride. Or how I've defined myself for the last fourteen years. See ya, Soccer Girl.

I should have realized my dismissal was imminent, having sat the bench for most of my two seasons on the team. Most players sat as freshmen, but when sophomore year came and went and I'd only played a few minutes total, I saw the writing on the wall.

Still, I hung on to that last optimistic thread of severed rope I'd been grasping, hoping I'd get my chance. Was I the most talented player? No. But I worked my ass off and practiced harder than anyone on the team.

Shaking my head to dismiss the thoughts, I check out the crowded field. Guys I've known for years are scattered across the grass. A few went to high school with Drew and me, but the majority are guys Drew played with on travel hockey teams. As the only girl who's ever been invited to play, you'd think I'd have dates for the rest of the year.

Nope. None of the guys have ever expressed interest in me. Granted, I'd been shy in high school and didn't speak up much, but still, not one of them found me even remotely attractive?

No wonder I went boy crazy when I got to Central State.

A few feet away from me, a guy jumps up and down tapping the top of his ball in an alternating pattern, left foot then right foot. It's someone I've never seen at the field before, but recognize immediately.

Aleksandr in all of his soccer-shorts-wearing, Mohawk-pulled-back-in-a-ponytail, ridiculously-muscled glory. His thighs and calves alone are a testament to how much time he spends working out. As my gaze travels upward, my mind flashes an image of his half-naked body. I blink a few times as if that will erase the memory of the magnificent work of art under his shirt.

Without thinking, I run up behind him and steal the ball.

"Hey!" Aleksandr calls, looking up with narrowed eyebrows as I dart away. His annoyance fades, and he smiles. "I didn't know you'd be here."

"I play with these guys all the time." I wave to a kid I'd gone to high school with then spin around and pass the ball back to Aleksandr. "Who invited you?"

"Your twin."

"Excuse me?" I don't have any siblings.

"Landon's brother, Jason. He looks just like you." He nods to the circle of guys juggling balls. The one next to Landon Taylor has dirty-blond hair very similar to my color, but I can't get a good enough glimpse to see if we have more similarities.

"Not mad at me anymore?" Aleksandr's question catches my attention in time for me to see him send the ball back to me.

I stop it with my left foot. "I'm over it. I just want to finish out the month."

Which is true. I'd taken Kristen and Gram's advice to heart. His prank could've been a hundred times worse. I can handle a few more weeks of his immature shenanigans.

"You're going to get back at me by kicking my ass out there, aren't you?" He nods to the field.

"Scared?" I ask. I can't be sure, but I think I puffed out my chest—chimpanzee-challenge style.

"Stand down, Berezin." Aleksandr holds his palms up. "I deserve whatever you give me."

"It's all in good fun, *Sasha*," I say, rocketing the ball at him. He jumps, and the ball bounces off his broad chest and onto the ground near his feet.

I'll be using the Russian diminutive of his name in public from now on. If anyone notices that *Audushka*, a makeshift diminutive of my non-Russian name, sounds like a feminine care product, they could tease him because his sounds like a girl's name.

Aleksandr kicks the ball. I follow as it sails over my head and drops in front of Drew.

"Game on!" Drew yells. He gives Aleksandr an evil-eye assessment. It reminds me of an overprotective father meeting his daughter's date for the first time, just before telling the poor kid he has a shotgun.

"That's English for, I'm about to kick your ass out there," I say to Aleksandr, then turn my back and dart to the other side of the field.

"Good luck!" Aleksandr calls to my retreating figure.

"I'm not the one who'll need it," I sing over my shoulder.

Confidence is so easy for me on the soccer field. Out here, I can ignore the ridiculous way my heart pounds around him.

The group divides into teams in a quick, militaristic manner. I'm playing opposite both Aleksandr and Drew. In any other situation in my life, I would be timid and nervous about not having a friend on my team, but this is soccer.

On the field, I step out of my body and ignore my hyper-vigilant, over-analytical mind. On the field, I talk trash and kick ass. If Aleksandr thinks he can beat me at my own game, he'd better think again.

It's an intense and fast-paced match—as it always is with these guys. I played center midfield for the first half, setting up one goal and scoring another. I'd railed through the defense without having to throw any elbows, as I'd expected.

This group plays no-referee soccer. No red or yellow penalty cards. The boys never take it easy on me, which I learned the hard way the first time I'd played with them and left the field with bruised ribs. The injury taught me to defend myself better and learn a few of their dirty tricks.

In the second half of the game, I move back to play defense. Despite my team racking up two goals, Aleksandr's team had scored three against us. The score held at 3–2 through most of the second half. We don't use a time keeper, so the game ends when both teams decide we've played long enough. And my teammates and I aren't finished yet.

Jason, the dirty blond that Aleksandr called my twin, took my place at center mid. He boots the ball up the field to catch one of our forwards on the fly. Drew sprints between the attackers, intercepting the pass. Soon, he's in our zone, dribbling the ball down field with a burst of speed and intensity. He passes to a teammate on his left without even a side glance. The ball rolls out-of-bounds off the foot of our defender.

As I walk backward toward the goal, I notice Aleksandr is my man to cover. We jostle for position as his teammate gets ready to throw the ball inbounds. If I do nothing else the rest of the game, I will not let Aleksandr beat me. It doesn't look as if he'll let me win either.

Fair enough.

When the ball sails inbounds, both Aleksandr and I jump up to head it. I plant my hands on his shoulders, hoisting myself higher since my five-foot-four frame could never beat a six-foot-tall man to the ball. After smacking the ball away with a brutal flick of my head, it sails up the field and into the possession of one of my teammates.

"That was bullshit," Aleksandr says between labored breaths, as we jog up the field to join the play.

"All's fair in love and war."

"Which one is this?" he asks, lips tilting upward.

"War," I growl, watching the play develop at the other end of the field.

"I disagree." Aleksandr races up the field, leaving me in the dust.

Literally. He kicked up so much dry dirt as he sprinted away, I feel like Charlie Brown's friend, Pig Pen.

My teammate misses a shot, at which point many of the guys start calling for the end of the game.

Aleksandr and I walk to the side of the field together. I take a long swig out of my water bottle before offering it to him. Drew and a few other guys come over as well, teasing and congratulating one another. A few guys slap me on the back or rustle my hair, welcoming me back and telling me they missed me.

Irritated, I pat my hair down as if my palms hold magical smoothing powers.

"Are you getting a ride home with your friend?" Aleksandr asks.

"Yep." I pull on my warm-up pants.

"Hang out with me. I'll drive you home." Aleksandr drags a tattered gray hooded sweatshirt over his head. On the upper-left chest, there's a small red flag with a yellow hammer and sickle below a star in the left corner.

There's a faded yellow stain a few inches below the frayed crew neck.

I imagine a young Aleksandr and his parents eating lunch at a picnic table in a park with the magnificent onion domes of Saint Basil's Cathedral looming in the backdrop. As the Varenkov's feast on hot dogs and potato chips, his father raises his hot dog to his mouth, and a dollop of mustard falls onto his favorite sweatshirt. Aleksandr and his dad laugh as his mother tries to blot it away, warning her husband that the stain will be there forever. Mr. Varenkov just smiles and says it will be a constant memory of the wonderful day he's had with his family.

The fake memory I've conjured highlights how American I am, even in fictional day dreams. I sincerely doubt Russians sit in Moscow's city center eating hot dogs and potato chips.

"You know the Soviet Union is no longer, right?" I joke, rubbing the goose bumps on my arms beneath my warm-up jacket.

He looks down at his chest and laughs. "It was my father's."

"Daddy-o still stuck in the Soviet era?"

"I guess you could say that. He's dead."

Chapter Nine
ALEKSANDR

"Oh my gosh, *Sasha*, I'm so sorry. I didn't mean to make fun of it—of him." The silly smile slips from Auden's lips as she apologizes. She rakes her hand through her hair, avoiding my eyes as if both embarrassed and horrified.

"It's okay," I assure her, grabbing her hands and tugging her to her feet. "It's old and stained, but it's the most comfortable sweatshirt. And it reminds me of Papa." I shrug.

Talking about my parents doesn't make me uncomfortable. It makes *other people* uncomfortable, but not me. Though still young, I was old enough to appreciate them and the time we had together. I'm eternally grateful we had a good relationship. They always supported me and my dream to play hockey.

Though death is part of life, it's still difficult to comprehend when someone is taken from your life unexpectedly.

I try to treat people in a way where my conscience is clear if something tragic happens. I guess it's my personal byproduct of trauma.

Which is why I need to apologize to Auden for my prank. I didn't mean any harm, but she took it personally.

Gribov told me And it's my duty to apologize when something I do offends someone—even if it was unintentional.

"I totally get it," she says, nodding. "I have this old softball shirt from when my mom was in an adult league with her friends. It's white, and the fabric is so thin you can see straight through it." She laughs. "But I love it."

"Can you wear it to the next game?" I wink.

"With anyone else I would be totally embarrassed right now," she admits.

"But not with me? Why not?"

"I've gotten used to your sense of humor."

"Are you sure that's it? Maybe you're thinking about how much you want to parade around me in a skimpy top."

My teasing—but true—comment strikes a major embarrassment nerve. When her cheeks turn pink, I almost apologize. But Drew interrupts our conversation before I have the chance.

"Ready, Aud?" Drew asks. He's jumping up and down to keep warm.

She bites her bottom lip as she thinks about her options. She wants to stay with me, but she thinks she should go home with him.

And I want to take that lip into my mouth...

"I'm gonna hang with Aleksandr," she says after a long pause. "He said he can give me a ride home."

"Auden?" Drew's voice lifts, scolding her as if she's a child.

She shoos him away with a wave of her hand.

"Whatever." He shakes his head and knocks into my shoulder as he blows past.

My jaw twitches and I count to five in my head. "Should I let that go?" I ask out loud, then nod and answer my own question. "Yes, I will let that go."

I watch him jump into his Explorer and slam the door before turning my attention back to Auden.

"I have protective friends," she says as if it's an explanation for Drew's rude behavior.

"He's just a friend?" I ask.

"So, you guys won last night." She ignores my question.

I chuckle. "How did you know?"

"Read it in the paper."

"It's kinda sexy that you keep track of me when I'm on the road."

"All part of the job," she assures me, though her cheeks don't lie. The rosy pink color is a telltale sign I caught her caring about me.

We trade the grass of the soccer field for a wood-chip-covered playground. A swing set with six black U-shaped seats swaying in the wind sit empty a few feet away from a tall, metal slide.

Auden drops her duffel bag on the dirt and claims one of swings. She takes a few steps backward to push herself off, but doesn't get a good start. I move forward and place my hands on her back, propelling her forward with a swift push.

She looks absolutely elated sailing through the air with the wind against her face, like she truly appreciates the childlike magic of a swinging. As she takes herself higher and higher using the pumping power of her legs—all I can think about is taking her higher and higher using the pumping power of my cock.

It's been hard to focus on anything else since I met her.

But I need to apologize for being such a douche before she'll ever start thinking about me the way I think about her.

"I'm sorry I embarrassed you the other night. I thought I was being funny."

My voice must interrupt her euphoria, because she drags a foot in the wood chips to slow down.

"It's fine." She shakes her head. "I'm the one who blew it out of proportion. Sorry for yelling at you in front of your team."

"I deserved it."

"No, you didn't. What I did was totally unprofessional."

"Unprofessional," I repeat, smiling wryly. "Of course."

"This is the first time I've ever gotten to work with a real person. Grandpa always had me translating documents before. I just want to prove I'm good enough."

"Good enough? You speak Russian better than Gribov." I laugh.

"Don't even talk about that guy." She shudders at the mention of my teammate. Which is weird because Gribov has always been popular with the ladies.

"A woman who doesn't want to talk about Pavel Gribov? I can't wait to tell him."

"He was an ass to me for no reason. I don't even know what I did to piss him off."

"Maybe because you don't stare at him in the locker room. Most women want to see him naked. He gets fan mail about it."

"I don't stare at anyone," she says quickly.

"Not true."

"Who do I—" she begins, but must realize I'm talking about myself. "I'll admit, when he has his teeth in, he's attractive. But there are plenty of hot guys who aren't nice people. Now all I see is the ugly. It works the opposite way, too."

"Which one am I?"

"Attractive. Inside and out."

"Whoa!" I sit up straight on my swing. "Does this mean I'm forgiven?"

"Yeah, but I still have to figure out how to get back at you," she teases.

I love that she's finally comfortable enough with me to let loose. "Wasn't wearing that black dress punishment enough? I need to keep my pants on when you're around."

She drops her eyes to my legs, which are covered by gray fleece warm-up pants.

"My hockey pants, I meant. I'm not usually excited by things in the locker room, you know? And my hockey pants keep, uh, they keep things hidden."

She smirks, rubbing it in that she's given me a taste of my own medicine.

I'm so comfortable talking to her, I feel like I'm talking to one of my boys. But I respect her too much to use any crude terms for an erection like I would around them.

Instead of keeping the boner-talk going, I change the subject. "Did you ever audition with that band?"

"I did." she shakes her head slowly. "And I made it."

"That's awesome."

"Thanks." She takes a deep breath and catches my eyes. Her hands twist in her lap. "I'm sorry I made fun of your sweatshirt. I didn't know about your dad."

"No worries, *Audushka*. How could you know?" I smile, but my mood dulls slightly. I hate that she feels like she has to apologize. She didn't know and I didn't take any offense. "What about you? What happened to your parents?"

"What about them?" She crosses her arms in front of her chest as if shutting me out.

It feels like we've taken one step forward two steps back in a matter of minutes. But we've come this far, so I persist.

"You live with your grandparents and you said something earlier about having an old shirt of your mom's. 'Happy families are all alike; every unhappy family is unhappy in their own way.'"

"Could you be any more stereotypically Russian?" she asks. "Quoting Tolstoy, drinking vodka, playing hockey."

A deep laugh straight from my belly bursts out. It does sound ridiculously Russian. "Don't be jealous because Americans can't quote great literature like Russians can."

"My dad ditched me before I was born and my mom was killed in a robbery when I was six," she blurts out.

"Shit! I'm sorry, *Audushka*." I don't know what else to say. I wasn't expecting anything like that.

"Don't worry about it." She shrugs as if dismissing me. "It's been a long time."

But I won't be dismissed—and I won't let her off the hook, either. If asking questions gets her this defensive, it means she needs to talk about it. "Did they find the person who killed her?" I ask.

When she locks eyes with me I can't tell if she's angry or—dare I say it—*touched* that someone asked. I assume most people change the subject when she tells them about her parents. Because that's what people do when they're uncomfortable don't know what to say.

But I want to know everything about her; her background, what makes her tick, what makes her eyes light up like they did when she was swinging.

"I don't think so. I doubt anyone is even working on it anymore." She drops her gaze to her feet, pushing at the wood chips under them. "Murders are a dime a dozen in Detroit. My mom's case is freezing cold by now."

"Never having any justice, any closure, has to be frustrating for you."

"I used to believe that the police would find her killer and my life would go back to normal, but that's not how it works. The damage has been done." She squeezes her eyes shut for a moment. "I have to live with a bad decision someone else made and hope karma really does exist." An empty, bitter laugh escapes her lips.

"Both my parents were killed," I murmur, reaching out to brush a strand of hair out of her eyes and tuck it behind her ear. "I wish I could believe some force in the world will provide justice."

"They were?" She bolts upright and backs out of my reach. "I'm, geez, I'm so sorry."

"It was a car accident," I clarify. "The traffic in Moscow is bad, um, heavy, yes? They were taking back roads trying to get somewhere faster. A bus turned onto the side street they'd taken and hit them head-on. They had no chance."

Her eyes widen and she swallows hard, which makes me think she's never had someone confide something so personal before. She's probably never known anyone who understands what she's been through.

"You didn't get closure either. You never got to say goodbye."

"No."

"Are you okay?" This time she's the one leaning toward me. Her fingers are stiff and alert as if she's ready to brush away tears.

"I am Russian. Cool head, blazing heart," I respond, tapping my temple, then my chest.

It's such a lame thing to say. I've cried before. I just don't do it in public. Taking a moment to embrace my pain and let it out is for myself, not for others.

Silence falls between us. As bizarre as it sounds, sitting together with our sorrow is comfortable. She drops her gaze to the wood chips at our feet while I stare at the cars on the street in the distance.

"Do you think about your mom a lot?" I ask, interrupting the tranquility of the moment.

"Probably more than I should," she says quietly.

"What do you mean?" I cock my head and turn to face her. Strands of hair that had fallen out of her ponytail during the game hang in her eyes.

"It's been fourteen years and I still think about her all the time. I should get over it, but I can't. I can't let it go. I can't stop thinking about how she left me."

"She didn't leave you, *Audushka*. She was taken from you."

"I was with her in the ambulance on the way to the hospital. Kids aren't allowed, but I wouldn't leave her, and I made her tell me she wouldn't leave me. She promised me she wouldn't leave me." As she speaks, tears glide over her cheeks. "I know she didn't leave on purpose, but tell that to a six-year-old. All I've ever known, all I can remember, is being left."

She drops her head into her hands, as if embarrassed.

I jump up, pull her off the swing and into my arms, whispering, "Shh" into her hair. Her shoulders shake as horrible thoughts that have plagued her throughout her life spill out—maybe for the first time.

I wish she would take solace in my arms, but she stiffens and tries to struggle out of my grasp. I've been in the same position she's in before, so I do what I needed at the time—I hold her.

"And now I don't remember her at all, *Sasha*. I don't remember her voice or her smell, not even what she looked like. I don't remember one single moment with her. It's like my brain has blocked out my entire life with her."

"It's okay," I whisper, using the palm of my hand to rub large circles across her back, wishing they could infuse strength into her.

"Have you ever seen that eighties movie Pretty in Pink?" she asks, lifting her eyes to mine. When I shake my head, unfamiliar with the title, she continues. "There's this scene where one character who talks about a friend who didn't go to a big school event when she was younger. She always feels like something is missing. She checks her keys, counts her kids. But nothing is missing." She pauses. "Some days I wake up and think something's missing. I check my keys. I check my wallet. Nothing is missing. Except my mom. She will always be missing. And no one understands the feeling."

"What about your grandparents? Have you spoken with them about it.

"Yeah, right. Every time they look at me, they see their dead daughter. I'm a constant reminder of their loss." She hangs her head.

Without thinking, I reach out and lift her chin, . "No! Auden, that's not how it works. They look at you and see life—not loss."

"I'm a horrible burden to them. They should have been able to enjoy their retirement, but they couldn't because they had to raise me."

"Your grandparents knew what they were doing when they took you in." I squeeze her tighter.

"But should a child have to feel like a burden?" she asks. "To live life believing that nothing is permanent? Believing everyone I love will leave me someday? Is that what my life is supposed to be like?"

"No, *Audushka*." I stroke her hair. "No one should ever have to live through what you have. You aren't alone anymore. I know what you're going through, what you're feeling. Talk to me. Lean on me."

"Oh geez! I'm sorry, I'm so sorry. I'm so fucking selfish." She wiggles out of my arms and covers her face with her hands. But I'm not letting her do that. I pull her back immediately, enveloping her as she shakes.

"You're angry and lonely. It's okay to show your feelings. It's okay to be scared and upset. We'll get through it," I assure her, rubbing her back.

She allows herself a few fleeting seconds but I can feel her discomfort. Suddenly, her body stiffens completely and she wriggles out of my arms again. Then she jumps up and backs away, stumbling toward the parking lot. She bring her hands to her face, wiping away tears and snot. She's only gotten a few feet away when I run to catch up.

I wrap my arm across her shoulders and squeeze her to me. "I'll take you home."

Her body is filled with a tension that refuses to release its paralysis of her body.

"Thanks," she mumbles, watching the leaves shrivel under our feet with every step.

The ride to her house is silent, with the exception of the directions she provides between snot-sniffs and hiccups.

When I pull into the driveway, I shift the Jeep into park and kill the engine. "I'm here if you want to talk. You can always call me." I put a hand on her leg, but her body goes rigid, and she grabs the door handle.

"Thanks for the ride."

I can't let her leave like this. Embarrassed and angry. Just as she's about to escape from an emotionally intimate situation neither one of us knew was coming, I reach out and grab her forearm. Her head snaps back and our eyes meet.

I move my hand to her face and stroke her temple with my thumb. Thankfully, she doesn't protest or pull away.

"Whenever I start a car, I see my parents' accident," I whisper. "I see it happening to me. Every time I turn the key something bad could happen, but I still drive." I drop my hand and twist the key in the ignition, revving the Jeep to life. "I can't change the past. Can't escape the fear. But I can't let that fear paralyze me. Sometimes you have to take a chance."

Chapter Ten

AUDEN

Ever since Aleksandr dropped me off, I can't stop thinking about the conversation we'd had. He seemed surprised that I didn't know much about my mother's murder or the investigation that followed. I'd been six years old at the time. How was I supposed to remember what had happened? My family doesn't share information with me now, let alone at that age.

My grandparents raised me to accept what I was told and not ask questions. They view questions as outright defiance, rather than curiosity. As I got older and more well read, accepting their unyielding perspectives proved difficult, resulting in constant head butting during my high school years.

My mind wanders, sparked by a curiosity I'd never felt before. I've done internet searches—and there's nothing except basic public information like birth and death records. If I want information, I need to look in the only place I might find some. Lucky for me, both of my grandparents are gone when I get home. Unsure of how much time I have until they return, I need to be quick.

Taking two steps at a time, I bound up the shag-carpeted steps to my grandparents' attic bedroom. I almost fall as I slide across the slippery wood floors at the top of the staircase. I cross the room, jumping onto the bed, and rolling to the floor on the opposite side.

Very stealthy.

A gray fire-safe cabinet sits against the far wall of the room, directly under a window. My grandparents keep their important paperwork and valuable jewelry and keepsakes in the cabinet.

I kneel in front of it and reached around the back, swiping my hand across the back until I feel a small, magnetic box stuck to it. "Bingo." I pluck the case off and slid the top open, scooping out a small key hidden inside.

The cabinet stores numerous treasures, tiny boxes and soft, black zippered cases. I know the bronze satin box holds Gram's engagement ring, since she'd let me see it before. I tried it on, but it doesn't fit on any finger except my pinky. Another ring-sized box, this one made of white cardboard, holds six silver charms from Western states. I recognize the charms because Gram had shown these to me as well.

My mom had bought them for me on a family trip out West. I was only a year old at the time, so I don't remember the trip, but I've seen pictures of myself in my mom's arms at a Grand Canyon overlook and standing on the Four Corners, where Arizona, Colorado, New Mexico, and Utah meet.

I peek into a few more boxes containing random pieces of jewelry belonging to my grandmother, before pushing them aside.

I twist my arm and reach deeper into the back of the cabinet, where I find three raggedy manila envelopes. The thickest packet contains my report cards for all the years I've lived with my grandparents. I skim them with amusement. I'd been a talker when I was young, but any low conduct marks were negated by A's and B's down the line after each subject. Oh, except the D in math in fourth grade. Fractions killed me.

I stuff the report cards back into their longtime home and lift another envelope. When a rectangular Mass card from my mother's funeral falls out, I know I've hit the jackpot—if I can call articles about a murder a jackpot. Since I'm in super-sleuth rather than abandoned-daughter mode, I decide I can.

I pore over the words, even though I've read an identical card hundreds of times. I folded my copy into a tiny square and shoved it inside the pocket of my soccer uniform shorts. Even though she never saw me play soccer, it was my way of having her at every game with me.

I set the card beside me and upend the envelope, emptying the contents. Various newspaper clippings from the Detroit Times and folded papers spill onto my lap. One of the articles even contains a sketch of the might-be murderer. Though it isn't very descriptive, looking at it gives me goose bumps. The face peering out from the newsprint doesn't look familiar at all. It's just one of millions of men.

I scan the articles but they don't mention any names, just a description of the events of that night and a plea to readers to contact Crime Stoppers if anyone had information. I don't remember anything about that night, which I should consider a good thing. It's bad enough that I was there to witness it. And as much as I want to know what happened, I don't think I could handle having the details burned into my memory.

Every article is from an inside section of the newspaper. Why hadn't my mom's murder been on the front page? Why hadn't there been organized manhunts for her killer, like there are for others? What kind of murder was good enough to be the lead story on the eleven-o'clock news?

She was one of many. We live in Detroit—not small-town USA. This city is in the running for murder capital of the country every year.

I pick up the Mass card from my mother's funeral again and reread her name until my vision blurs.

I was so young when she died that I don't remember anything about her. I only know what she looked like because I'd raided all of my grandparents' photo albums in search of her.

There aren't any pictures of her displayed in their house. Why have a picture on display when it could increase the likelihood of someone asking about her? Especially if that someone was me, a disregarded daughter desperately craving snippets about what my mother was like when she was alive.

Was she excited to be pregnant with me? Was she sarcastic and wisecracking like the rest of my family? Would we have fought or been best friends? What would my life have been like if I had been raised by my mom?

Was it horrible and ungrateful to think that way when my grandparents had sacrificed the best years of their retirement to take care of me?

Would I have loved my mom as much if she were alive as I loved her dead?

But I realized a long time ago that life moves on despite the "I wonders" and "what-ifs." The only choice I have is to go on, hoping I'll realize I was strengthened by it all.

How long would it take to get there?

How long would it take for me to stop wishing I was the one who had died that night? How many times have I wanted to take her place, instead of being forced to live without her?

Unsure of how long I sat staring at the words printed on the back of the Mass card, I snap back to reality when I hear a car door slam. I shove the papers into the raggedy envelope, ram it back into the metal cabinet, and lock it. Then I slide the key into its plastic box, attach it to the back of the cabinet, and run around my grandparents' bed.

As I rushed down the stairs, I smack right into Grandpa, unable to put on the brakes in time.

"Sorry," I apologize, taking a step back up the last stair.

"What were you doing?" he asks, looking past me, as if someone else will appear.

"Trying on Gram's boots," I lie. "I wanted to wear them out this weekend."

Lying comes fairly easy for me. I don't do it often, but when I do, it's believable. Another defense mechanism I'd built up to hide my feelings and not allow people to get too close.

"Boots, eh? Not snooping for Christmas presents?" he asks, backing away from the staircase so I can jump off the last step.

"Come on, *Dedushka*! Would I do that?" I laugh.

"Of course not, *Audushka*," he says and rolls his eyes. "Stay out of there until after Christmas. I know how you like to peel back the wrapping on the side of presents."

"I did that one time." I edge past him, scowling in exasperation. "I was eight!"

People in my family never forget anything they can use against you later.

Chapter Eleven

AUDEN

"He was such a jerk." Kristen leans forward to switch the radio station as I drive us through the streets of Grosse Pointe Woods, a suburb of Detroit. She lands on the country channel.

"Country? How are we even friends?" I ask, reaching over to turn the dial back to the local alternative station. "My car, my music." I bat her hand away as she leans in to change the channel again.

Kristen falls back against the passenger seat. "Fitness instructor, kid lover, charitable giver. I thought he'd be like you—but a guy, you know?"

"I told you, he was only helping at the center because of some frat's community service hours," I say. "And for the record, I'm not sure how I feel about you comparing your dates to me."

"Chill. It's not like I want to jump your bones. I just thought he'd be like you, all Mother Teresa and shit."

"Get out of my car." I shoot her a sidelong glance.

"Mother Teresa wouldn't have talked to me like that." She snickers and pulls down the visor to fluff her curls in the mirror.

"Well, of course not. I don't think she had a car either."

"Ha-ha," Kristen deadpans. "Have you changed your mind about doing bad things with Crazy Hair?"

"He's a client. Viktor would kill me." Which is true, but allowing myself to do bad things with him is no longer an option after my breakdown at Kerby Field.

Breakdown at Kerby Field has a nice ring to it. I'll have to keep that title in mind in case anyone wants to make a made-for-TV movie based on my future book, *Memoirs from the Psych Ward.*

"Can *I* do bad things with him?"

"No!" I protest. Too quick and too loud. Am I scowling at her?

"You totally want him."

"But I can't have him."

"We'll see," she sings. I turn up the volume on the radio to cut off the conversation.

We're on our way to pick up Scott, Lacy's boyfriend, and one of his friends whom we don't know. They're hitching a ride with us so they can meet up with friends of theirs in Canada. Even though Lacy is in Marquette visiting her grandparents, we agreed to give him a ride anyway. I don't know what she sees in him. Scott is one of the biggest jerks I'd ever met.

"Hey, girls," he greets us as he climbs into the backseat. "Jeremy, girls. Girls, Jeremy."

"Thanks for the ride," Jeremy slurs, collapsing next to Scott.

Great. As if Scott isn't annoying enough, he and his buddy have already been drinking.

"Why do you go to Canada when you don't even drink?" Scott tugs on a piece of my hair that hangs over the headrest. I flick my head to make him stop.

Since he's always hanging around our apartment, Scott has observed me restrain myself on many nights, and he never passes up a chance to tease me about it. He still hasn't graduated from junior-high dickhead mentality.

I shrug. "I can still enjoy our neighbor to the south without getting plastered. A packed dance floor helps."

I drink, but not very often anymore—a couple of beers here, a vodka and club soda there. I think I've been buzzed a few times, but I haven't been drunk in over a year. I got bored with the getting-drunk-and-hooking-up part of my life before I even turned twenty-one. Plus, my sobriety ensures that we'll have a safe ride home after partying in a foreign country tonight.

Especially since no one else ever volunteers to be DD.

Did my choice to rein in my drinking as a junior in college make me more mature or more depressing? Maybe that's what Gram meant when she said I was an old soul.

"Isn't Canada our neighbor to the north?" Jeremy asks.

"You have to go south to get to Windsor from here." Scott holds the back of his fingers to his mouth and stage-whispers, "Jeremy's from Ohio."

"Ohhh." I nod.

At the same time Kristen says, "That explains it."

"Fuck off." Jeremy shakes his head, but he's smiling. No love lost between Michiganders and Ohio—ans?—people from Ohio.

"Does Ohio have enhanced licenses?" I ask, tucking my hair behind my ear, concerned about Jeremy's ability to get in and out of the country.

Michigan offers an enhanced driver's license for residents to go back and forth between Canada and the U.S. without needing a passport. I would have never thought to apply for one, but my grandparents surprised me with a trip to the Hockey Hall of Fame in Toronto for my seventeenth birthday. It's come in handy for going to bars since turning nineteen.

"Nah, I have a passport," Jeremy answers.

"Ooh. Where have you been, world traveler?" Kristen twists in her seat toward Jeremy.

"My dad got remarried in Saint Thomas a few years ago. It's a US territory, but we all got passports just in case."

"I want to go to the Virgin Islands." Kristen grabs my knee. "Save up for spring break senior year."

"I can't even afford a cell phone, KK. How am I gonna go on a tropical vacation?"

"Florida then?"

"Good compromise." Scott scoffs.

Time to change the subject. Unlike Scott, not all of us have parents who can afford to pay for international spring break trips every year.

"I remember my uncle talking about a bar Don Cherry owned. Is that place still open?" I ask. Scott always brags about how often he hangs out in Canada, so I figured he's the one to ask about the status of the bar.

"That place has been closed since we were kids."

"Who's Don Cherry?" Kristen asks.

"How are you two even friends?" Scott asks.

"He was a hockey coach. Now he's a commentator," I explain. "You know, Coach's Corner?"

"The guy with the high collars?" she asks.

"High five!" I hold up my hand. "I'm proud of you, KK. Very, very proud." The obscene amount of Hockey Night in Canada I'd subjected her to in our two and a half years as roommates had paid off.

Though the conversation continues, I tune out the chatter and my mind zones to Aleksandr. Thoughts of him have filled every crevice of my brain since the moment we met. Talking with him feels so comfortable, which must be why I completely overshared after the soccer game. But he didn't react the way most people I know would have. He didn't make up an excuse to leave or change the subject. He listened and even understood and comforted me.

That nagging voice in the back of my mind is why I can't get him out of my head. I'm attracted to him and he showed me attention—the insecure girl's favorite combination for heartbreak.

When we get to Windsor, I drive straight to Wicked, our favorite club. A prickling sensation sizzles through my body when we leave the chill of the December night and enter the warmth of the building. Exposed, matte black pipes form a maze across the ceiling while columns and blood-red walls envelop me in industrial comfort.

The best part? Writhing bodies already pack the dance floor, and it's only ten-thirty. A lively dance floor early in the night is the saving grace for a designated driver. If I'm dancing, I don't have to dodge the "Why aren't you drinking?" question all night.

"Let's dance!" I shout, after Kristen and the guys tip back shots. We all grab a drink before bouncing through bodies to the middle of the dance floor.

"You like to dance?" Jeremy asks as we claim a somewhat open spot on the floor.

I touch his arm, leaning close to his ear so he hears me. "Love it."

Jeremy spins around and grabs his crotch in what I can only describe as a drunk Michael-Jackson-wannabe move. Of course, I take it as a challenge and come back with the Swim, alternating my arms in front stroke movements before holding my nose and wiggling to the floor.

Within minutes, we're entrenched in a battle of retro dance moves. For every Kid 'n' Play and Shopping Cart he throws out, I return a Tootsie Roll or Sprinkler. I can't remember the last time I'd had so much fun.

"What are you drinking?" Jeremy asks, still breathing heavy from our dance-off.

"Just a club soda, thanks." I appreciate that he'll brave the crowd at the bar for me.

After less than a minute to catch my breath, "The Wobble," a song with its own line-type dance moves, blasts through the speakers. Kristen clamps a hand over my arm and drags me toward a bar on which a few girls had been dancing during the previous song.

"Not tonight, KK." I try to pull away, but she's persistent, even pulling a bar stool aside to give me something to boost myself up.

"Oh, come on. You teach this dance. You have to get up there," she coaxes.

She's talking about the children's cardio hip-hop fitness class I teach at our university's student center. I use "The Wobble" as the cool-down song in my class.

Sighing in defeat, I climb up a rickety bar stool, and hoist myself onto the alcohol-slick bar.

Totally sober. In a curve-clutching black minidress and stilettos.

Super classy, Auden.

I haven't always been a good dancer. I used to have to count the beat and lip-sync through the numbers. But teaching a class helped me understand and get better. Plus, "The Wobble" is even easier than the Electric Slide, so I don't have to worry about messing up.

Jeremy waves to get my attention, then points to the drink he's placed on the bar for me. I mouth thank you and give him a thumbs-up. I watch as he and Kristen start talking, then wander away from the dance floor. So much for my Wobble partner.

Halfway through the song, I get bored and carefully step onto the bar stool I'd used to get onto the bar. I stop to grab my drink before setting out to find Kristen.

"Don't you work tomorrow?" a voice yells in Russian.

"Geez!" I tighten my grip on my drink so it won't slip out of my hand. My heart betrays me, accelerating more from the excitement of seeing him than the surprise attack. The correct move is to quash that feeling. "Didn't realize I had a curfew."

"Why are you mad at me again?" Aleksandr asks.

"I'm not mad. I'm embarrassed," I admit, crossing my arms in front of my chest. Why don't I have a filter when he's around?

"Does my presence piss you off?" He nods toward my stand-offish stance.

I drop my arms, but now there's nothing between us and he's standing too close. "Just wondering how we ended up at the same bar in Windsor again."

"You have good luck?" Aleksandr's mouth is so close to my ear that his lips touch it every third word. I'm keenly aware of the soft tickle against a very sensitive body part.

"I get enough of your jokes at work. Can't you tone it down during my leisure time?"

"I can't seem to tone myself down around you at all. I thought we established that." Now I feel his lips on every second word. And this time his nose brushes the skin behind my ear.

His presence has the bees buzzing in my stomach like they'd mistaken Death Wish coffee for nectar. I take a slight step to the side, silently reminding myself that Aleksandr is a player, not someone I should get involved with. He'd told me himself that he's with a different puck bunny every night.

And I don't want to step into an uncomfortable, immature pattern of hooking up with someone I still have to see every day. Even if the feeling of over-caffeinated insects wreaking havoc on my insides has its own agenda.

Aleksandr moves closer. His firm, flat stomach presses against my arm when he bends to speak into my ear again. "You are beautiful."

"You are drunk."

He laughs, a sexy, husky growl that makes my knees weak. "I am, but I'm not blind. You looked so fucking hot dancing on that bar." He isn't yelling this time. His voice is just above a whisper, with a guttural rasp.

Instinctively, my shoulder rises to my ear, itching at the tickle of his breath. I try to stay composed, despite being turned on by the knowledge that he'd been watching me.

"Thanks." I take a long gulp of my drink to halt the words on the tip of my tongue.

Confessing that I think he looks hot every minute of every hour of every moment I spend with him might give him the wrong impression. I can't respond to his flirting. Not when all I am is a conquest to screw and dump.

"Blah." I rake my teeth against my tongue a few times, trying to get the taste off. Nothing like being saved by a disgusting drink.

"What is it?" Aleksandr asks.

"I asked him for plain club soda. They must've put gin or something in it."

"Who's 'him'? All the bartenders are women," Aleksandr asks, taking the cup from my hands and bringing it to his nose.

Of course he'd know all the bartenders are women. He's probably had an orgy with all of them.

"The guy who came with one of our friends bought me a drink."

Aleksandr tosses my cup into a nearby trash bin and grabs my hand. His warm fingers lace through mine, squeezing so we won't disconnect as he weaves us through a group of people hanging out in front of the bar.

Aleksandr nods his head at a bare-bottomed bartender. "A shot of vodka and a plain club soda with three limes."

Skimptastic winks at him before turning around to get cups. Her shorts, which were barely there in front, are nonexistent in the back, just two high-cut half-moons that show off her ass—et. Sure, she has fishnet stockings underneath, but do holey tights leave anything to the imagination?

No reason to be jealous. He's not yours, I remind myself. Rather than picture Aleksandr and Skimptastic screwing on the bar, I root around in my purse, hunting for my wallet.

Aleksandr puts a hand on my arm, stopping my search.

"You don't pay when you're with me."

"Why wouldn't I pay for my drink?"

"Consider it a gift for putting up with my shit." He smiles, that perfect white smile, which I now know is partially dentures.

"Sorry." I shake my head, holding out a ten I'd found. "Can't accept gifts from clients."

"Please," he says. "It's a club soda. She won't even charge me."

When Skimptastic comes back with our drinks, Aleksandr accepts them both before handing one to me.

"Thanks, *Sasha*."

"I'm *Sasha* now?" He pokes me in the rib cage as a smile creeps across his face.

"Yes. When you do nice things like get me a new drink," I respond, pushing his arm away with an elbow. His teasing makes me want to giggle, but giggling is not an option.

"I'll do nice things more often. I probably shouldn't be a jerk to my beautiful translator."

"Yeah, let's get back to that." I turn to face him, ignoring the shiver of lust that shook my body from him calling me beautiful. "You never begged for my forgiveness."

"I wouldn't beg for forgiveness." Aleksandr leans closer. His fingers skim the back of my leg where the hem of my dress hugs my thigh, and I gasp. "Your permission? Definitely."

Damnit! Why do I have to react to his touch right in front of him? Am I so hard up for a guy's hands on me that I can't hold in a damn gasp?

Yep. It's been over a year since I've hooked up with anyone—around the same time I stopped drinking so much. Interesting how those two things go hand-in-hand.

"Why did you order me three limes?" My lame subject change is obvious.

Aleksandr chuckles before answering. "You always have three limes in your drinks. Figured that's how you liked it." He shrugs and tips back his shot, like knowing how to order my drink is no big deal.

Maybe it isn't for him. Maybe he's one of those annoying life-of-the-party, people-pleaser type guys.

"Thanks for the drink. I've got to find Kristen." I nod to the dance floor.

Aleksandr barely registers my goodbye, since his eyes have narrowed in on someone at the end of the bar. I watch him slam his shot glass down before stalking toward his prey without a second glance at me.

A part of me wishes he would have waited until I left the vicinity before finding another girl to hit on, but, *oh well.*

I stumble away, suddenly feeling light-headed and dizzy. Crossing the crowded dance floor proves to be more of an adventure than it should be. I bump into more people than I can count as I search for Kristen. I had one drink when we got to the club over an hour ago, then switched to plain club soda. One sip of that last one shouldn't have caused me to be so unbalanced.

I stop to get my bearings and scan the crowd, but I can't focus. A glob of colors swirl in front of me as faces blur into one another. When I take another step, my stomach rolls and the floor drops. Throwing out an arm, I catch my balance on the shoulder of a guy dancing. After a wave of apology, I elbow through the crowd, willing the vomit rising in my throat to stay put until I make it to the bathroom.

As I push open the door to the women's bathroom, I panic at the length of the line. Thankfully, the girls can tell a puker when they see one, and they all let me stumble into the next open stall. One girl even follows me in and holds my hair out of my face as I heave into the toilet.

My legs shake and I grip the wall for assistance as I stand. I thank the girl who helped me before I stumble to the sink to wash my hands. As I rinse my mouth, Kristen barrels through the bathroom door.

"Aud! Are you okay?" she asks, pushing sweaty, stringy hair out of my face.

"I got sick," I tell her, making a face in the mirror.

"Why do we come to Canada again?" She fishes a travel-sized bottle of mouthwash out of her purse. As I take a swig and swish it around, she retrieves a powder compact from her purse.

I hold a hand up and bend to spit before she presses the soft puff across my forehead, nose, and cheeks. Neither the puking nor the makeup make me feel better. I still feel light-headed, as if I could pass out.

Kristen lowers the compact. "You still don't look good. You want to get going?"

I nod, holding my forehead with my palm, unsure if I can walk to the car.

Kristen grabs my free hand, weaving us through the bar with expert precision. She leaves me near the door so she can close out her tab. A few minutes later, Jeremy bounces into my peripheral vision.

"Come back out there with me," he coaxes, grabbing my arm. I shake my head, but he's strong, and his tug wrenches me away from the wall.

"I do not think she want to dance right now," an accented male voice growls.

Jeremy drops my arm. "What the fuck, man?"

"Maybe I do," I tell the voice.

I know the voice. I'm trying to be a hard-ass. A swirly stomach, light-headed, just-puked hard ass.

"Then you dance with me," Aleksandr commands, encircling me in his arms. The song blasting through the speakers isn't slow, but I don't care. I immediately feel safe wrapped in his embrace, swaying to the music. Resting my head on his chest, I shiver in anticipation of breathing in his sweet scent of clove cigarettes and mountain-fresh soap again.

Instead, he reeks of stale beer, which annoys me because he always drinks vodka. I want to strip off his smelly clothes and push him into the shower. I want to run my hands over the muscular swell of his arms and the ripples of his chest and abdomen. I want to push him up against the cold tiled wall and taste his tongue as hot water pelts our skin.

"Are you okay, *Audushka?*" Aleksandr asks against my ear.

I can barely hear him with the thump of the bass in the background. I shrug against his chest, nestling deeper into his arms, enjoying the fantasy while I have the opportunity.

"I need to get you home," Aleksandr whispers, warm breath tickling my neck. The same part of my brain that's having shower fantasies about him wants me to cover his mouth with my own, but I'm unable to lift my head.

"*Audushka?*"

His voice sounds miles away. Why is he leaving me?

"*Audushka!*"

My chin drops to my chest and my head rolls to the side, as strong limbs push me away from the warm mountain I'm clutching. Suddenly the floor disappears, and I'm wheeled through the air, as if on a Ferris wheel. I hold on tight to the pole in front of me, in case I fall off.

"Get your fucking hands off her!" someone yells.

The pole I'm holding staggers back a few steps before staggering forward. I feel the force of hitting something, but I don't feel any pain. It's the last thing I remember before everything goes black.

Chapter Twelve
AUDEN

A forceful knock on my window wakes me up, though I have no recollection of how I got into my bed or when I fell asleep in the first place. My head pounds and my mouth feels like I chowed down on the stuffing in a Pillow Pet.

I pull the covers over my head, convinced that the wind and a tree branch caused the noise I'd heard, until the heavy rap starts again. My hands shake as I continue to hide, curling my fingers around my blanket.

If you ignore things they go away, I remind myself.

Then I laugh, because ignoring everything is my family's pathetic mantra. It's never worked before, but, for some strange reason, I hoped tonight would be an exception. Soon the rap turns to scratching and fumbling as someone tries to open the window.

"Auden," a voice calls in a loud whisper from outside.

Awesome. Whoever it is knows my name. I lay still for a moment, deciding it's probably a positive sign, but still.

Just go away, I silently will the intruder.

"*Audushka*, open the window. It's fucking freezing!"

My heart speeds up as I throw the blanket off and kick my feet until it lays in a pile of fleece on the floor. Stumbling out of bed, I lurch toward the window and pull up the shade to find Aleksandr jumping up and down, rubbing his hands together.

"What are you doing?" I ask, after unlocking the latch and shoving the window upward. Though I know my bed head is untamable, pushing the hair away from my face makes me feel better.

Aleksandr clutches the windowsill and attempts to propel himself through the opening but fails and falls back to the ground. Literally falls. Not that the drop is very far.

"I needed to see you," he says while brushing dirt off his butt. "I couldn't wait."

I glance at the clock: 3:06 a.m. "You couldn't wait until I get to the arena later?"

"No. I could not." He hoists himself up again. His knuckles change from pink to white as he grips the window, and his feet scratch against the house like he's scaling a flat rock wall.

Grabbing hold of his biceps, I jerk him inside, unapologetic about causing his graceless face-plant onto my floor. Serves him right.

I poke my head outside before sliding the window shut. A person jumping in through the window of a house at three a.m. might be a normal occurrence in many parts of Detroit, but we still have a few good neighbors who would be alarmed.

"Is this what you sleep in?" Aleksandr reaches for the hem of my pink plaid boxer shorts, which I've paired with a vintage Sergei Fedorov T-shirt. His eyes aren't focused.

Is how I look at three a.m. that repulsive?

"You expected lingerie?" I deadpan. What the hell is he doing here?

"No, it's perfect." He smiles. His hand misses the hem of my boxers and grazes my bare calf.

"Holy!" I jump when his Popsicle-fingers touch me. "Get up, would you? What's your deal?" I fake agitation, but excitement is probably the best word to describe my feelings. It's not like guys sneak into my bedroom all the time.

Or ever.

Collapsing onto my bed, I lean over and snatch my blanket from the floor before whipping it over my shoulders and snuggling into it.

The temperature of my room must've dropped ten degrees with the arctic winds swirling in through the window.

Aleksandr crawls to my bed and climbs in next to me. Suddenly aware of my cold and braless state, I pull the blanket tighter around my shoulders.

"You look perfect," he slurs, closing his eyes and leaning toward my face. When I scoot back, his face falls into my lap, which isn't the kind of kiss I'm looking for either. I inch back again, accidentally banging his head with my knee.

"Fuck." He rubs his chin.

"Sorry!" I reach out to touch his face, as if my palm, like a mother's kiss, can take away the sting. "I'm so sorry. I didn't mean to do that."

He catches my hand and pulls me toward him, wrapping me in his arms and pressing his lips to mine. This time, I don't pull away. I let the warm, firm touch of his lips devour me.

He pushes me onto my back and crawls over me, pinning me down, without taking his lips from mine. As he lowers himself onto me, the metal zipper of his leather jacket touches the bare skin of my stomach where my shirt has ridden up, and a tremor shakes my whole body.

When something hard under his jacket jabs my rib cage, it's the wake-up call I need to stop things from going too far.

"*Sasha!*" I shove him back, and try to slow the erratic heartbeat. "What is up with you?"

"I needed to make sure you were okay," he says, caressing my side from under my arm down to my hip and back up again. Then he leans down and presses his lips to my collarbone.

"We shouldn't do this," I whisper, as a shiver courses through my veins. I'm about to lose all control when something pokes me in the ribs again. "What the hell is in your jacket?"

Aleksandr sits up, digs into his coat, and removes a half-empty bottle of vodka. Then he unscrews the cap and takes a long pull before offering it to me. I shake my head.

"Forgot I brought this." He screws the cap back on the bottle. "I love when you call me *Sasha*."

Aleksandr seizes my lips again, his tongue plunging into my mouth to explore. Then he catches my lower lip with his teeth and tugs.

While he kisses me, he squeezes my hips as if my love handles can save him from drowning.

Despite my intention to keep things platonic between us, I get completely lost in his touch. His fingers slip under my shirt, and his calloused thumbs skim the skin of my stomach. When his hands creep under the waistband of my boxers, I jump like a mischievous cat who's been squirted with water.

Aleksandr pulls his hands out and jerks his head up. "What's wrong?"

"Did you think we were going to have sex because you got drunk and climbed in my window?"

"We don't have to have sex, *Audushka*. There are other things," he says, placing his fingers where they'd been a magnificent moment ago. His lips curve into a sexy smile, causing the skin around his eyes to wrinkle. "Unless you want to?"

Hell yes, is the truthful answer, but I won't admit that in the position we're in.

Or ever.

"What are you doing here?" I ask instead.

"I wanted to make sure you were okay," he repeats, releasing my boxers and rolling onto his back, fumbling to remove his coat. After a few sloppy yanks at the sleeves, he finally tugs off the jacket and throws it to the end of the bed.

Did I miss something?

I don't get a chance to ask because I hear my grandparents' bed creak, and bolt upright. Startled, Aleksandr sits up, too, scanning the room for an invisible attacker.

Shit.

Please don't come down to use the bathroom, I mentally will whichever grandparent is stirring. It wouldn't have surprised me if one of them heard the window incident because they aren't very sound sleepers.

I place my fingers over Aleksandr's mouth to keep him from speaking, and sit sculpture-still on the bed while I listen for more noises. After a few minutes of silence above us, I chalk it up to someone rolling over rather than getting out. When I lower my hand, Aleksandr clotheslines me at the waist, taking me down to a lying position.

I giggle, though I still can't relax. My mind is all over the place. "*Sasha*, how did you get here?"

"Jeep is outside." He closes his eyes and pats the bed in search of something. When he finds my hand, he laces his fingers through mine. "I think."

"You think?" I ask, pulling my hand away. I'm too paranoid to continue this surreal experience.

"I maybe have driven. I am home, then I am climbing through your window."

"Are you joking?"

"I don't know," he says, opening his eyes in confusion. "I might be."

I jump out of bed and rush into the living room. Pushing up on my tiptoes, I crane my neck to see out the tiny window in the front door. His Jeep isn't on the road. It isn't in the driveway either.

At least he hadn't driven. How the hell had he gotten here? And how was he getting home?

Somewhat relieved, I turn to return to my room and run smack into Aleksandr.

And he's almost naked.

Evidently, the treacherous ten-step journey from my bedroom to the living room was more than his clothes could handle. His discarded T-shirt lies a few steps behind him and his jeans pool around his feet.

The hard planes of his chest and defined stomach muscles take my breath away. His tattoos, which I've noticed during shirtless interviews with the media but never had the opportunity to see in depth, are amazing.

Intricate, swirling Cyrillic script spans the length of both his sides; bold, haunting, beautiful. Maybe I'll ask him about them on a day when we aren't at each other's throats, or in a situation like this— which I still can't explain.

Pushing aside questions about his tattoos, I rub my face with my hands to regain a semblance of composure.

That's when he decides to drop his boxer briefs.

"Jesus, Mary, and Joseph," I hiss, using one of my grandma's favorite expressions.

I stand in front of him, mouth agape because I've never seen a naked man in real life.

Near-nude men fill the Aviators locker room while I translate, but strategically placed towels always cover any indecent parts.

I've seen tons of photos of models wearing their pants so low you can see the V of their pelvic bones and the "happy trail," but I've never seen where the trail led. Sure, textbooks from health class have drawings of male parts and how they function, but a scientific drawing doesn't prepare me for seeing the real thing. It's actually not that intimidating, but then again, it's not "ready for battle."

Stop looking, Auden!

"*Sasha*, my grandparents are upstairs," I whisper. "You need to get dressed."

"No. I need to take a piss," he responds, scratching his head.

Hoping Aleksandr understands the universal sign for shhhh, I put a finger to my lips. Then I grab his hand and lead him to the bathroom, stooping to scoop up his clothes on the way.

I stand outside the door and let him complete his business. When he stumbles out, I place my hands on his back and direct him toward my room. He raises his arms and stretches as he walks, his muscles ripple under my palms. A shiver of lust courses straight to that sweet spot between my legs.

Thankfully, Aleksandr has the decency to slip on the boxer briefs I stuffed into his hands before he climbs into my bed and passes out. Cold.

I scan my room for the next best sleeping option: dresser, desk, or floor. I'm sure as hell not going to be the one on the floor.

I grab one of Aleksandr's arms and try to pull him out. When he doesn't budge, I remember from reading the Aviators media guide that I'm tugging on two hundred pounds of dead weight.

I step back from the bed and cross my arms over my chest as I strategize. Then I snap my fingers and climb over him. This time, I place my hands on his back and push with all my might, but quickly realize I have the same problem as pulling. I think about leaning against the wall for leverage and pushing him out with my feet. But that isn't a good idea because of the noise his body hitting the floor would make.

I sigh in defeat and, because I have no other option, shimmy under the covers. I snuggle up to him, laying my head on his chest since his massive body takes up my entire twin-sized bed. With his steady heartbeat as my personal lullaby, I let the rhythm of my head rising and falling with his shallow breaths rock me toward sleep.

Is it possible for the peace inside him to transfer into me? I reach out and brush my hand through the Mohawk I love so much.

When I hear another creak from upstairs, I freeze.

When I hear footsteps, I bolt up.

I shake Aleksandr's shoulder a few times, but he's still dead to the world. "Oh, come on!"

I'm worried because my grandparents usually check on me during the night. It's either still a habit from when I was a kid, or they want to know if I've made it home from the bar.

I shake Aleksandr again, harder this time. No response.

My heart races as I contemplate what I should do next. Pull the covers over him and run to the closet? Climb on top of him to give the illusion of only one bump? Time is running out with each heavy footstep pounding the stairs.

I yank the blanket over Aleksandr's head and sling my arm and leg across his body, so it looks like I'm hugging one of those long body pillows. I don't own a body pillow, but it's not something whichever grandparent looks in on me would register at this hour.

Sure enough, I hear the door swoosh against the shaggy red rug in front of it. There's no light on in the hallway, so I have complete darkness going for me. I squeeze my eyes shut, which doesn't make me invisible, but makes me feel better. I wouldn't be surprised if whoever stood there could hear my heart as it bumps hard against my chest, attempting to escape. I hold my breath until the door shuts again, then let it out slowly.

I stay motionless until I hear the toilet flush, the faucet turn on and off, and heavy steps plod up the stairs. I'm not sure if I move until I hear the familiar creak indicating someone has gotten back into bed.

This sucks.

All the kids in high school who bragged about how exciting it was to sneak people into their rooms were big fat liars. Who could handle the pressure? It's not fun. It's not rebellious. And it's definitely not worth the stress. It's not like I would do anything with Aleksandr in my bedroom while my grandparents were upstairs.

Although he *was* naked at one point. And we had been making out. Some people might consider that "doing something."

I remove the covers from Aleksandr's head, hoping I haven't accidentally suffocated him.

Nope. Still breathing.

Time to get comfortable. I press my body against his, wrap an arm around him, and hug his back. It feels awkward, and I'm not sure if I can sleep that way. I turn around, so my back touches his, and curl up. But sleeping like this doesn't feel comfortable either.

What's my problem? It's not like he'd be mad if he woke up and I had my back to him. And why should I care if he wakes up angry? Let him be pissed. He's the one who knocked on my window at three in the morning, drunk.

I yank my pillow out from under his head and flip it to the cool side before nestling into it.

Chapter Thirteen
ALEKSANDR

"What the fuck?" I whisper through a yawn, lifting up to my elbow as I try to figure out where I am.

"Nice language."

Auden's voice grounds me in reality and I realize I'm in her room. In her bed, to be exact. The night before comes rushing back.

"Oh, hey." I say, looking down at her. Then I smile and laugh nervously as I survey her room.

"Morning," she replies. Her eyes are bright and her hair frames her face in soft, messy waves.

"Damn, girl. You are really hot first thing in the morning." I lean over and press my lips to hers.

Evidently, she didn't expect that sort of greeting because her eyes are wide in surprise.

"Are you still drunk?" she asks when I pull back.

I laugh, wondering how a human so gorgeous doesn't even realize it. "Probably, but I would've done that anyway."

"Well, you shouldn't have done that. Doing something drunk is one thing. Doing it sober is totally different."

"Good thing we've established I'm still drunk then." I look around the room before stopping on the window I vaguely remember climbing in through last night. Embarrassment floods me. "Oh shit, Auden. Did we? Did I?"

"Absolutely not," she assures me. "All we did was sleep. You climbed in my window, made out with me, and stripped before passing out cold."

"I climbed in the window?" I ask, rubbing my face with my hands.

"Don't worry about it." She pats my bicep. "Happens all the time."

I raise one eyebrow, calling her bluff. "Really?"

"Yep, just another fun night."

"I took all my clothes off?"

"Uh, yeah." She rolls her eyes. "You dropped trow in the living room."

"Drop trow? What is this?"

"You dropped your boxers. Like, took them off completely."

I pause, vaguely remembering following her into another room and then having to take a piss. "That's right. And you liked it, if I remember correctly."

"Your memory deceives you," she says, pulling the covers up to her neck. "I didn't even look."

She's totally lying. I can tell be the way she won't meet my eyes.

"Sorry about that." But I'm not. I just wish I would have remembered doing it so I could have caught her reaction.

Her mouth curves, and that tiny little dip in her lip appears. I love that I put the real-smile dip there. I love that she isn't faking when she smiles at me, even if she is just being a flirt.

No. No. NO.

No more loving things about her. Coming here last night was one of the worst drunk ideas I've ever had.

Except, I'm not sorry because I was really worried after Landon dropped her off. I knew that prick she thought was a friend slipped something in her drink. And I didn't know how it would affect her.

She shakes her head and narrows her eyes. "No, you aren't."

"True," I admit, stretching my arms toward the ceiling. "But I am sorry I don't quite remember it all."

Suddenly, her entire demeanor changes, and she looks panicked.

"How the hell are you going to get out of here?" She runs a hand through her bed-head, until it gets stuck in a snarl.

My dick jumps when I think about how fucking sexy she'd look with sex-hair.

"Same way I came in?" I ask, squinting at the window.

"Yes. Do that. Now."

She pushes my shoulders, pressing her palms into the sable ink on my chest and pushes me as hard as she can. I fall onto the floor, landing on my ass with a thump.

"Thought you were trying to be quiet," I deadpan.

She leans over the bed, chewing her bottom lip. "Sorry."

"I'm sure." I roll my eyes and crunch myself into a sitting position. Her eyes widen and she swallows hard. "You've got a little drool there." I point to my own chin.

"Shut up," she says, holding the blanket over her. Which I don't understand, because I know she's not naked.

Using my unfortunate position to take action, I scan the floor for my jeans and grab them. I'm sliding my jeans up my legs when I hear heavy footsteps descending the stairs.

"Get in the closet," Auden says in a panicked whisper, pushing me toward the door with her foot.

I bat her toes away. "You're kidding, right?"

"Please, *Sasha*. It's just until *Dedushka* goes into the kitchen to have his coffee," she pleads.

It's a good thing I like this girl, because there are not many women that I would hide in a closet for. I swipe my shirt from the floor, before stumbling into the tiny space.

And I *do* mean tiny. I can barely fit with all the clothes hanging and shoes all over the floor. I kick a pair of boots to the side and stand on a pair of flip flops because they're the flattest thing on the ground.

"Sorry," she says through the door.

"I bet," I mumble.

It's actually kind of comical. I've never been with a girl who had to hide me from her parent—or grandparents. But I know this is a unique situation, as she's home from school for a month-long break.

I push the hangers out of my face, then dig into my pocket for my phone. As soon as I press the flashlight, her closet comes alive—and it's a whole lot of black.

I flip through a few coats and hoodies before finding something that feels like leather. Intrigued, I remove them from the hanger and find another thing underneath.

A red lace tank top.

Damn. This girl has a super sexy side.

I've still got the clothes in my hand when I hear Auden come back into the room, so I drop them quickly.

When she opens the closet door, she hands me a weird dry rectangle-shaped thing and a glass of orange juice. "I got you breakfast."

I stuff half of it in my mouth, chewing for a moment before frowning and looking down questioningly at the "food."

"It's a Pop-Tart," she responds, evidently noticing how puzzled I am.

"You call this food?"

"You've never had a Pop-Tart before?"

I shrug and take another bite. Even the inside—which I assume is supposed to be the "good part"—is absolutely disgusting and now my mouth is so dry it feels like I've been walking in the Sahara for days. No wonder she brought something to wash it down.

After downing the orange juice in one gulp, I crouch down and grab the clothes I dropped. "When do you wear this?"

"Church," she answers quickly, grabbing the sexy gear and throwing them back in the closet.

"Seeing you in that could make me a believer."

She hip-checks me out of the way and shuts the closet door. "Time for you to go. I need to get showered."

"Can I join?"

"Still drunk?" she asks again.

"Definitely," I agree, setting the empty glass on her desk.

Time to get out of here the same way I came in.

I finish getting dressed quickly, then open the window and swing a leg out.

"*Sasha.*" She grabs my arm.

I look up, searching her light blue eyes.

"Last night you said you came over to make sure I was okay. Why would you think I wasn't okay?"

"You don't remember?"

She shakes her head.

"That Jeremy guy put something in your drink. You got really dizzy and sick. I carried you to the car. Landon drove you home."

"Are you kidding?"

Her eyebrows knit together as if she's trying to remember what happened at the bar. I doubt much of it will come back to her. Roofies are pretty good at erasing someone's memory. And any guy who uses them on a girl deserves to get fucking beat down.

Which is what I did to Jeremy, but I don't want to tell her that. I'm not a violent guy, but I was so absolutely livid at what he'd done to her, I couldn't stop.

"It was completely fucked." I shake my head and start out the window. Then I pause and turn around. "I'm glad you're okay, *Audushka*."

"Thank you." When she touches my hand, I lift my gaze and our eyes meet again. The sincerity of her gratefulness is apparent. "Seriously."

Without thinking, I lean in and peck her lips.

She responds with a flustered huff, which makes me laugh. "I swear I'm still drunk," I say, swinging the other leg over the sill and jumping out.

When I look back, she's leaning out the window watching me retreat, so I shoot her a wave before bursting into a jog.

It's been a while since I really liked someone. After my last girlfriend stomped on my heart, I put my sole focus on hockey.

Relationships are a distraction.

But Auden is different. She's beautiful, wicked smart, speaks amazing Russian, and she's got a beautiful heart.

I unlock my Jeep and climb in, pausing before I start the engine. Which makes me think about my parents and the love they had. They rarely fought, and when they did, it ended with kissing—and usually sex.

Not that I watched or anything, but we lived in the same one-room apartment with my grandparents. There was no other place for them to go. I think they waited until I was asleep when I was a kid, but when I got older, I'd just put the covers over my head and pretend to be asleep.

Maybe that's why they had me try out for a hockey program that had us in barracks eleven months of the year.

Papa told me he fell in love with my mother the first time they met, and he wouldn't stop at anything until she was his.

If Auden thinks she can resist me, she has no clue the force she's up against. My father's blood runs through me and I'm a professional athlete. When I know what I want, I won't stop until I get it.

Chapter Fourteen
AUDEN

"What's going on with you and Aleksandr?" Kristen asks when I pick up the phone, instead of the usual hello in which most people begin conversations.

"Nothing," I say through a yawn, holding the phone to my ear with my shoulder. I should have ignored the ringing, but I knew my grandparents would wake me up for the call anyway.

Why didn't anyone want me to sleep today?

"Um, yes, there is something. He left here last night completely plastered saying he had to check on you. And he didn't come back until this morning."

I spring up, grabbing the phone before it fell. "Excuse me? What do you mean 'here'? Where is 'here'?" I ask, ignoring her interrogation by starting my own.

"Landon's."

"You're at Landon's? You spent the night with Landon?"

"He drove us home last night. I didn't want to make him drive all the way to New Baltimore."

"You could've stayed here."

"Shut up and answer my original question."

I smile. Kristen and Landon. It's not an odd combination, since

Kristen is a grade-A knockout. I just didn't expect to hear her say it. I'd never even seen them have a conversation. Which doesn't mean much, since most of the night is absent from my brain.

"He said Jeremy drugged my drink." I fall back on the bed, closing my eyes as I inhale Aleksandr's clove scent wafting from my pillow.

"Yeah. I can't believe Scott would even bring that frickin' psycho."

"You can't?" I ask.

While I don't believe Scott brought someone to hurt us intentionally, I'm not surprised he has the kind of friends who would drug girls. I've seen enough crazy shit at college to know some guys have zero morals when it comes to getting what they want from a woman.

"I'm so glad Aleksandr beat his ass."

"What?"

"He punched Jeremy out. Like, punched him out cold," Kristen explains.

Though I don't condone violence, my heart swells knowing that Aleksandr punched him for me.

When I hear the rumble of a vehicle pulling into the driveway, I cut the conversation short. "I gotta go, KK. Uncle Rick's here."

"Scratch Max's belly for me," she replies. "And call me later."

I pause to put on a bra and sweep my hair into a messy ponytail before trotting out to the living room. I assume the visitor is my Uncle Rick, since he comes over every weekend with Max, his golden Lab.

But when I look out the window, I see Aleksandr hopping out of his black Jeep Wrangler. He looks up from fumbling around in the passenger side and winks, before resuming his task. When he emerges again, he closes the door with his hip, as his hands are full. He carries a bouquet of flowers in one hand and a package wrapped in plain brown paper in the other.

"Who is it?" Grandpa asks.

"My client," I answer. My heart pounds so hard, it feels like the offspring of unicorns and elephants are banging against my chest cavity.

"Let the boy in the house, *Audushka*," he commands, looming behind me.

I step back, before Grandpa brings out the mosh-pit elbows on me.

Aleksandr steps over the threshold and into the house before greeting Grandpa in English.

"Viktor Vladimirovich, is nice to finally meet you. *Zhenya* and *Audushka* tell me many good things." After speaking with my grandpa, he steps to the side and leans over to kiss Gram on the cheeks three times. "Mrs. Berezin."

Points for the Russian: Using Grandpa's patronymic and speaking in English so Gram can understand, and kissing her cheeks in greeting.

Points against the Russian: His hair. I watched Grandpa's eyes lock on Aleksandr's head for a few seconds before he backed away. He doesn't say anything, but I know he's judging.

Aleksandr must have noticed where Grandpa's eyes lingered, because he smooths a hand over one shaved side and shrugs. "Prank on rookie."

"Oh my." Gram covers her mouth, hiding the curve of a smile.

"For you." Aleksandr doesn't miss a beat, holding out the paper-wrapped package to Gram.

"Thank you," she says, peeling back the wrapping to reveal a loaf of dark brown bread.

"Is black bread," he explains, seeing her eyebrows lift in question at the gift.

"Where did you get black bread here?" Grandpa interrupts.

I swear Grandpa is salivating. He's told me stories of how much he loved his mother's black bread, but I've never had it before. My great-grandma passed away before I was born, and Gram isn't a baker. A few years ago, I looked up a recipe to make the dark rye bread for Grandpa on his birthday, but immediately filed it under the impossible-for-my-skill-set category. I must've inherited Gram's baking capabilities.

"I make this," Aleksandr explains.

Three pairs of eyes widen as we all stare at him like he's crazy. And a liar.

"I made this bread," he continues, "but I cannot tell you how this taste. I hope like *Babushka's*."

"You bake?" I ask peeking at him from over Gram's shoulder.

"Not really. But I watch *Babushka* so many times, I make this in my sleep." Aleksandr smiles. "I can cook."

"Well, it was very thoughtful," Gram tells him, before turning to give me a pointed look.

I guess it's rude to ask a guy if he can bake.

"Come sit down," she says, closing the door behind Aleksandr. "Can I get you something to drink, dear?"

"No, thank you." He shakes his head. "I will not stay long. I come to meet you. Tell you *Audushka* is amazing translator. She, uh, professional and fast."

Aleksandr hands me the beautiful bouquet of red roses and kisses each of my cheeks, then the left again, just as he had Gram. I bring the flowers to my nose, inhaling the musky scent that reminds me of Gram's favorite lotion. Holding the bouquet in front of my face masks the color flooding my cheeks, but it won't stop the thrum as my heartbeat accelerates in my chest.

"I'll take that," Grandpa says, holding his hand out for Aleksandr's pea coat. Grandpa nods to the couch. "Take a seat."

A few strands of loose hair fall in front of Aleksandr's eyes when he settles on the couch.

Grandpa keeps glancing at Aleksandr's head as he hangs the pea coat in the front closet. He hates his hair.

"Let's put those in some water." Gram motions for me to follow her into the kitchen. I nod, though I'm uneasy about leaving Aleksandr alone with Grandpa.

Gram and I set to our tasks in the small kitchen. She unwraps the bread and sets it on a cutting board, as I grab an empty vase from the cupboard above the sink and fill it with water. I separate each rose with care from the extra greenery and arrange them in the vase. Eleven roses. I count again. Still eleven. Jerky florist gypped the guy from a dozen roses.

"*Audushka* tells us you are from Serpukov." Grandpa's voice booms from the living room. Then I hear the distinct creaks as he lowers himself onto his worn, gray recliner.

"Yes," Aleksandr answers.

Hurrying to the living room, I set the vase of flowers on the coffee table and scoot around it to sit next to Aleksandr on the couch. Sitting next to him doesn't mean anything except that we have a good working relationship. We're friends.

Friends. Keep telling yourself that, Auden.

"How often do you get to go home?" Gram asks, placing the bread on the coffee table in front of Aleksandr and me. She's set a small ramekin of butter and a knife next to the now-sliced bread. Gram takes a piece, butters it, and hands it to Grandpa before doing the same for herself. "Your parents must miss you."

"My parents, they are killed in car accident. But I have many aunts, uncles, cousins. Never enough time for these visits when I am home." He smiles.

"Oh dear, I'm so sorry," Gram tells him, her eyes soft with empathy. No doubt in my mind, she's already saying the rosary for him in her head.

"I have my parents eighteen years. I miss them, but I come here like I plan. I just hope I make them proud, yes."

"This bread is wonderful, Aleksandr," Gram says, looking from Aleksandr to Grandpa. "Isn't it wonderful, Viktor?"

If Gram is doing a quick subject change, it means she's about to cry. And Irish Catholic Catherine is just as stoic as Russian atheist-turned-Catholic Viktor when it comes to crying. They rarely let loose in public.

"Very good," Grandpa answers while still chewing. He's already motioned for a second piece, so I believe him.

"Thank you," Aleksandr tells them.

The conversation continues, but I tune out because I can't take my gaze off Aleksandr. His blue eyes are bright, highlighted by the cute wrinkles surrounding them. He wears an easy, genuine smile during a conversation in which I'd expect him to be stiff and uncomfortable. He seems anything but uncomfortable. Should the power go out, we could use the glow of happiness radiating from him as a generator.

This confident, sometimes arrogant, man just wants attention and praise. I keep forgetting he left everything familiar back in Russia to start a new life here. He's made a huge transition, and I need to cut him some slack.

"Aleksandr, I'm glad you came to spend time with us. Thank you so much for the delicious bread. I have to excuse myself to finish up some work." Gram rises from her chair.

Aleksandr stands. "Is nice to meet you. Thank you."

She rubs his shoulder as she walks past him to the kitchen.

Whoa, now! Back off, Catherine!

A minute later she's pecking away on her typewriter. (Yes, typewriter.) As the secretary of her Thursday-night bowling league, it's her duty to put the score sheet together from the previous week.

I wait for Grandpa to make his exit, too. Instead, he pushes back on his recliner, getting more comfortable.

"I think you got gypped at the florist," I tell Aleksandr in Russian, ignoring my nosy grandpa who's most likely listening to every word.

"What do you mean? You liked them, yes?"

"Oh, yeah! They're gorgeous. But there's only eleven."

He smiles, and shakes his head.

"Oh my gosh, that was so rude. I'm sorry." I'm a class act—insulting the only person to ever give me flowers over one measly flower. As if I haven't put him through enough in the last twenty-four hours.

"In Russia we do not give even-numbered flowers as gifts."

"Why not?" I thought something as simple as giving flowers would be the same across the world.

"Even numbers are for the dead."

I pause, unsure how to answer. "Well, then, I'm really glad the florist gypped you."

"Me, too." Aleksandr laughs, glancing at his watch. "I need to get going."

"Oh, okay," I mumble, jumping up to retrieve Aleksandr's coat from the front closet. My cheeks flush as I watch him pull it up his arms and over his shoulders. His movements are so easy, so self-assured. Leave it to me to get excited over someone putting on clothes.

"Thank you so much, *Sasha*," I say, throwing my arms around him. My hug must catch him off guard because he stumbles backward.

"Thanks for letting me stop by," he responds, recovering from my attack. I pull back, sneaking a peek at his reaction. He's smiling—a white-teeth-showing, bottom-lip-dipping smile.

"Aleksandr?" Grandpa calls just as Aleksandr is about to open the door.

"Yes?" He lifts his head to meet my grandpa's eyes.

"I can't help but notice that you have a good handle on the English language." Grandpa says, mincing no words in Russian. He pushes down the footrest on his recliner and stands up.

Oh shit. I put a hand over my mouth.

"I do, yes," Aleksandr admits.

"Then why do you need a translator?"

The story of what happened in my first night translating must've gotten back to Grandpa. Gram never could keep a secret.

"I don't like speaking with the media. I haven't mastered reining in my thoughts, giving the correct answers." Aleksandr shifts his weight from his left foot to his right. Then, he must think better slouching, because he straightens up.

Viktor's going in for the kill. I can feel it.

"I understand that. You're young and relatively new in the country. How the Aviators spend money is not my business, but I will not allow my granddaughter to be embarrassed and disrespected by a dishonest young punk. You should consider her services a favor since she is assisting you in a situation you don't want to be in."

"Yes, Viktor Vladimirovich." Aleksandr's swallow is audible.

"I am changing *Audushka's* title and job duties to translator and tutor. We will let everyone, including the media, know that in addition to translating, she will help you learn the English language so you will be able to handle your own interviews. It makes sense as she is only in town for the next month."

"Yes, that's a good idea." Aleksandr nods.

That glow he just had—yeah, that's gone.

"Thank you. And if I ever hear of you embarrassing my granddaughter when she is being professional and helpful, I will personally pay you a visit. And believe me when I say, I don't think you'll enjoy it."

Aleksandr nods. "I'm very sorry, Viktor Vladimirovich. Please accept my apology as I hope *Audushka* already has." He studies the floor.

"Please, call me *Dedushka*." Grandpa claps his shoulder before shuffling off to the kitchen.

Call me Dedushka? He sounds like a frickin' mobster. Viktor Sopranov.

"And, *Sasha?*" Grandpa turns around.

Aleksandr whips his head up. "Yes?"

"How about coming over tomorrow to help an old man with some outdoor work?" he adds before walking away.

Aleksandr nods.

"Sorry," I say, lowering my hand from my mouth. "I didn't know he was going to say anything."

"I deserved it." Aleksandr opens the door and jumps from the porch to the grass. When it's clear he's not going to turn toward the house again, I shut the front door.

All the time I'd spent trying to keep my attraction to Aleksandr under wraps to avoid creating an uncomfortable work situation—turns out it wasn't necessary at all.

Thanks, *Dedushka*.

Chapter Fifteen
ALEKSANDR

When I arrive at the Berezin's house at noon the next day, Viktor greets me at the front door. "*Sasha*, it's good to see you. Go around back, I'll meet you at the gate."

At first, I didn't think much about the prank I pulled on Auden the other day because hockey players play pranks on each other all the time. But the more I thought about it, the more I realized that she isn't just one of the guys. She's a professional hired by the team to provide a service.

I never thought she'd rat me out, but I'm glad she told her grandfather instead of someone in the Aviators organization. I can handle an old Russian dude putting me to work, but embarrassing my team with some stupid antics wouldn't have looked good for me with the media or the team.

A few of my teammates told me to blow him off, but there wasn't one part of me that thought about ignoring his request. Not when I can't get his granddaughter out of my head. If I plan on getting closer to Auden, the last thing I want to do is piss him off.

I jump off the porch and shuffle across the lawn to the driveway where Viktor waits at the gate.

"We're getting ready to put the house on the market in the spring," he tells me, leading me into the garage. "I've started painting already, but I still have two sides that need to be scraped." He hands me one of four scraper-things on his workbench and points to the wall. "You can start on that one."

I've just started scraping at the old chipped paint, when Auden barrels out of the back door and swooshes past me. She's wearing tight black yoga pants that hug her thighs and make her ass look out of this world. I shake my head and return to my work on the wall.

"I'll help," she tells her grandfather as she pulls on a pair of old leather gloves.

Viktor, who's stirring a can of bright white paint, lifts his head to flash her an irritated look.

"Come on!" she cajoles, undeterred. "I'm great at home improvement stuff."

"He does not seem excited about your skills," I say as I dig under a lifted piece of paint and fling it to the ground.

She shrugs. "He's probably thinking about the time I tore the carpet off my bedroom floor, rolled it up, and dragged it out to the curb."

I stop to stare at her. "You did what?"

"This is not a story you should be proud of," Viktor warns.

Ignoring him completely, she jumps right into the story. "I'd spent the night before binging one of those house-flipping shows. Almost every single episode showed beautiful hardwood floors underneath the old carpet. Not knowing any better, I assumed that's what was under the gross, old carpet in my room. So, one Saturday morning when my grandparents were out of the house, I ripped it up."

"I really hope you were right," I mumble, glancing at Viktor who still doesn't look amused, even though the story must have a good outcome.

She tilts her head at me. "I was! The floors were beautiful, but they needed a lot of love to bring them back to their glory. My Uncle Rick covered them with a coat of stain, installed quarter-round molding, and —boom—beautiful wood floors, just like I'd imagined."

"You can help with the scraping." Viktor hands her the tool with a wide, flat metal head. She takes the scraper, but glances at the paint can.

"Painting can't be that hard. I mean, it's a garage, how good does it have to look?" She takes a spot next to me and begins assaulting the paint that's bubbled and cracked over the years.

"That attitude is exactly why you are scraping." Viktor winks at me and carries the paint over to the other side to get started.

"Rolling my eyes would get me smacked," she whispers to me, glancing over her shoulder to make sure her grandfather is out of earshot.

"He's right," I say, still scraping away. "Just because it's a garage doesn't mean it's not important. Should still look good. *Dedushka* has pride in his home."

"That attitude is why he already likes you better than me," she says in a voice that sounds eerily like Viktor's.

I hip-check her. "Likes me? He's punishing me for playing a prank on you, and you say he likes me?"

"You gotta know Viktor." She laughs and resumes scraping.

While I don't think he likes me better than his own flesh and blood, I understand what she's saying. If Viktor hated me, his granddaughter wouldn't be my translator right now. Viktor would have put a stop to it without hesitation.

After we've been at it for a couple of hours, I look over at Auden. Her cheeks are rosy and flushed from the cold December day. Sunlight shines down, brightening the tip of her nose.

She must notice my gaze, because she turns to me and says, "I'm really sorry about this. I didn't know Grandpa would put you to work. You probably think we're weirdos."

"Stop apologizing, *Audushka*. The joke I pulled was stupid and unprofessional. Your grandfather was right to put me in my place." I laugh quietly and shake my head. "It's exactly what my father would have done."

I wipe at my runny nose with the back of my hand and smile. Thinking about my parents used to upset me, but right now I can't help but smile as I think about the last time Papa really laid into me.

"There was this one time, a few years before I come to America, I climbed onto the roof of our apartment and slapped hockey pucks trying to make it onto the roof next door. I'd made most of them, but there was one stray puck that I didn't get a good handle on."

"Oh no," she says, hooked on my story.

I raise my hand and make an arcing motion of the puck sailing through the air. Then I bash my fist against my palm. "Boom! It smashed through a window on the top floor."

"Yikes! Was anyone hurt?"

"No, thankfully. But my father was so pissed. He made me work to pay it off."

Viktor dismisses us from scraping, Auden takes my tool and throws it onto the workbench with hers, before grabbing my hand and leading me to the sliding glass door to the house. I follow her inside and we head straight for the bathroom to wash our hands.

Though she makes it to the sink first, I reach over her to grab the soap and flip on the water.

"Hey!" She bumps my hip, knocking me away as I try to run the bar under the stream. She wets her hands quickly and holds them out for her turn with the soap. I ignore her, and lather my hands and arms instead. When she tries to grab it, it slips through her fingers and falls into the sink.

"Let me help you," I say, dotting her nose with suds.

She twitches like a rabbit, before wiping it away with her arm. We playfully bump each other's shoulders out of the way, vying for who gets to rinse the stray flecks of dried paint away first.

We're still laughing when we make our way to the kitchen where Catherine stands at the stove stirring a saucepan. The luscious smell of chocolate wafts through the air, transporting me to Sweden as a teenager—the first time I'd tried hot chocolate. They offered it in the lobby of the hotel we were staying at during a tournament in Stockholm. At the time it, was the most delicious thing I'd ever tasted.

My gaze slides to Auden's lips and suddenly I'm struck by the thought that she might take the trophy for most delicious if I ever get the chance to taste her like I want to.

"That smells amazing," she says, hugging her grandmother from behind. "Thanks."

"There's a plate of graham crackers and apples over there." The older woman nods to the counter near the sink, as she pours the steaming liquid into two mugs.

"Do you want to hang out or do you need to get going?" Auden asks as she shakes tiny white squares into her drink. I read the label on the container—marshmallows.

I glance at the clock on the microwave. I have a game tonight, but there's plenty of time before I have to be at the rink.

"I will stay a little bit," I say, studying the tiny dried marshmallows she drops into my mug. "Thank you, Mrs. Berezin."

"Thank *you*. You helped us out so much," Catherine says, as she rinses out the pan.

Auden picks up her mug and the plate of food and leads the way downstairs. I follow with my drink and two napkins Catherine shoves at me as we walk away.

When I get to the bottom of the stairs, I have a full view of their beautiful basement. "Wow! This place is great."

There's a couch, an old recliner, and a TV in one section and a huge, mahogany pool table that takes up most of the far side of the room. There are also some bookcases and a tall chest of drawers near the pool table.

"Thanks." She sets her drink and the plate of food on the table next to the couch, then press the *power* button on the TV. The old box hums, warming up for about a minute before the picture pops up.

I reach over and grab a graham cracker from the plate, dunk it in my hot chocolate, and take a bite.

"Ever since I was a kid, my grandma has made me hot chocolate, apples and graham crackers as a snack after coming in from doing something on a cold day." She shakes her head and drops her gaze to the floor, as if embarrassed. "Seems really childish."

"It's not childish. She cares about you. It's her way of offering comfort."

She bites her bottom lip, as if she hadn't thought of it that way before.

"You have Atari?" I ask as my disbelieving eyes focus on the dusty, black rectangle on the floor next to the TV.

"I didn't realize anyone would be impressed by that old thing."

"It's a classic! I have only seen this on the internet."

"Are you a gamer?" she asks as if accusing me of something.

"No. I play with the guys sometimes, but I don't have a system."

Some girls really hate when guys spend their time gaming. As if it consumes their life so they won't be a good boyfriend. I get it, to an extent. But, I mean, if a guy chooses video games over his girl—they probably aren't the right fit.

I can't imagine ever wanting to play a game over having sex. If Auden were mine, nothing on TV would stop me from being inside her at every possible minute.

"Do you want to play?" she asks, snapping me out of my thoughts.

"Uh, yes!" I set my drink and the napkins on the table. "I have never seen one of these in real life."

We settle on the floor in front of the TV, because the joystick cords aren't long enough to reach the couch. I sit close to her, the outside of my thigh touching hers.

Being with Auden is comfortable, like we've known each other for longer than we have. There's comfort in being around a stern Russian man again. I've been away from home and my family for so many years, I almost forgot what it was like to have family.

"Watch out for that snake!" I say, grabbing her knee, as she expertly maneuvers her Q*bert character around, illuminating the blocks of the pyramid game board.

"Don't worry, Coily will eat my dust," she brushes off my warning.

I laugh. "You name this snake Coily?"

"No. That's his name. The snake is Coily, and the green dude with the sunglasses is Slick, which is totally lame, but who am I to argue with Q*bert's creators?" She shrugs.

I stare at her with wide eyes for a few seconds before laughing. "You're the best, *Audushka*." My eyes catch on a familiar uniform on the wall—one I've seen countless times before I wore a similar version myself. "Is that Tretiak?"

"Yup." She nods without taking her eyes from the TV screen.

Posters of Vladislav Tretiak—the greatest goalie of all time—along with Bobby Orr, Henri Richard, and Detroit's Production Line (Gordie Howe, Sid Abel, and Ted Lindsay) adorn the basement walls.

"You keep surprising me."

"Why? You knew I was a hockey freak." She glances at me out of the corner of her eye.

"I knew that, yes, but I don't know any girls who have posters of hockey legends on their walls. And I don't know any Americans who have a Tretiak poster at all," I say.

"What can I say? I've always had a thing for Russians," she murmurs without looking at me.

That's when I decide I won't be ignored. I tackle her, wrapping my arms around her and pressing my mouth on hers. She drops the joystick and clutches my shoulders to keep from falling over as I part her lips with my tongue and enter her mouth.

The tinny swearing sounds of Q*bert dying ring out in the background, but neither of us care. I pull her closer until she's in my lap and intensify the kiss, rolling my tongue over her, pressing harder, softer, then harder again. Her back arches and her chest slams against mine when I tug at her lower lip. Suddenly, she pulls away.

"Sorry." I smirk while sliding my fingers through my hair. But the only thing I'm sorry about is having to stop.

She looks so fucking sexy with her messy hair, bright eyes and moist, red lips. It takes every ounce of self-control to stop myself from devouring her.

I want to, but the last thing I need is to start getting hot and heavy and have either of her grandparents walk in on us. I can't remember the last time I had to think about parents—or grandparents—when I was making out with a girl.

"Dude, you killed my guy," she says with a shy smile, turning her eyes to the screen. A new Q*bert stands at the top of the pyramid ready to bounce.

"You can play mine." I push my controller toward her, then climb onto the couch, hoping she'll follow.

She tries to come across as a hard-ass, but she's so skittish, I know better. I have to take things slow and let her come to me when she's ready.

"Nah. I have Atari hand," she says, rubbing the spot where the base of her thumb and index finger come to a curve.

My cock gets hard and my balls tighten just watching her. All I can think of is how else she could hurt that part of her hand—by jerking me off.

But I can't think that way when her grandparents are upstairs. *If only we were at my place.*

As she leans over to shut off the game console, my heart beats rapidly, hoping she'll make the move to be near me. There's a flash of hesitation in her eyes, before she crawls up to the couch to join me. As soon as she gets on, I grab her from behind and drag her into me. I'm enjoying the sweet almond scent of her hair when she flips around to face me.

"I don't know if we should start this, *Sasha*," she says, her nose brushing mine, our lips inches away from another intoxicating kiss.

"We already have, *Audushka*," I whisper.

Doesn't she get it? Why would I have come over if I didn't want to be with her? I would have let her grandfather take her off the job and let the Aviators find me a new translator. An ugly old dude who didn't make my dick jump every time I saw him.

"Can we just, I don't know." She shakes her head and exhales. "Take it slow?"

"I'm in no hurry." I press my forehead to hers and drop a kiss on her nose. Then I slide one arm across her stomach. We settle into the couch—and into each other.

She feels perfect in my arms. As I adjust my own breath to the rhythm of hers, I fall asleep within seconds.

"*Audushka*," I whisper, rubbing her back in a soft swirling motion. "*Audushka*, you have to wake up."

"Hmm?" She stretches her arms, her body pressing against the length of mine—which ignites every nerve in my body.

"And you have to stop doing that." I kiss her neck, just below the jawbone. "Unless you want Viktor to kick my ass."

She giggles and drops her cheek to my chest. I want to hold her forever, but I have a game.

"I need to go, sweet girl. I've got to get to the rink. I'm already late."

"Oh shit." She bolts up, swinging her legs to the ground.

"Thank you for a wonderful afternoon," I whisper into the side of her neck, punctuating my sentence with a kiss. Then, I get up quickly and jog to the stairs. "See you tonight."

She looks dazed, but still lifts a hand and gives me a small smile. As I climb the stairs, I glance back. She falls back onto the couch, brings the back of her hand to her forehead, and raises her eyes to the ceiling.

When I first hit on her, I thought she was hot. When I found out she was my translator I was excited to be in such close quarters. At first, a sexy make-out seemed like the perfect solution, as it's the only way I know of to release the feeling of caffeinated bees attacking my insides. Unfortunately, the more I kiss and touch her, the more I want her. The more time we spend together, the more time I *want* to spend together.

I wouldn't consider myself a player, but I've hooked up with a few girls. If I know I'm only in it for the sex, it's easy for me to keep my feelings separate. But this time, I realize I really like this girl. I want to protect her and show her the world. I'm getting emotionally attached —and if we continue down the physical path, I know she will be too.

But her insecurities are strong. She still doesn't believe I like her for who she is. And I don't know if I can be with a girl who keeps up thick walls. My job is intense and it takes up a lot of my time. And no matter how much I tell her I want to be with her, I'll always have to leave. Insecure women and professional athletes don't go together.

I don't know if I can trust that she won't run away to protect her heart, but I'm not ready to walk away.

Chapter Sixteen
AUDEN

What's that old saying? It's better to have loved and had your heart raked across hot coals and stomped on than never to have loved at all?

That's the route I've decided to take, because saying no never even crossed my mind when Aleksandr invited me to go to the Detroit Red Wings game with him.

The Aviators had a five-day break over Christmas and Aleksandr wanted to see the Red Wings, since he hadn't had a chance to get to a game yet.

As I crunch across the greenish brown lawn to his Jeep, I remind myself to be calm and cool.

But calm and cool get kicked to the curb when I lift my eyes to Aleksandr, with his Mohawk gelled into a petite pompadour and a five-o'clock shadow dusting his strong jaw. I climb over the gearshift to straddle him before intertwining my hands behind his neck and planting my lips on his.

"Best. Greeting. Ever." Aleksandr says when I pull back. He sweeps away a few strands of hair that had fallen forward when I'd attacked him. "You always surprise me."

A stupid girly giggle slips out as I climb back over to the passenger seat. As I buckle my seat belt, the realization of what that kiss meant hit me.

There's no turning back. I've already secured the parachute to my back, hopped on the plane, ascended to an altitude of 12,500 feet, and jumped out.

Now, I'm falling.

"First Red Wings game. Smile!" I snap a picture of Aleksandr in Little Caesars Arena's dark, dank parking garage.

"Shouldn't we wait until we can see the arena?" he asks, blinking rapidly.

"Sorry," I say as I shove my camera into my purse. Then I grab his forearm and hop up and down. "I'm just so excited for your first game."

Aleksandr laughs and places his hand over mine so I can't let go of his arm as he leads me toward the walkway to the arena.

After snapping Aleksandr's picture in front of the arena, we enter the building and weave through the crowded concourse to find our section, Aleksandr comes to an abrupt stop.

"Did you know he was going to be here?" he asks, nodding toward a stand where an older man holds up multiple game programs. I follow his gaze and see Drew exchanging a ten-dollar bill for the program.

"No," I say.

Drew's parents have had Red Wings season tickets for as long as I can remember, but he never told me he'd be at the game. Although I haven't spoken to him since the soccer game.

Aleksandr presses a kiss on the top of my head, and I let out a breath of relief. Just as I turn to enter our section, I hear Drew call my name.

I had every intention of pretending I hadn't heard him until I notice the tall brunette at his side, fingers intertwined with his. It's Shannon Richards, one of my friends from high school that I'd lost touch with during our freshman year at college. At first, we'd kept in touch by e-mail. Then life got busy, and e-mails became less frequent, save the occasional birthday message, until they stopped altogether.

"Let's go," I whisper. I wave to Drew, then point toward the bulky, crimson curtain separating the concourse from the seating area. "We're going to head in. See you at intermission?"

Instead of waiting for a response, I poke Aleksandr in the rib cage to prod him forward.

"'See you at intermission?'" Aleksandr asks when we settle into the rigid red seats. "Why would you say that?"

"We can't say hi to my friend during the first intermission?" I ask.

"Not when your friend is in love with you."

"He is not!" I laugh out loud as I lean over, setting my purse at my feet. "He's here with a girl."

Aleksandr shakes his head and turns to watch the Red Wings and their opponent, the Chicago Blackhawks, skating around their respective nets.

I love watching to see if any players have superstitions, like tapping the goalie's pads or the crossbar of the net.

"Do you have any pregame superstitions?" I ask, sliding my hand under Aleksandr's dark waves to rub his neck at the hairline. My pulse quickens when I feel the tension ease from his shoulders and his body shiver under my touch.

His lips quirk up and he throws me a quick glance. "Can't tell you."

"Seriously?" I ask, halting my massage.

"Don't want to jinx it." He wiggles against my hand like a dog that won't let you stop petting him.

I laugh and resume my caress. I understand player superstitions. I used to sing and dance to "Gettin' Jiggy Wit It" before every soccer game in eighth grade. I'm still convinced it worked because we'd gone undefeated and won the city championship that year.

When the horn sounds to mark the end of the first period, I turn to Aleksandr. "Are you coming with me?"

"*Da.*" He emphasizes the yes in Russian. At least he'd remembered I'm his translator, and he's not supposed to know much English; I sure hadn't. In my eyes, this is a date.

After making our way to the concourse, I excuse myself to use the ladies' room.

I hear a female voice call my name as I take my spot at the end of the line. I scan the area for the voice that had beckoned me when I see Shannon step out of the line and walk back to where I'm standing.

"Hey, girl!" She has her arms around me before I can respond.

"Hey," I say as I break away. "How's State?"

"So frickin' hard," she says, though her smile tells me she doesn't mind. "Tell me why I went into prelaw, again?"

"Because you're smart as hell and like to argue with people," I answer, returning the grin.

"That's not true." She nudges my arm with her elbow. "See what I did there?"

"Stop laughing at your own jokes. That's my thing," I tease.

Shannon doesn't seem to have changed much, physically, since high school. She's still rocking long, dark brown hair and bronze skin, even in the middle of December. Since her dad owns a chain of tanning salons around the metro Detroit area, her skin stays perfectly sun-kissed. In addition to being pretty, she's also wicked smart. Almost too smart.

Sometimes it seemed like she didn't know how to tone down her intelligence to talk to people. She'd always get an eye roll or a big sigh from classmates when her arm shot up to answer a question. Every. Single. Question.

Our friendship worked because we both let the other one be herself. Shannon was smart and a little awkward, whereas I was athletic and a little awkward. Neither one of us drank in high school, so instead of going to football games and parties on Friday nights, we hung out at the local civic arena and watched Drew's hockey games. Shannon didn't even like hockey before she met me, but it beat sitting home on the weekend, so she rolled with it.

"How've you been?" she asks, stepping forward as the line moves.

"Great. Just working on my social work degree so I can help people before they become your future clients."

"You don't think I want to be a prosecutor?"

"Nope." I glance at the concrete floor, wondering if I should even ask the next question.

Ah, what the hell. "I saw you with Drew when we first got here. What's up with you guys?"

"We saw each other at a party on campus freshman year and we've been dating ever since." We inch up a few more steps as a few women leave the restroom.

"You've been dating for three years?" I ask. I'm sure my voice holds more surprise than I mean to express. Drew has been dating Shannon for three years? And he never told me?

"We both have really busy schedules. I'm always studying, and he's always practicing or traveling, but, um, yeah." Shannon looks at the girl in front of us in line, effectively avoiding my eyes. "It's kinda weird running into you while I'm with him, ya know?"

"Why?" I ask in confusion. Had I done something to offend her, other than let our friendship slip away? Maybe that's a big deal to some people. To me, it's just the cycle of life.

"I don't know, I just—I know you liked Drew a while back, and I would never want to hurt you." Shannon finally looks at me. Her relief is almost tangible. "Are you mad?"

"No," I say. "Seriously, I'm here with someone."

Would I have been angry with Shannon if I were here with Kristen instead of Aleksandr?

Yes and no.

While, I don't have feelings for Drew anymore, it's not a total slap in my face.

But there's a stupid, ridiculous attention-craving part of me that hurts knowing he picked her over me, even years later. What did she have that I didn't?

My internal thoughts need to tone down the cattiness before I grow karmic whiskers.

"You're sure you aren't mad because it's Drew?" Shannon asks. She looks so nervous I almost feel bad for her, but I'm too busy thinking about how pathetic her nerves make me seem.

"Oh my gosh. That whole thing I had for Drew was lame. Just a crush a long time ago," I tell her with certainty as we shuffle forward.

"It's good to talk to you again," Shannon tells me, leaning in for another hug.

I hug her back before she enters the restroom.

When I walk out of the ladies' room, I spot Drew and Aleksandr talking. Well, talking might not be the correct word, since Aleksandr and Drew are almost nose to nose and Aleksandr has a fist clenched at his side.

Drew's lips are moving as he watches me approach, but I can't make out what he said.

I rush to Aleksandr's side, taking hold of his fist, so he won't use it. His breathing is audible, and his shoulders are heaving. How the hell could someone who supposedly can't speak English get so angry?

"Stay the fuck away," he tells Drew in heavily accented English.

"What's going on?" I ask.

"*Neeshtoh*," Aleksandr spits out, grabbing my hand and pulling me toward our seats.

"Yeah, that looked like 'nothing,'" I mutter as I follow him.

"You all right?" I ask Aleksandr during the first break in play of the second period. I'd given him some time to cool down from whatever had transpired between him and Drew in the concourse by letting him watch the hockey game in silence.

"*Da*," he responds.

No eye contact. One word answers. Definitely not all right.

"You seem upset."

"Tell me the truth about him, *Audushka*." He swivels to look at me. "I deserve that, don't I?"

I nod. "Drew and I have been friends since birth. I had a crush on him years ago, but he made it clear he never liked me in that way. I'm over it. I've been over it. Now he's dating someone who used to be a good friend of mine. It's no big deal."

"He likes you in that way now."

"No. He doesn't."

Aleksandr laughs. "I can't tell if you're lying or clueless."

"Seeing as I've never had a boyfriend and the only guys who've ever showed interest in me just wanted sex, I'd say I'm completely clueless." In raising my voice to emphasize my point, I've drawn the attention of roughly thirty of the twenty-some thousand people at Little Caesars Arena watching the hockey game. Though we'd been conversing in Russian, I still slink back into my seat trying to curl up like a roly-poly bug.

"You're too beautiful to be completely clueless," Aleksandr mumbles, his eyes returning to the action on the ice.

Beautiful? I have fairly good self-esteem now, but the B-word has never been on my radar.

"I'm not beautiful. I'm average. I'm the wing woman, not the one guys go for." I sigh. "I guess that makes me a realist."

"You are clueless. You don't even know."

"Know what?"

"The effect you have on me." He meets my eyes again and shifts toward me. "The effect you have on others."

Holy crap. My effect on him? A tight ass for him to ogle while I translate his words for the media?

Does this guy realize the effect he has on me? Does he know that every time I look at him I see stars? Or that his voice is my new favorite song? Does he know his presence makes me feel more comfortable and calm than I've ever felt around anyone in my life, including my best friends?

Probably not. And I can't tell him any of those things.

"I have no effect on anyone. I'm a ghost. Forgettable."

"A ghost is haunting, possessing." Aleksandr places his hand on top of my thigh as he leans closer. His lips brush my ear as he speaks. "You are anything but forgettable. You are so beautiful, the sun dims when you're around."

I don't understand his angle. I've already chosen him. I don't want Drew. Is he throwing the kitchen sink at me to get in my pants?

"Let me break it down for you. Kristen and I were walking across campus one day and there was this guy driving around yelling things into a megaphone out his car window. He said, 'Wow, you're hot!' When Kristen and I both smiled, he corrected himself. 'Not you. The one in purple.' I was wearing red."

"I'm not even gonna respond to that story. That guy was an idiot. I'm not an idiot. And I'm not letting you go."

"Not letting me go?" I ask. "You think you have me?"

"Yes." He leans in all the way and plants his lips on mine. I sink into the kiss, my eyes fluttering shut as he presses harder.

"Seeing your friend with him upsets you, doesn't it? Just like seeing you with me upsets him."

His voice causes my heavy lids to flash open. Why can't he just stop at having me? I'd let him have me in the arena's grimy bathroom or on the beer-soaked floor. I don't care where we are as long as his lips are on mine again.

I try to brush it off. "It doesn't matter."

"It does. You shouldn't have to tiptoe around your friends."

"I avoid conflict. I fly under the radar. Everyone is happy." He carried the conversation into uncomfortable territory, even for someone I feel comfortable being myself with.

"That's fucked up."

"Exactly."

"I'm sorry."

"Why? You didn't do anything." I look at him. His eyes are sad but gray—the sky before a thunderstorm.

"I'm sorry you've never been able to share your feelings with your friends because you think they'll be mad at you and end the friendship."

"It makes life easier." If my eyes could give off laser beams, there would be a puddle of water at center ice.

"Does it? I would think that's a lot to keep up. Must be exhausting."

"I keep the peace."

"At what price?"

I shrug again.

"I think the flying-under-the-radar bit is a total smoke show. It's fake. You want people to notice you, to care about you. You think you have to suppress your feelings because you don't want to lose anyone else. You don't want people to think you're looking for attention, yet you desperately crave attention because you are missing the two fundamental people who fill that need for a child. It's okay to say what you want and feel what you feel, *Audushka*. It's not weak. Keeping people at a distance will lead you to a very lonely life."

"I'm gonna take a walk." I get up from my seat. I need to get away.

Aleksandr grabs my hand and pulls me back down. "You don't have to run away from me. I won't be mad if you open up."

"I don't open up, so don't take it personal." I ball my hands into fists—in frustration—I'm not going to punch him or anything.

"Is talking about something that scary?" Aleksandr asks, uncurling one of my fists and lacing his fingers with mine.

I nod.

"I would be jealous if a girl I liked chose someone else over me."

"But that would never happen because you're a hot Russian hockey god."

Aleksandr chokes out a laugh. "What?"

Tension relieved. Exactly what I wanted.

"*Sasha*, I'm not interested in Drew anymore, haven't been in years. It was the realization of who he was dating that shocked me. He's dated girls before. But for him to choose one of my best friends. I don't know. It's weird."

"Yeah, I'm sure that sucks."

"Isn't there an unwritten friend rule? You can't date the person your friend had a major crush on for years?"

"I have no room to talk. I stole Gribov's choice."

"What?" My head snaps to face Aleksandr. Just hearing Gribov's name makes me think of his rude gesture in the locker room. What kind of guy jiggles his junk at someone?

"He called dibs on my new translator if she was a hot female. But I stole you, so I can't say I follow that rule. You're the one who said all's fair in love and war."

"Gribov called dibs on the next warm female body. I can't say that's very flattering."

"You should be very flattered. He said the first translator *Zhyena* interviewed was a dog. And she modeled for someplace or other, so she said."

"This is a ridiculous conversation." Although a twang of pride hits me, hearing him say they'd interviewed another translator yet still chose me. I thought I'd gotten the job because *Zhenya* and Grandpa were such good friends.

"You're right. I don't want to talk about him." Aleksandr leans over and brushes his lips across mine so lightly it's painful. "Just promise me you'll always tell me what you're feeling. I'm not going to leave you if you speak your mind. Trust in me, *Audushka*."

I nod, my lips sweeping across his as my head bobs.

"I don't want you to be on tiptoes around me. Not unless you're reaching to kiss me."

I press my lips to his firmly. I have no other answer. I appreciate his effort, but he can't erase a lifetime in a few minutes.

After the game ends, Aleksandr drives me back to my grandparents' house. He pulls into the driveway, puts his Jeep in park, and turns off the engine. Then he reaches around and pulls a small plastic bag from the backseat.

"Your Christmas present," he explains as he hands it to me.

"*Sasha*, you took me to the game. I don't need anything else."

"Please."

"Why not give it to me on Christmas? You should come over and have dinner with me and my family."

"I have plans."

"Oh, well, okay. I was worried you'd be alone." I play with the hem of my Red Wings jersey to hide my disappointment.

Aleksandr cups my chin between his thumb and forefinger, lifting my face to his. "You worry about me?"

"Yeah. I mean, I know you don't celebrate Christmas on the twenty-fifth, but it's still a day for family time, and since you don't have any family here, I wanted you to have somewhere to go." I try to look away but can't, since he's still holding my face.

Aleksandr moves forward to kiss me. "Thank you for thinking of me, *Audushka*. You have no idea what that means to me."

"It's not a big deal." I shrug out of his grasp.

"Here." Aleksandr pushes the bag into my hands.

Inside is a small black box—the same size and shape as a ring box. Don't get me wrong, I'm not jumping to any crazy conclusions; ring box is the best description. Definitely a jewelry box. I lift the lid to find a small, gold Aviators logo charm.

"This is awesome," I whisper, touching it with the tip of my finger. "I love it. Thank you."

"You always wear the same chain and charm, so I thought this might fit on there with it."

And just like—that I'm done for.

I put my hand to my neck, fingering the gold chain with the delicate owl charm that belonged to my mother. I had to assume my mom liked owls because there was also a latch hook owl hanging on the wall in the basement of my grandparents' house that she'd made. Personally, I'm not a huge fan of owls, but it's the only piece of jewelry I own that belonged to her.

"This is the most thoughtful gift I've ever received," I tell him, meeting his eyes.

"It was something I knew you'd like."

I lean over, giving him a tight thank-you-for-the-best-gift-ever hug. When I pull away, I glance out the car window to see all the lights on in the front room of my house. I'm positive my grandma is watching through the window.

"Thank you for this." I shake the box. "And for a wonderful night. Tonight was great."

"You're welcome."

I don't want to get out of the car without acknowledging what I'd realized.

"Thank you for trusting me enough to tell me about your parents and your fears. Thank you for understanding and being patient with me. You're the kind of friend I didn't even know I needed."

"Friend?" His shoulders shake, and a low laugh leaves his lips. "Well, you are the friend I needed, but hadn't been able to find."

"See ya later, *Sasha*." I swing open the door and heave myself out.

Chapter Seventeen
AUDEN

"I can't fit one more thing in my stomach," I groan, leaning back in my seat at our kitchen table after finishing my second piece of pumpkin pie. The first slice should have been enough after the huge meal Grandma cooked, but I'd taken such a tiny sliver, I went back for more.

"I can tell. Those pants are pretty tight," my cousin, Liam, teases.

"Shut up." I grab a homemade buttermilk biscuit out of the basket next to my plate and whip it at him.

Uncle Rick reaches out and, with amazing catlike reflexes, nabs the biscuit from the air. "Well, now, just because you're full doesn't mean you have to waste food." He bites down on it.

"I'm gonna barf just watching you," I tell my uncle, covering my mouth with my hands.

There are ten people gathered at my grandparents' house for Christmas dinner. We're all laughing and teasing each other, like normal, but in the back of my mind, I wonder how many of us felt a twinge of sadness knowing it would be the last Christmas dinner we'd ever have here.

So many vibrant memories live in this house. The house where my grandparents raised my mom and Uncle Rick. The house where they'd raised me.

The house should have been on the market years ago. There've been multiple home invasions in the neighborhood recently, as well as a shooting a few houses down. My grandparents could no longer make the case that they still felt safe. We all knew moving was inevitable, but like a girl who still couldn't get over the fact that her soccer career was over, none of us are ready to let go of the memories.

"Merry Christmas." I hear my grandma say in the distance.

"What?" I turn back to Liam, who had asked me something as I listened to see who Gram was talking to.

"I said, where's lover boy? I thought for sure you'd have him here to show off."

"'Show off?'"

"You're dating a famous hockey player, I'd show him off."

"We aren't dating. I'm his translator slash tutor," I correct.

"Yeah, I had a tutor once. Totally banged her."

"Nice Christmas talk," Uncle Rick says, slapping Liam upside the head.

"Auden! Phone!" Gram calls.

Phone? So that's who Gram was talking to. My family's chattering must've drowned out the ring.

I push back from the table and run up the stairs to the kitchen, where our main house phone is mounted on the wall. And, yes, it's a rotary.

"Hello?" I ask after Gram hands me the receiver.

"*Audushka*? Merry Chrissmas," Aleksandr slurs.

"Merry Christmas, *Sasha*. What are you doing?" I play dumb, since I can practically smell the vodka through the phone.

"I am sitting in this very nice establishment having dinner and I realized I did not call you and wish you a merry day. I do not celebrate this day, but I know you do, so I am calling you."

"Well, thanks. Are you okay?"

"Okay? I am very okay, Auden. However"—he pauses to belch in my ear—"I think they would like me to leave."

I pull the phone away from my ear with a grimace. "What makes you say that?"

"They told me to go home."

"You're not driving, right?"

"No, no, no. They won't let me. This nice gentleman said he would call me a cab, but I told him I had a ride."

Silence.

"You need me to pick you up, don't you?" I ask after a moment.

"Yes."

"Where are you?" I sigh, grabbing a pencil and piece of paper from the second shelf of a tiered plant stand in the corner of the kitchen.

"A very nice establishment."

"Yeah, you said that. Where is it?"

"No clue."

I raise my eyes to the ceiling. "Is there someone I can talk to who knows where you are?"

I wince at the loud clang and scrape in my ear. He either dropped the receiver as he handed the phone off or got hit by a semi. I hope it isn't the latter.

"Are you coming to pick this guy up or what?" a rough male voice asks.

"Yeah, I just need to know where to go."

I write down the address he rattles off, thanking him before I hang up.

Blowing past Gram and Aunt Sharon at the sink rinsing dishes, I run to my room to grab my coat. I shove my driver's license into the back pocket of my skinny jeans, and return to the kitchen.

"Was he drinking, Auden?" Gram asks, looking at me over her shoulder and not missing a beat as she rinses those dishes.

"Yep," I say, sliding an arm into my pea coat. "I'm going to pick him up."

"Make sure he takes some Advil," Gram orders. "And roll him onto his side this time."

"I will." I wrapping a mock Burberry plaid scarf around my neck before I realize she'd said "this time." I try to recall another time she would have seen him drunk—

Oh my gosh! My grandmother knew Aleksandr had been in my bed after the night in Canada. As I snatch my keys off the hook by the back door, I dare to glance over my shoulder. Aunt Sharon is putting dishes in the dishwasher, but Gram catches my eye and winks.

* * * * *

Aleksandr must've been pulling my leg when he'd told me he was at a "very nice establishment" because when I pull up to the scary, dilapidated building on the outskirts of downtown Detroit, I don't even want to get out of the car. I really hope the jacked-up guy in a long, black leather coat and black knit beanie taking up the whole doorway is the bouncer. He looks like he could challenge Sylvester Stallone in the next Rocky film.

"ID?" Rocky's opponent demands.

"I'm just here to pick someone up," I tell him.

"ID."

I fish my driver's license out of my back pocket, thankful I'd remembered to grab it before I left the house.

"I'm under twenty-one. I just want to pick up my friend. He's really drunk."

"Dude from the Aviators?"

I nod.

"Wait here. I'll get him." He starts through the door, but I grab his arm. The muscle tightens under my grasp. His gaze travels from my hand to my eyes.

"Sorry." I release him. "Can I, um, can I just take one step inside?"

I check over my shoulder. The street is devoid of people and cars, other than my own, but I'm still freaked out. I'm a complete wuss, and the bouncer knows it. Which is fine with me as long as he doesn't make me wait alone on the streets of Detroit.

His mouth turns up in an amused smile, but he holds the door open for me to follow him inside.

If the steel door with a blacked-out window wasn't foreboding enough, the smoky haze and urine smell when I enter is.

"Isn't smoking banned?" I tug the collar of my sweater up to shield my mouth and nose.

"Don't make me regret letting your underage ass in here," the bouncer calls over his shoulder without stopping his pursuit.

Yeah, it doesn't seem like a place that cares about smoking fines.

I watch the bouncer weave his way through a small room crammed with a half dozen people and two pool tables. He taps Aleksandr's shoulder and points my way. When he swivels on the bar stool and catches sight of me, his face lights up.

At least he's a happy drunk. Cheers for small victories.

"And I feel fine," Aleksandr sings as the bouncer leads him by the arm. "Remember that song?"

"There's no song like that, man." The bouncer shakes his head, unamused with Aleksandr's ditty.

"There is. Tell him, *Auduska*."

"The Beatles?" I guess.

"The Beatles! Ha!" Aleksandr pokes the bouncer in the chest.

"Take him before I punch him," he tells me, releasing Aleksandr's arm. "Drive safe."

He wobbles on his feet, so I shove my shoulder under him and wrap it around his back. He tries to take a step, but falls onto me. I have to take a step back for leverage.

"Sorry, *Audushka*." He squeezes my bicep. "Damn! You're strong."

"My car is right there." I point with my free hand, which I've extended for balance.

"I can walk," Aleksandr says, shrugging out of my grasp and straightening. "I just wanted you to touch me."

"Get in." I shake my head as I walk around to the driver's side.

"Thank you, *Audushka*," he says, pulling his seat belt across his chest.

"No problem."

And it isn't. I'm happy he'd called me instead of trying to drive himself.

We drive in silence though the questions in my head are loud. Why had he chosen to get drunk at a bar by himself tonight rather than come over and have dinner with my family? I knew he didn't celebrate

Christmas, but it was more about eating and hanging out with us than celebrating the holiday.

"See this?" Aleksandr breaks the silence. When I glance over, he's pointing to the scar on his cheekbone, inches below his left eye.

"Yes."

"You know how I got this?"

"High stick?" I ask.

"No. This one was a high stick." He points to a freshly scabbed-over gash above his right eyebrow, before trailing his finger back to the original scar he'd pointed to. "This was a bottle of vodka. Two years ago today."

"How did it happen?" My grip tightens on the steering wheel. Bar fight is the first thought that comes to my mind.

"I threw the bottle at a mirror. One of the two came back." Aleksandr diverts his eyes to the window. "I was getting dressed for a game. Then my coach walks in with my aunt. I knew something was wrong immediately since my aunt hadn't been to a game in years." He pauses to swallow. "She told me my parents died in a car accident on the way to my game. She said it just like that. Didn't prepare me, didn't ease me into it. I ran out of the locker room in full gear and drove to the hospital, but they wouldn't even let me see the bodies. So, I went back to my apartment and got drunk. I got angry. I threw the vodka bottle. All I could do was sit on my bed and cry and scream and throw bottles. My parents were killed trying to get to my game. They would be alive if it weren't for me."

"It wasn't your fault," I say, reaching out to place my hand on top of his.

Why was it so easy to tell other people something, but not believe it yourself?

"No, but I was the reason they were looking for a faster way to the arena. My hockey games. My hockey practices. Their lives revolved around my hockey career. And it killed them. I swore I would never play hockey again, and didn't—for a week." He looks at our hands, twisting his so his palm is cupped toward mine. "Then I remembered that hockey was the only thing I had left."

"I'm so sorry, *Sasha*. I didn't mean to—"

"Stop apologizing, *Audushka*." He lifts his eyes to mine, intensity poking through the haze. "I brought it up. I wanted you to know. For you, I'm an open book."

I squeeze his fingers before resting our joined hands on top of his thigh. Our situations are mirror images of each other. He'd retreated into hockey to numb the pain of his parents' death, just as I'd retreated into soccer to numb the pain of my mom's.

"Will you stay with me tonight, *Audushka*?" Aleksandr asks, still staring at our joined hands.

We both already know the answer, so I don't hesitation when I say, "Yes."

We drive the rest of the way to his apartment in silence. Though I'm enclosed in the warmth of the car, the winds whipping outside seem to be slicing through me, carrying away the final bricks of the walls I've built.

The condo Aleksandr rents in downtown Detroit is part of the Westin Book Cadillac, a historic building which had undergone a major reconstruction a few years back. It currently houses a restaurant on the main floor, the Westin hotel, and luxury residential condos on the top eight floors. No doubt numerous other amenities are hidden between the walls of the building, but the restaurant—and the valet service that parked my car—is all I know.

Luxury is the ideal word for the condo that Aleksandr shares with Landon Taylor. I'd expected the condo to resemble one of the hotel rooms on the floors below, but the space is huge and gorgeous, an unexpected surprise. The entryway leads directly into a kitchen that would make Gordon Ramsay salivate. Though I can barely scramble eggs, I'm completely mesmerized by it.

The cabinets are a medium shade of brown, slightly darker than the hardwood floors and all the appliances are stainless steel, including a gas range and double oven. A wraparound bar and glossy black granite countertops serve as the exclamation point of the gorgeous kitchen. But as impressed as I am, I'm practically drooling when I glance to the left of the entrance, where the space opens to a substantial living room with three large windows along the pristine white wall.

Eager to see what Detroit looks like from the twenty-eighth floor,

I rush past the gourmet kitchen to the living room and peer out of the middle window. Instead of the city, I'm rewarded with a stunning view of the illuminated Ambassador Bridge. The lights of the bridge cast a reflection onto the rippling Detroit River, which proves, if studied from the right angle, Detroit can be beautiful.

"Take a seat." Aleksandr nods to the black leather couch I'm leaning against. Instead of sit, I watch him extract a small white bottle from the cabinet above the huge stainless-steel sink, shake a few pills into his hand, and throw them into his mouth. He swallows them before filling up a glass of water and guzzling it. "My head hurts already."

"This place is amazing. It's huge," I say as I turn back to the view of the river. Warmth spreads through me, knowing that Canada, the place Aleksandr and I met, lays directly across that body of water.

"Yeah, I guess it used to be two smaller condos, but someone bought them and tore down the separation walls and renovated it into one large space."

"That person was a freaking genius," I whisper mostly to myself. I tear my gaze away from the window to check out the rest of the condo. The living room is on the left side of a long, narrow room. The middle section holds a four-person dining table, and the area to the far right has a stationary bike, a weight bench, and a rack of dumbbells in various weights on the wall next to it.

"Want anything? Beer? Water?" Aleksandr asks as he fills his glass again.

"I'm good. Thanks." Since he's already gotten the ibuprofen himself, it looks like my job here is done, so I take a step back from the window. "I should get going so you can rest."

"No. You said you would stay." He moves toward me, stumbling over a pair of black dress shoes on the floor near the bar. Aleksandr stops in front of me, close enough that I can feel the heat radiating from his body next to the draft of the window.

"*Sasha*, I know what I said, but you should sleep it off." I take his hand in mine and give it a light squeeze. "I'll see you tomorrow."

"There is no tomorrow."

Aleksandr bends down, wraps his arms around my thighs, and hefts me over his shoulder.

Though I pound on his back, he doesn't stop walking until we've entered a large room with snow white carpet. Being upside down, the carpet is all I can see until he deposits me onto a king-sized bed. *His* king-sized bed.

"Please, *Audushka*, I need you here with me," he says as he climbs on top of me, pinning me below him.

I don't have to ask why because the answer already slapped me in the face during our conversation in my car. He needs to be held, and I want to be the one to hold him.

How many times had I wanted someone to stop talking and just hold me? Hold me until I didn't need the comfort anymore. Hold me until I was the one ready to step back, rather than being released first.

"I'll lay with you for a few minutes," I compromise, snuggling under the protection of his body.

We both lift and twist to allow Aleksandr to tug the luxurious silky fabric of his gray paisley duvet over us. Then he wraps his arms around me and hugs me to his chest. I feel his stomach expand and contract against my lower back, his thighs molded against my thighs.

Aleksandr's breathing slows and soon our chests rise and fall in unison. I rub one of his forearms in appreciation. He nuzzles his face into my hair, kissing the back of my head. Then he presses his pelvis into my backside.

It's not a sleepy move.

I respond by pushing back into his groin.

"*Audushka*," he whispers hoarsely, lowering his hands to my hips and grinding himself against me again.

"This isn't gonna work," I tell him, my heart racing as I wiggle out of his grasp and twist around, so we lay chest to chest. When I lift my gaze to his, it's immediately clear that I hadn't chosen the safer option. The heat in his eyes is so intense, if he were to cry, his tears would burn my skin.

Aleksandr rises onto his elbow, never taking his steamy gaze away from mine. He pushes my shoulders against the bed and throws one leg over me while holding himself up on his forearms. His lips are feather light as he lowers them onto mine, but when he invades my mouth with his expert tongue, I arch my back, and my chest slams against his.

Goose bumps prickle my arms when his tongue flicks over my neck. He rolls his hips against mine, sliding every hard inch against the sensitive spot between my legs.

I let out a series of soft gasps, but Aleksandr doesn't relent, doesn't give me one second to catch my breath, as he continues to rub himself against me. The intensity of the friction he's creating is going to put me over the edge.

Though I've had a few heavy make-out sessions in the past, no one has ever come close to bringing me to orgasm. I hadn't felt anything but alcohol-induced lust for the guys I'd been with, so I'd definitely never felt comfortable enough to let myself go.

Being comfortable with Aleksandr isn't a question. The question is: Will I be able to reel myself in before we go too far?

I realize I'm shaking when he rubs his hands up and down my arms, as if to warm me up.

"I'm not cold," I tell him, trying to calm my breath.

"I know. I'm trying to keep my hands busy," he admits before driving his hips into mine again, the friction escalating the throbbing sensation throughout my core.

I squeeze his biceps. "Why?"

"Because I want to touch you."

Aleksandr disappears under the comforter. His warm body slides down my skin before settling between my legs. While pausing to kiss the sensitive skin below my belly button, his deft fingers unbutton my jeans and pull them down my legs. I shudder with nervous energy and lust. Then lace my fingers in his long, dark locks while lifting my hips off the mattress to give him a better angle to pull, and end up thrusting my pelvis at his face.

"Fuck," he groans. The rush of cool air from his curse hits me at the same time his fingers brush between my legs.

It's then that I realize how different this situation is from anything I've previously been involved in. I can't control my desire, which trumps all common sense at this particular moment. Even though he's wasted, I want him to tear my underwear away and push himself into me.

Vision after vision rips rampant through my mind. "Danger Ahead" signs. A paper heart bearing my name being ripped to shreds by hockey gloves. A feeling of absolute isolation and emptiness vibrates through every bone.

I should ignore the Debbie Downer thoughts and side with my raging and ready hormones. I don't care if I wake up alone and used, my dignity like tin cans tied to the car of newlyweds, dented by each jolt against concrete. Being with Aleksandr is worth it, isn't it?

No.

Though I'm as ready as I've ever been, when it comes down to reality, I don't want my first time to be while he's drunk. I want him to have control over what he's doing, rather than a sloppy, painful interaction I might regret later.

Not that there's been anything sloppy about his current actions. He's the most nimble drunk I've ever encountered.

"*Sasha*, I don't want to do this when you're drunk," I protest.

"I don't either," he says as cold air takes the place of the warmth where he'd been holding my thighs. Though we're in a king-sized bed with four humongous pillows, when he emerges from the depths of the comforter he rests his head on the same pillow as I, his face inches from mine. He grips my hips, his hands slipping under the fabric of my underwear as he pulls me closer.

"*Sasha*," I warn when he rolls me to my back, pressing his body weight against me. I could've kicked myself for telling him I wanted to wait until he was sober. It wasn't really true. I want him inside me now.

"We don't have to have sex, *Audushka*," he whispers, nipping my earlobe with his teeth. "I know you're close."

Hearing him verbalize how aware he is of my current state of excitement makes me squirm, giving away any poker face I'm trying to keep. His mouth lifts into his trademark smirk, but I don't want the smirk, I want that mouth all over me. While I'm insanely comfortable with him, I'm not bold enough to tell him.

"Just say yes."

Teetering on the edge of the ultimate release I've only ever accomplished by myself must sway me in the direction of extreme selfishness.

"Yes," I whisper, letting Aleksandr take me into oblivion.

The last thing Aleksandr does before falling asleep is kiss the top of my head and curl his body around mine. Deep breaths and counting sheep, my usual remedies to calm down, aren't having any soothing effect on my rapid heartbeat. Being wrapped in his arms with nothing but my shirt and underwear between us keeps my pulse pumping for completely different reasons than I normally feel with guys.

In previous experience, lying in a guy's bed made me feel trapped like a firefly in a mason jar. I'd lie there, anxiously waiting for the opportunity to slink out as fast as I could. I'd always been able to walk away.

But I don't have any such claustrophobic feelings with Aleksandr, and it freaks me out. He has a hold on me. A hold much stronger than the heavy arm draped over my waist.

I never want to let myself slip into thinking I can't live without someone, because I know it's a lie. When you grow up without the most important people in your life, you know you can—and will—live without anyone.

Chapter Eighteen
AUDEN

Two days after Christmas, I'm back in my seat at "The Hangar," which is Robinson Arena's nickname. As I wait for the game to begin, I survey the crowd. There are the normal jersey-wearing hockey fans—men, women, kids. And then there are the puck bunnies.

I'm not talking about normal women who like hockey but don't want to wear a jersey to the games. I'm talking about the girls wearing tight tank tops, skirts barely covering their butts, and knee-high boots. The girls who are obviously not there for the love of the game but for catching the attention of the players.

As I continue scanning the crowd, I spot the BFAs—Bunnies for Aleksandr. One girl wears a replica of Aleksandr's Aviators jersey and Daisy Dukes—I assume. I only see legs sticking out from under the jersey, so I hope she has some kind of shorts on underneath.

Another wears an Aviators T-shirt with Aleksandr's name and number on the back. The shirt is so tight, I'd bet my car the tag inside would have a capital Y denoting a youth size. She'd cut the front into a deep V and used shoelaces to tie it together, creating great cleavage. It was also cut and tied on each side, revealing tight, smooth abs. I'm slightly jealous at her killer stomach.

When the announcer introduces Aleksandr, I jump from my seat and clap like Pavlov's freaking dog. So, when I catch myself staring at him as he stands at the blue line shuffling his skates, I lift my gaze and scan the arena again. Unfortunately for my self-esteem, my eyes go straight back to the bunnies, with their big breasts bouncing in their seductive altered T-shirts and their plump, painted lips screaming his name. I lower myself into my seat, casually inspecting my hands.

The guy next to me leans over. "Don't worry about them. Varenkov only has eyes for you."

I roll my eyes and scoff. "Whatever."

"You've got his eye right now." He nods to the ice.

Aleksandr isn't paying attention to the man in military regalia singing the national anthem in a rich baritone. His eyes are on the section of seats where I'm sitting. All the bunnies are sitting behind the goal, which is far right of where I am, so he's definitely not looking at them. Turning my head slightly, I steal a glance at the people occupying the seats behind me—a couple of old guys and a kid.

Aleksandr brings his gloved hand to his lips, then pounds his heart twice, before he drops his arm back to his side. He doesn't smile, which is good. He needs to focus. What the hell is he doing looking up here anyway?

"Are you his girlfriend?" the man next to me asks.

"Uh, no." I laugh his comment off, though I feel my cheeks burning. Despite how close we'd grown in the last two weeks, Aleksandr and I haven't discussed our relationship status, so I can't assume he's my boyfriend. "Why would you ask me that?"

"This is where the wives and girlfriends sit." He thrusts his hand at me. "I'm Jason, by the way."

I shake it. "Auden."

"The translator. That's right." Jason nods, leaning forward and grabbing his beer from the cup holder.

The translator. Of course, I'm just the translator.

"Which one are you?" I ask.

"Which what am I?"

"You said this is where wives and girlfriends sit, so which one are you?" I wink.

Jason laughs, deep and hearty. "I'm Landon Taylor's brother." He points to the ice. "Number six. I try to see a game whenever I'm in town."

"Where do you live?"

"Bridgeland."

"I go to school there. Central State."

"No way."

"Way." I laugh. Then realize I'm not talking to Drew.

"Wayne's World was a little before your time, wasn't it?" Jason's eyes scan my face, as if estimating my age.

"Yours too, but you got the reference."

"Uh, yeah. It's a classic."

"Party on, Jason." I hold my fist out.

"Party on, Auden." He grins, bumping his knuckles with mine.

The pale blue eyes peeking out from under the faded navy Detroit Tigers baseball cap on his head are kind and familiar. It doesn't feel like I'm talking to a stranger, more like hanging out with an old friend. It's not like I'm looking to ditch Aleksandr for him, but I'll bet Jason Taylor gets his fair share of the ladies.

Not that Aleksandr is mine to ditch. A Christmas gift and a drunken make out session probably don't mean much to a guy like him. We hadn't spoken since I'd snuck out of his apartment early the following morning. Waking him up at six-thirty just to say goodbye seemed rude, so I left.

No big deal. That's what I keep telling myself. But I probably messed everything up by sneaking out. Stupid, ingrained flight mentality.

"Have you ever been to Johnny's?" I ask. "I'm a server there."

"I knew you looked familiar. I thought it was because I saw you send Aleks down in flames when he hit on you in Canada."

"Someone has to put him in his place." I laugh. "Ask for me next time you're there. Coffee's on Johnny."

"Coffee's always on Johnny. I'm a cop. She keeps us awake for free."

That's true. Johnny always let the cops drink coffee for free. She says it's her civic duty to help them stay focused on protecting and serving the community, but I think it's because she has a thing for guys in uniform.

The Aviators and their opponent, the Providence Bruins, skate into their positions for the opening face-off. Aleksandr is the left wing on the first line. When the referee drops the puck, I scoot to the edge of my seat and stay there for the first twelve minutes of the period, watching the furious pace of the game.

"Shit!" I slam back against my seat when the Bruins score.

"You're pretty intense," Jason says.

I jump, having forgotten Jason was there—and conversing with me. "Oh, yeah, sorry. I get excited. Edgy," I explain, hoping my cheeks aren't announcing the wave of embarrassment washing over me.

"No, it's cool. I can see why Varenkov picked you over any of them." He nods to the bunnies. "Plus, you can understand what he says."

"Well, I doubt he does much talking with bunnies anyway."

"True." Jason shrugs, taking a sip of his beer. "He usually just ignores them."

"Don't most guys, after they've slept with someone?" I joke, remembering Drew's warning that Aleksandr was a dick to bunnies he'd slept with. Was I in for the same treatment?

When I glance over, Jason is staring at me like I have snakes wriggling from my head. Guess he didn't like my grouping "most guys" into the jerk category. "Some guys?"

"Aleksandr doesn't sleep with bunnies. He doesn't even talk to them," Jason says.

"Sure." I wink conspiratorially. "When we met, he told me he could have a different bunny every night of the week."

Jason nod. "Yeah, he *could*. But he doesn't."

"He's a total player," I argue, sliding to the edge of my seat.

"Who told you that?"

"I, he, I don't know. I just assumed by what an ass he is and how many sexual comments he makes."

"You assumed he was a player because he acts like a twenty-one-year-old male."

I open my mouth and close it without speaking because Jason is right. I'd assumed Aleksandr was a player because of his stupid pickup line at the bar and his cockiness. He had the similar arrogant air of the guys I'd been burned by in the past.

"Look, I don't know Varenkov as well as my brother does, but Landon told me he's never brought a girl back to their place. Especially not one of them." He nods to the bunnies again.

"Oh," I say, though it comes out so soft that Jason may not have heard it. I lean back into my seat and focus on the action on the ice. I should probably stick to hockey—what I know.

How the hell has the hot Russian hockey god never hooked up with a bouncing-breasted bunny?

When the game ends, Jason and I both stand and cheer with the rest of the arena at the final score. Aviators 4, Bruins 3. Aleksandr scored one goal and assisted on two others. My heart fills with pride for him.

I wait, watching as Aleksandr skates off the ice with his team before tapping Jason's shoulder.

"Thanks for the chat," I tell him, as he stuffs his arms into his coat.

"Yeah, you, too. I'm sure I'll see you at Johnny's." Jason winks.

Translating for Aleksandr during interviews after the games gets easier and easier as our time draws to a close. Not just because I'm getting more comfortable with it, but also because Aleksandr started answering parts of the questions. Though it's only been three games since my grandpa called him out on knowing English, he's taken the reins on speaking to the media himself. I'm there as backup when he has to pretend he doesn't understand something they ask or doesn't know the English words to respond.

Obviously, he can't go from not speaking any English at all to being fluent. During practice he speaks in broken English and clipped sentences, because he has that skill mastered. Still, learning English is a slow process. I'm more than happy to go along with his act, because I only have two and a half weeks before I go back to school, and I like having an excuse to spend time with him.

Just when I start to think that way, my brain reminds me that he hasn't called since our intimate night together.

I feel like an old cartoon character carrying a fictional little angel and devil on each shoulder. The little white liar, so ecstatic I'd met my match, jingles wedding bells. The red realist reminds me how good an actor Aleksandr is, as demonstrated by his ability to fool the media into thinking he barely knows English.

As if he can hear my internal monologue, Aleksandr stands up and reaches over me to grab something off the top shelf of his locker.

"Thank you for being with me on Christmas," he whispers in my ear, as he retrieves a towel.

Though I try to contain my outward emotion, my insides are flipping like a gymnast during an uneven-bars routine. He doesn't regret our night together.

"It was my pleasure." The words slip out in English, as I'm too flustered to come up with a response in Russian. At least I'd remembered to keep my tone professional, though I doubt anyone believes we're talking about the game, with his mouth so close to my ear.

Someone beside me snickers. When I turned to see who it is, Landon's shoulders shake while he rubs a towel over his wet blond waves.

Nice word choice, Auden.

Aleksandr leans into me, ignoring Landon. "Come over tomorrow. I'll cook dinner for you. We'll watch a movie. I'll kiss your beautiful lips again."

"Sure, I can tutor you tomorrow." I adjust the strap of my messenger bag on my shoulder. Guys always talk about mentally reciting baseball rosters or picturing their fat aunt Edna to keep from getting too excited. Talking about tutoring is my fat aunt Edna equivalent.

"See you tomorrow." He skims my hip with his fingers as he edges past me to the shower.

I shiver. Of course I shiver, it's damn cold in the basement dungeon locker room. It has nothing to do with the fact that he wants to hook up again. Or the fact that he remembers it though he'd been drunk. Nothing to do with wanting to feel his lips on every part of my body.

Nope. Nothing to do with any of that.

Chapter Nineteen
AUDEN

"You're on math duty," I tell Aleksandr as he pulls his Jeep to the curb in front of a small church that houses the after-school program I'd started. It's only ten-thirty a.m., but Detroit's public schools had a day off for a teacher workday.

"My English isn't good enough to tutor children?" Aleksandr asks, shifting the Jeep into park and sliding out of his seat.

"It's not supposed to be," I remind him as he opens the door for me. "Numbers are numbers. No language needed. Plus, I'm not good at math."

"Not good at elementary school math?" He raises his eyebrows, taking a puff of his clove cigarette.

"Dude, stomp the cigarette. We're supposed to be good influences, remember?" I nuzzle my face in his neck, inhaling deeply to get a good whiff of him as he mashes his cigarette into the sidewalk with one of his black-and-white checkered Vans.

One of Aleksandr's unwritten off-ice duties as an Aviators player is to participate in community-service projects in the area. Since he's been in Detroit for only two months, he hadn't found a specific charity he wanted to get behind yet. So I invited him to join me.

"Hey, guys!" I call to the dozen or so kids seated in folding chairs at a long table. My heart melts when their eyes brighten and their lips curl into smiles upon seeing me. All of them start speaking at once; yelling hello, calling my name, talking a mile a minute about whatever it is they have on their mind. It's the best greeting ever, but I put my finger to my lips. "Shh. I just wanted to say hi."

"Sorry, I got them all riled up, Case." I pull Casey Johnson into a hug, before taking a step back. "I brought our first celebrity volunteer. Aleksandr Varenkov, from the Detroit Aviators."

"First celebrity? What about me?" Casey's lips spread into a large smile, revealing bright but slightly crooked teeth. Upon first glance, the former Central State football player's six-foot-five, 245-pound frame and bald head look intimidating, but his effortless and genuine smile squashes that within seconds. Watching him interact with the kids reinforces my decision to recruit the gentle giant to run the Detroit program while I finish my degree at Central State.

"That's right. I forgot," I say, snapping my fingers. Casey just rolls his eyes.

"Thanks for coming, man. It's great to meet you." He shakes Aleksandr's hand. "I'm sure Auden told you all about the program."

"No. The only thing she tells me is I cannot teach English to these kids," Aleksandr says in his fake broken English.

"Well, I guess she has a good point." Casey laughs, deep and loud. "What we do here is provide year-round, free activities for children who can't afford to pay for programs in the community. We have volunteers to tutor, to play, or just to talk with them. We try to make the environment fun. We want the kids to enjoy coming here, so they stick with it and don't turn to the streets. During the school year, it's homework first, and they know that, so don't let them sweet-talk you into going into the gym and shooting balls around until they're finished. Right, Luis?"

"I'm working, Casey. I'm working." Luis, a nine-year-old boy whose been part of the program since we started it, holds up a halfway-completed math worksheet as proof.

Casey winks at Aleksandr. "They're all good kids. Some of them come from messed-up situations. Unfathomable situations. A few of them eat breakfast and dinner here. It's something we didn't offer at first until we saw a need for it. There were kids who were eating one meal a day, the lunch they got at school, because their parents aren't around."

Aleksandr's face goes from amused interest to concern and sadness within seconds. Though I know the situations of most of the kids who utilize the club, every time Casey or I tell someone new, it upsets me all over. I can't imagine not knowing when I would eat next. I can't imagine my grandparents not coming home for days on end. And I definitely can't imagine going to school through it, laughing through it, and playing through it.

The kids who attend the Central Club amaze me with their resilience and tenacity in the midst of their everyday struggles. It's a great feeling knowing the club gives them a place they can get help with homework, have fun, and be safe. And, judging by the record number of people who'd signed up to volunteer, these kids finally have people who care.

Aleksandr and I slide into seats across from each other, in the middle of the table where the kids are working on homework. Within seconds, we're both bombarded. Aleksandr gets more attention than I do because he's fresh meat. The kids love to show off for new people. All at once, boys and girls come up to us, shoving drawings, math problems, and stories in front of us.

Sean, one of my favorite little boys, climbs into my lap and puts his arms around my neck, giving me a tight squeeze. I smile and hug him back.

"I'm glad you're here, Miss Auden," he tells me. "I missed you a lot."

Come on, how can anyone not melt from that?

After Aleksandr and I help with homework, we walk into the gym attached to the church. For over an hour, we play every game imaginable, from basketball, dodgeball, and kickball to jump rope and hand-clapping songs. It's past noon when we say our reluctant goodbyes to the kids and Casey.

"How did you get involved in this?" Aleksandr asks, stopping to light a cigarette before he gets into the Jeep.

"I did a study about after-school activities for kids in my community in one of my first classes. The findings gave me the idea to start the Central Club. The attention and positive reinforcement they get here is something some of them may never have at home."

"Wait. You *started* this group?" he asks.

I nod.

"How did you pay for the building and all the equipment?" Aleksandr asks.

"I applied for a grant. I did fundraisers. It was an insane time, especially with soccer and all my other classes," I say, shaking my head as I remember how stressed and stretched I'd been. "But I wouldn't change a thing. I learned so much, and since I've done everything as part of my major, it's been really beneficial. My advisor said I probably won't have to take my capstone class next year. All the work I've done on this program would take its place."

"That's awesome, *Audushka*." Aleksandr squeezes my hand. "I can tell you love those kids."

"I do. I mean, I can relate to them in a way. I see what could have been if I didn't have a family that cared about me. They need to know there are people who care. There are people who want to help, want to see them succeed. Maybe if they see that now, they'll make good decisions in the future," I answer, blinking a few times to stop the tears. They aren't angry tears. They're fighting tears. I need to fight for those kids.

"You are amazing," Aleksandr tells me. "You are an amazing person."

"I'm not amazing." I shake my head. "I'm a human being who doesn't want to see more kids messed up because they were born into a situation that was out of their control."

"Back to my amazing-girl comment. When we go to service projects in the community, some of the guys on the team complain. They don't see how helpful even a few hours can be to someone."

"That's sad. Those kids help me just as much as I help them."

"Can I invite some of the guys to come with me next time? Landon would love it."

"Of course."

"Want to come over and nap with me today?" Aleksandr asks, squeezing my knee. My body tingles, a reflexive response to his touch.

"You probably need to learn the English words for nap and bed. As your tutor, I don't really have a choice." I wink though I know I should say no, because he needs to rest and mentally prepare for the game.

"No, you don't. I need you."

How do you say no when someone says they need you?

"Of course, I'll come over," I agree, because deep down, as much as I try to deny it, there's one specific reason I want to join him for a nap.

I love spending time with him. I love how being with him makes me feel. I love how he treats me.

I love him.

And it scares the hell out of me.

* * * * *

I'm on the edge of my seat for a completely different reason later that night at the Aviators game.

My grandparents occupy the seats next to me, as Aleksandr and his teammates take on the Chicago Wolves. I wondered when Grandpa would attend a game to critique me on my translating skills. He'd be in the locker room tonight, standing among the reporters.

After the game, I lead my grandparents to the locker room. Grandma waits in the hallway, while Grandpa enters after me. It feels like a major test—the SAT of translating. Grandpa is an intimidating figure in general, but I now understand the sheer terror his students must have felt stepping into his office for the oral part of a Russian language exam. My palms are clammy, and perspiration keeps beading up on my forehead no matter how many times I wipe it away.

It's your grandfather. He's not going to skewer you, I tell myself. I just wish I could believe it.

The questions are almost always the same, and I'd gotten into a good rhythm with Aleksandr by now. Thankfully, he plays it straight and comes up with different but similar-sounding responses every time.

The reporter with John Lennon-style spectacles holds out his tiny recording device and speaks. "You'll play your first game in the NHL tomorrow. How do you feel about being called up to Charlotte?"

The world around me stops. I can't speak, stunned into silence. The only thing I notice is the reflection of the overhead lights in his stupid, outdated glasses.

Aleksandr is leaving.

Leaving Detroit.

Leaving me.

Chapter Twenty
ALEKSANDR

How the hell had a reporter from the Detroit Press find out I was called up when I only found out while getting dressed for tonight's game?

Auden is visibly shaken, silent as she processes the question. I tap her hip with my shoulder, bringing her back to the task at hand. Her voice cracks as she translates the question for me. I motion to stop her halfway through to let her know I understand, and give her a break.

"I am, uh, excited about this, yes. I do not like seeing any guys hurt, but, you know, is chance for me. I get in Charlotte and, uh, do this work hard and I take my shot."

Her usual professional, crisp demeanor has faltered to a glassy-eyed stare. When she swallows hard and shifts her gaze to the floor, I decide to end the questions.

Making sure she's okay after the shitty way she found out about my getting called up to the NHL is much more important than anything the reporters have to ask me. They know what they need to know for now, and the story will be out everywhere soon and I'll be interviewed when I get to the arena in Charlotte tomorrow.

"Thank you. This is all," I dismiss the reporters in English.

I watch Auden shake her head as if lifting from a fog, then glance at the door where I see Viktor leaving the locker room. When a flash of disappointment crosses her face, I know exactly what she's thinking.

Stumbling over a question. Falling in love with her client. She's thinking those are good reasons for her grandfather to never let her translate for a human again.

She thinks she fucked up. She thinks she disappointed him. She thinks she's not good enough. But I know all of those things are the furthest things from his mind.

She's absolutely amazing.

"I need to catch up with *Dedushka* and talk to him about—"

"*Audushka*—" I interrupt, reaching out to touch her arm.

But she shrugs me off, reaches down to grab her messenger bag from the floor and hurries toward the door.

"*Auden!*"

But she doesn't turn back.

"Nothing is forever," Gribov hisses in Russian as she rushes past his locker. Thankfully, she doesn't give him the satisfaction of acknowledging his comment.

I jump up from my seat and snap, "For once in your life, shut the fuck up!"

"She's weak. Let her go." He shrugs as if nothing bothers him. Because nothing does. His heart is as cold and desolate as a Siberian winter.

"Heartless motherfucker," I mumble as I shove the locker room doors open and search the hallway for Auden.

She's with her grandparents, who are huddled near an exit door. I hold back, watching their exchange instead of interrupting it.

"Thanks for coming," she says, before stepping into Catherine's outstretched arms. When she releases her, Auden inches toward Viktor, but hovers awkwardly as if she's unsure of his reaction.

"You did very well, *Audushka*," Viktor says as he brings her into his arms. "Very well."

When Viktor lets her go, her grandmother pulls her in for another hug, whispering something against her hair. Auden nods, then pulls away and straightens her shoulders.

"I'm glad you came to see me in action. Think I can have a dignitary next time?" she jokes. Her lip quivers as she tries to smile through tears.

My stomach tightens. I caused those tears. I let her down.

"We'll see." Viktor winks, then fails to dodge Catherine's arm smack.

"Sasha should be out in just a minute," Auden says, throwing her thumb over her shoulder to point behind her.

Viktor glances at the door and our eyes meet. I can't tell if it's anger or understanding swirling in them, but I stumble back into the locker room anyway.

Never in my life have I showered and gotten dressed so fast. I'm back in the hallway less than fifteen minutes later. I probably still stink, but that's not my concern at all. If I could have, I would have skipped the shower all together.

I raise my arm to get Viktor's attention since Auden still has her back to the locker room door. He waves and shoots me a smile.

Suddenly a female voice calls out, "Aleksandr!"

When I turn my head to look at who'd called my name, a familiar bunny who always hangs around outside the locker room, throws herself at me and plants her red lips on mine. Because of that split-second reaction to turn my head her lips didn't land on my cheek.

"Jesus!" I push her away and hold her at arm's length. Anger zaps through my veins, and I hold her tighter than I should. "Don't ever fucking do that to me again. Get the hell out before I have you dragged out."

Her stupid smile falters and when I release her, she stumbles back as if I'd struck her. Then, she throws her shoulders back, she flips her long blond hair, and strides past Auden with a big smile on her face. As she passes, she touches her fingers to her lips and smirks, giving her a quick sidelong glance through false eyelashes.

This is absolutely not the time for bullshit drama.

Auden brushes past her grandparents, and slams her palms against the exit door. She's almost out the door, but I didn't waste a minute following her, reaching her in time to grab her arm and reel her back into the arena.

"*Audushka*, please," I say.

She drops her gaze, refusing to meet my eyes.

"Good game, Aleksandr," Viktor interrupts, clapping me on the back.

"Thank you for coming." I say with genuine appreciation. I'm not trying to add to Auden's discomfort, but I respect Viktor too much to ignore his presence. "She's a brilliant translator, yes?"

"She makes us very proud." He nods and at his granddaughter whose expression lacks any sort of emotion. Even after the praise from the man she wanted to impress the most with this gig. "We'll give you two some time to talk."

Viktor puts his hand on Catherine's back and leads her out the door Auden tried to escape out of.

That will be Auden and me someday. Forty-something years into marriage and still holding hands and doing romantic things.

With a renewed passion to let her know how I feel about her, I close the distance between us, and speak softly so she has to lean toward me to hear. "I'm sorry I didn't tell you, *Audushka*. I found out *as* I was getting suited up for the game. There was no time. I swear."

"Let's go outside," she says when she notices a few of my teammates filing out of the locker room and heading toward the exit we're blocking. She takes a step back as if she doesn't think my teammates know about our relationship.

Which is hilarious because I haven't shut up about her since we met. I haven't told any locker room tales, but they definitely know I'm completely captivated by her.

When we get outside, we start walking toward the parking lot.

"Please don't be mad at me. I don't want to leave you, but I have to go to Charlotte," I plead, holding the passenger door open for her.

"I'm happy for you, honestly," she tells me as she climbs into the Jeep. "And I'm so proud of you."

"Then what's wrong?" I turn the key to start the Jeep.

That's when I realize—I didn't pause.

I have everything I've worked for: the NHL, an amazing relationship. I'm glad she's not mad about me leaving or how she found out. I knew she wouldn't be, but I also thought she might feel rejected.

"Nothing."

As we sit in silence, I throw my arm over the back of her seat and look out the rear window as I back out of the parking spot.

"Last-ditch effort," I say.

"Hmm?" she asks, confused.

"She kissed me because it was her last chance to try. It didn't work. It will never work," I tell her, cutting through the bullshit, as I try to catch her eye before focusing on the road ahead. "Girls like that don't care who they hurt."

I'm too exhausted to play the infuriating "What's wrong?"/"Nothing" game.

"Please speak to me." I remove one of my hands from the steering wheel and grab hers, clutching it tightly.

"How do I know it was nothing when she just kissed you? How do I know that's not happening with other girls when you're on the road?" she asks, almost accusingly.

She knows. She's just looking for a fight—to protect her heart.

"You don't. You just have to trust me."

When she shrugs, I know I have to say something to get through to her because I don't have much time.

Cranking the wheel to the right, I jerk my Jeep onto a random side street. She reaches up, clutching the dashboard for dear life. I pull to the curb, shift into park, and kill the engine before turning to face her.

"I don't fuck bunnies, *Audushka*. I barely even talk to them. All I say is, 'Leave me alone. Not interested.' I'm sure they get pissed off because I don't pay attention. Some of them do stupid shit to try to get you angry. I haven't made it a secret I'm with you." That doesn't knock her out of the funk, so I continue. "I haven't had a girlfriend since I was eighteen. She dumped me a week after my parents died because she said I was too depressed and moody."

She grabs on to my hand. "You're kidding."

"I'm not."

Her face shows the perfect amount of horror, so I lace her fingers through mine, my thumb rubbing circles into her palm, hoping to sooth her tension. "I don't fuck bunnies. I haven't even been interested in getting involved with another girl until I met you."

She swallows hard and hair falls into her face, covering her eyes.

"Do you trust me?" I ask.

She nods, but doesn't look up. That's when I know I have to take it to the next level. She needs to understand what I feel in my heart—and my head.

I release her hand, reach behind the passenger seat, and rummage along the floor until I find the gray and black plaid scarf I threw back there last weekend.

She raises an eyebrow, curious because she's already wearing a scarf.

I lift her chin with my forefinger, lining up our faces until our gazes meet. Then I slowly wrap the scarf around her eyes and secure it in a knot behind her head.

There's a thick silence in the air. I know she wants to ask me what's going on, but I also know she's too nervous—or anxious—at the loss of control.

Yet, I can tell by the flush of her cheeks that she's turned on.

"Where are we going?" she finally squeaks when the Jeep's engine roars to life.

"You'll see."

"Actually, I won't. You've got my eyes covered up here, buddy."

"I'm giving you an annoyed look right now," I tease.

She leans backs against the seat as if trying to relax.

"Tell me what you feel."

"I'm nervous, but not scared," she begins. "And I'm amazed by how my other senses compensate when my sight isn't available."

"Like what," I ask. "Explain this to me."

I want her to get used to communicating with me. The genius idea to blindfold her came to me a few moments ago. She has to learn to communicate with me and lean on me when she can't see me. I want her to know that she can trust me even when we aren't near each other.

She reaches up and grazes her fingers over the fabric at her eyes. "The scarf feels like cashmere. It's silky and snug against my skin."

Her voice is velvet and I have to swallow hard to keep from pulling the car to the curb and kissing her senseless.

"This part resting on the bridge of my nose," she points to it. "Every time I breath in, I'm inhaling your scent."

"What's my scent?" I ask, glancing at her, though she can't see me.

"Mountain-fresh soap and cloves."

I laugh. "Well, that's better than I expected you to say."

"I want to keep the scarf forever, without washing it or exposing it to any elements that would change its fragrance. I want to be able to breath you in whenever I want."

Damn.

I stop the car and scramble out, jogging to the passenger side to open her door. Instead of taking her hand to assist her out of the car, I lean in and scoop her into my arms. I tromp through wood chips until I reach the swings we sat on after that fateful soccer game.

The moment that sealed my feelings for her.

When I remove the blindfold, she scans the familiar playground. The pretty pink flush pales and her eyes widen in a look of sheer horror.

"This was where I realized that you were the most amazing, kind, funny, intelligent, and sexy woman I'd ever met," I tell her before she can question my destination decision. "You were so vulnerable, so honest."

"So psycho," she interrupts in English.

"It wasn't psycho. It was pain and vulnerability, *Audushka*. I knew where it was coming from." I drop to my knees in in between her legs and slide my palm over her cheek. My thumbs rub her temples as I weave my fingers into her hair. "Everything changed for me after that soccer game. I knew I'd fallen in love with you."

"What?" she gasps, obviously freaked out by the L-word.

I've never felt more real, more exposed, or more vulnerable. And it's the best feeling in the world.

"I told you that after my parents died I had nothing left but hockey. That's not true anymore. I have you now. Everything I do and everything I am is all for you, *Audushka*. I am so in love with you. I love you."

She blinks a few times, as if confused. Then her lips morph into a silly smile and she gushes, "I love you, too."

Knowing she feels the same why makes my heart swell and my dick burst. Rather, my dick swells and my heart bursts.

When my dick bursts I want it to be inside her.

I lean into her, taking her face in my hands kissing her over and over on her cheeks, brows, and eyelids, before settling on her lips.

The kiss quickly turns from elated to hungry as I press harder, sliding my tongue into her mouth to tangle with hers.

"Can I get something out on the table, since you officially love me and all?" she asks, pulling back breathlessly.

"What's that, love?" I lean over, taking her earlobe into my mouth, then trailing soft kisses down her neck. Her breath speeds up and she clutches the lapel of my pea coat.

"Don't ever cheat on me, okay?" she asks, moving one hand to stroke my hair. "All the stuff with that bunny is—whatever. I know girls are going to throw themselves at you, that's just part of your life. But when you're in Charlotte, I won't be around when you come home from a game or a road trip. So, if you ever feel tempted, I'd rather you tell me and break it off than cheat on me. It's the one betrayal I could never forgive."

"We both know that's not true."

"What does that mean?" She stiffens and I can almost see her brain's command to engage her "brick-wall" coping mechanism.

"The one betrayal you can't forgive is being abandoned."

"Leaving is your job. I've known from the start you'd leave me."

"Take yourself out of it, *Audushka*. I need to leave for my job, and yes, that means leaving you, but I'm not leaving *because* of you. You understand the difference, yes?"

She nods. "Logically, I understand the difference, but you leaving takes the same toll on my emotions whether or not I can separate the two."

"Yeah, I know. And I also know you're opening up because you think this is the end. You thought I'd be out of your life in a month, so why not?" I raise an eyebrow and smirk. "But it's not that easy to get rid of me."

"Nothing is forever, Sasha," she responds, smoothing out the collar she'd been clutching a moment ago.

I hate that she let fucking Gribov get into her head. All his stupid comment did was reinforce a lame idea she already had. If she's alone, no one can abandon her. In theory.

"That is where you are wrong, my sweet, silly girl," I say, shuffling to my feet. Then I lift her off the swing and into my arms, patting her rear to prod her to hop up.

She obeys immediately, like she always does, wrapping her arms around my neck and legs around my waist. I clasp my hands under her butt, cradling her with ease—and excitement.

"When we met you could've acted like a different person, hiding yourself from me. You could've fallen all over me, coming to my games in my jersey and boots and nothing else."

That makes her laugh out loud. It's a sound I love, but I tilt my head as if to say, *"Work with me here."* She presses her lips into a tight line, her smile dissolving—sort of.

"But you didn't. You made fun of me, and you put me in my place and you opened up to me about things you don't talk about to anyone. You trusted me enough to bring down the walls you'd built. You allowed me to see the real you and you like me for who I am."

"Love," she interrupts.

"You *love* me for who I am," I correct before dropping a kiss on her nose. "I'm not leaving you. I'm not cheating on you. I am madly in love with you. It's very hard to get a Russian man to back down once he finds his true love."

She raises an eyebrow, cocking her head to one side.

"You didn't know this about Russians?" I ask, with a sly smile.

"I thought you were all stoic bad-asses?"

"Well, yes, we are," I confirm, wondering if she can feel the pride pounding in my chest. "Until it comes to love. In love, we are passionate and stubborn. My father was thirteen when he met my mother. He fell in love that day and never, *ever* had a second thought. I never understood it until I met you."

"You have to leave tonight, don't you?" she asks.

I nod. "I'm meeting the team in Pittsburgh."

"I'm so proud of you." She squeezes me tightly. "Go kick some Penguins ass!"

"I love you, *Audushka*." I lean in *thisclose* to her face, stopping shy of her lips. I understand her need to be in control, and I want her to be the one to close the gap. I want her to trust in my love. Her breath is warm on my face as her lips hover in front of mine.

"I love you, Sasha." She finally leans in, meeting my lips with hers—sealing our bond.

Chapter Twenty-One

AUDEN

"Nasty," I grumble, wiping my gravy-covered hand on the towel draped over my shoulder. After I've gotten most of the congealed brown slime off, I resume my task, placing dirty dishes into a large plastic bin sitting on the table I'm cleaning.

"Saving that for later, sweetie? I can get Chef to make you a plate, you know?" Loretta, one of my fellow servers, jokes, plucking a large chunk of bread off my rear end as she passes.

"Ha-ha," I deadpan, laughing as I straighten up, hefting the bin of dishes off the table and carrying it through the kitchen doors. How the hell had a roll gotten stuck to my ass?

I've been back at school for over a month. It's been a month and a half since I've seen Aleksandr. He's still in Charlotte playing for the Monarchs, which is amazing for him but hard on me. The original objections I had for not getting involved with him swirl in my head. Separation was inevitable, whether he got called to Charlotte or not. There's no professional hockey team in my dinky little college town, and I can't transfer anywhere in my junior year.

Absence must be easier for my brain to comprehend when I'm the one walking away.

How can I even think about transferring schools for someone I've only known for a little over a month? Thank goodness I've never been in love before. I probably would have been on the first season of Teen Mom.

"Apple pie, coffee, and a fruit plate, right?" I ask my grandparents, who had taken a seat in one of the booths in my section at Johnny's. They're in town looking at apartments. They'd put their house in Detroit on the market after the first of the year and they'll be moving to Bridgeland when it sells. They want a safer city, slower pace, and to be closer to me.

And here I am fantasizing about moving to wherever Aleksandr happens to be. Looks like I won't be in the running for the Number One Granddaughter Award. Again.

"Did you get your loan check?" Grandpa asks. For someone who isn't helping me pay for college, he's overly concerned about my finances.

I was well aware of my grandparents' stance on financing higher education. If I wanted to pursue anything past a high school diploma, I was on my own. I'd been okay with that because I'd had my small athletic scholarship to play soccer. The academic scholarship I received for my grades and test scores, coupled with student loans, covered the rest of my expenses.

I know Grandpa is concerned for me because I lost my soccer scholarship, but having to answer to someone who's not helping fund my education annoys the shit out of me.

"Should be here any day," I tell him. "I saved most of the money from translating for Aleksandr." Then I add, "I do well here, you know."

"What about that opening at the steakhouse Kristen told you about?" he presses.

I should never have told him about that. Johnny's Diner was my first waitressing job.

Sure, tips would be bigger at the steakhouse, but the diner is only open for breakfast and lunch, so the hours are great for working around my class schedule.

"It's always busy during my shifts. Good tips and quick turnover works for me. Plus, I've got customers that come back just to see me." I wink at my grandma.

"I'm sure you do," she says, glancing at my purple shirt. Did my grandma just check out my rack?

"Hey! I'm the reason you guys will be regulars, right?" I ask, casting my eyes downward to make sure my uniform polo is buttoned up. Don't want my grandparents to think I do shady things to get my tips.

"No, *Audushka*, it's the cooking. You can't get home-cooked food like this at those chain joints," Grandpa says as he peruses Johnny's menu. His wheels are turning, probably planning on dragging my grandma back here again tomorrow before they leave town.

He hates chain restaurants. He loves dumpy little diners like this one claiming they serve "home-cooked" meals. My grandma deals with it because she hates to cook. Don't get me wrong, she cooked throughout my childhood, but once Grandpa retired, her cooking became scarce. I have a feeling that once they move to Bridgeland, they'll be eating out quite a bit. I don't blame her. Almost forty years of putting meals on the table every night had to have gotten old.

"I have to run and get an order. I'll be right back." I spin around, flitting to another table, letting the two older men sitting there know I'll be right back with their lunches.

When I push back through the doors of the kitchen with the sandwiches, I notice another one of my regulars has taken his place at a table in the back of the restaurant. It's the same table he always chooses, back against the wall, facing the restaurant. I figure it was a cop thing.

Jason Taylor has become a regular after we'd met at Aleksandr's game. In our short interactions, I'd uncovered a few things about the strapping hunk of law-enforcement eye candy. He moved to Bridgeland after graduating from college because he didn't want to be a cop in Detroit. He comes from a big family. And he coaches a youth hockey team in town.

"Be right with you, Officer," I call, flashing him a smile as I deliver the sandwiches. I wouldn't call him a friend, but we get along well and he's a good tipper.

Jason waves in acknowledgment.

"Who is that, *Audushka*?" my grandpa asks, staring at Jason.

"Officer Taylor. He's another regular," I tell him as I fill a glass for Jason. Cola, no ice. Every time.

"Are you gonna switch it up today?" I tease, setting Jason's drink in front of him. He always orders a Cola without ice and a club sandwich with mustard instead of mayo.

Jason smiles and shakes his head. "Not today."

"Come on, man, live a little." I wink as I jot his order onto my little green pad. I'm not interested in him, but he's too cute not to flirt with. I spin around and take the ticket to the kitchen.

My grandpa is still staring at Jason when I come back to the table with my grandparents' desserts.

"*Dedushka*, please stop looking at him. He could arrest you or something," I plead, though I don't think Jason can arrest him for staring. But he could stop eating at Johnny's, and I could lose a regular customer who tips me well.

"He looks familiar." Grandpa leans back so I can set his pie in front of him, but he doesn't take his eyes off Jason.

"He's from Detroit. His brother played with *Sasha* on the Aviators. Landon Taylor." I glance at Jason as I speak. Voices travel, and he can probably hear us talking about him.

"Enough, Viktor. Let the boy enjoy his lunch." Grandma pokes Grandpa's wrist with her fork.

"Ow." He laughs, shaking and flexing his hand.

I see him shoot Jason one more look before he digs into his pie.

"He's handsome," Grandma says, spearing a strawberry from her plate and bringing it to her mouth. "Reminds me of you when you were young."

Did Grandpa just blush? Time to find something to do. Thankfully I'm at work, where I have multiple excuses to take my leave.

Oh, look, table six needs to be wiped down.

"Are you coming to dinner with us tonight?" Gram asks.

"Nope. I have band practice."

"Band practice?" she repeats, taking a sip of her water. Grandpa stops chewing.

"Yeah. This guy heard me sing at karaoke and asked me to be in his band. Pretty cool, eh?" I answer, stretching to wipe the far end of the booth behind my grandparents.

"Your mother was in a band," Gram says.

"Excuse me?" I whip around, knocking my funny bone as I stand up. It takes every fiber of my being not to curse in front of my grandparents. Instead, I grab my elbow and rub it briskly.

"In high school. She had a beautiful voice." Gram shakes her head as if coming out of a daze and spears a melon from her plate.

This is a Twilight Zone moment for me. My grandparents rarely offer information about my mother. And I never heard that my mom had been in a band during high school, not even from my aunts and uncles. I'm not surprised to find out another thing I didn't know about her, I'm surprised Gram actually shared the information.

"Well, now I know where I got my voice. I mean, I've heard *Dedushka* sing in church and I knew I didn't get my pipes from him."

That gets a smile out of both of them, so I spin around and retreat to the kitchen.

Joking is my favorite defense against awkwardness. You'd think by age twenty I'd jump on the chance to talk about my mom by asking more questions, especially since Gram is the one who brought her up. But no. She caught me off guard, and I tucked my tail between my legs and avoided the situation. If I try to revisit the conversation at a later time, I'm sure their mouths would be closed tighter than a brand-new pickle jar.

The ever-revolving door of grief.

Chapter Twenty-Two

AUDEN

"Here." I thrust a small stack of papers at Greg. Using Gram's rare revealing moment as inspiration to open up, I just handed one of my bandmates, someone I'd met less than two months ago, a collection of deeply personal and emotionally raw poems. As soon as they leave my hands, I want to snatch them back. And burn them.

An eyebrow caterpillar creeps across Greg's forehead as he scans the first page and flips through the others.

"I write poems," I explain, casting my eyes to my feet. My scuffed black boots had never been so interesting. "Not good poems, but, um. I didn't know if you could use them for lyrics or whatever."

Poetry has been a passion since I was a kid, but because they were an insight into my warped mind, I'd never been brave enough to share them with anyone. Slicing open my emotional wrists and allowing others to see the blood flow had never been a desire.

Then I met Aleksandr, and removing the piano-sized weight of pent-up repression from my shoulders sounded like a good idea for the first time in my life.

Greg shakes the papers at me. "This is awesome, Aud."

I raise my head to meet his eyes. "That tune will change when you actually read them."

He laughs. "I just meant it's great that you write. And, yes, I can use them."

"Thanks," I mumble.

Greg drops to the floor in the living room of the house he shares with the guys. He pats the carpet. "Pull up a patch of"—he pauses as he inspects the area—"gross, green, shag carpet from the seventies. We're jamming tonight."

Aaron is already on the ground, his long jean-clad legs sprawled out in front of him as he leans against the most hideous sofa I've ever seen.

"Oh my." I hold a hand to my mouth, eyeing the couch as I plop down in between him and Greg. "That's an unfortunate piece of furniture."

Aaron lets his head fall back against the light green fabric littered with gaudy pink flowers. "My great-aunt died last year and this old girl is what my mom saved for me."

"It's ugly as shit, but none of us had any other furniture, so—" Greg shrugs.

"You have other furniture," I say. "I see a lovely modern piece over there." I point to a black, faux-leather beanbag across the room.

"That's mine. I'm the one with style," Josh jokes as he walks into the living room carrying three white pillar candles. He squats slowly, drops to his knees, then sets each candle down in the middle of the circle of seating we've formed. It looks like a preteen sleepover and we're about to have a séance.

"Are we gonna call on the spirits of rock legends gone too soon?" I ask as Josh settles into an Indian-style position.

"No," Josh snorts. Then he lifts his eyes to Greg. "You think it'd work?"

"Shut up. Shut up. Shut the fuuuck up," Aaron sings, using guitar chords to emphasize his point.

I stick out my tongue. He winks and strums the opening riffs of "Making Believe."

"No way? You learned it?" I shriek, and pound the carpet in excitement.

"Thank Greg," Aaron says, casting his eyes Greg's way. "He told us to learn it for the next gig. It is an awesome song, though."

Greg flashes me a smile. "After you mentioned it in your audition, we had to learn it." Then he frowns and yells at Josh. "Dude, come on."

"What?" Josh asks as he lights his cigarette from one of the candles on the floor.

"I love you guys already," I say, laughing at their banter.

"Hear that boys? She's saying we have a chance." Aaron winks again.

"Fuck you, man," Greg mumbles. Josh releases a gust of smoke toward Aaron's face.

I don't get the inside joke, but I assume Aaron's teasing me because he still needs time to get to know me before he feels warm and fuzzy. I knew from the start he'd be the one I'd have to win over.

When I'd returned to school after winter break, I'd braced myself for the harsh reality of a schedule with no soccer activities. The humiliation of being cut still thrummed through my veins, but it was actually refreshing to be rid of countless practices, meetings, and games thrown on top of classes, studying, working, and starting the after-school program in Detroit.

By taking a step back, I finally saw how grueling my first two years at Central State had been.

But if I thought joining a band would be easier on my schedule, I was wrong. I'd assumed the guys would give me a break because I didn't know my ass from my elbow when it came to making music. Instead, they pushed me harder and made me practice more.

When I wasn't in class, at the library, or at the diner, I was practicing with the guys. They even got me a vocal coach. "Vocal coach" being the fancy title Josh had given to a girl in his music program whom he'd bribed into helping me prepare. My vocals were coming along well, but my stage presence was a different story. I still remember the first time it finally clicked.

"*Tap your foot. Shake your hair around.*" *Aaron's face turned a deeper shade of red every time he yelled at me. It would have been comical if I hadn't been the one he was angry with. When he stomped up the stairs, I thought I'd finally broken him, but he returned a minute later with a full-length mirror.*

"Start again," he ordered, leaning the mirror against the wall in front of me.

Greg and Josh started the song from the beginning, and Aaron joined the song. I stared at the microphone as I swayed from foot to foot. Anything to avoid looking in the mirror.

"Do something. Move!" Aaron yelled, waving his hands in front of his chest, abruptly halting his guitar riff. I rolled my eyes, holding them up as I took a few deep breaths. "Look in the fucking mirror." Aaron's voice was a glacier, slow and icy.

"Jesus," Josh muttered. I couldn't tell if he'd directed his exasperation at me or at Aaron. Probably me. I wasn't used to having to practice something to be good at it. Not to sound cocky, because I worked my ass off, but soccer came easy for me. The skills needed to stand in front of a crowd of people waiting for me to sing out of key did not come as easily.

"Stop being a dick," Greg told Aaron.

"Fuck off."

"Chill out!" I yelled back. Kicking me while I was down was not the way to boost my confidence.

"No, I won't chill out," Aaron snapped, but the bitterness from before was gone. "You can do this, Auden. You're good."

I stole a glance at the other guys. Greg and Josh were both nodding, giving me hopeful half smiles.

Accepting compliments had always been difficult. In a generation of everyone-gets-a-trophy sports teams and parents who make sure their kids know how wonderful they are, I grew up with grandparents who didn't believe in any of that "generation of spoiled, entitled bullshit."

Compliments and praise were just words in the dictionary to my grandparents, who raised me to be humble and modest to the extreme, since pride is one of the deadly sins. Don't get me wrong, they didn't make me feel bad about myself on purpose, but accomplishments weren't talked about.

Asking if I looked nice in an outfit or if I played well was met with a "Don't be so vain," or "You're good at soccer, don't rub it in other people's faces." It was just how I grew up, and how my grandparents grew up, and so on. A mirror was for making sure I looked presentable. Hair combed? Makeup out of place? Was everything buttoned, tucked, and zipped?

"I'm sorry, okay. Can we start again?" I asked. I cranked my neck side to side and rolled my shoulders back. Time to approach singing the same way I *approached soccer. Be confident. Own it. But don't make a big deal of being confident and owning it. Just do it and shut the hell up.*

After taking a deep, cleansing breath, I lifted my eyes to my reflection. As I stared at the athletic girl standing tall in a long black tank top, dark blue skinny jeans, and her favorite beat-up Doc Martens, something clicked. I wasn't the quiet ghost floating through the halls of my high school, just hoping to get by without disturbing the peace. I wasn't the average girl on the soccer team, hidden among better players. I wasn't Kristen's wing woman. I wasn't a professional hockey player's girlfriend.

In that mirror, I saw myself as Auden for the first time, and plain old Auden was beautiful. I wasn't simple, or fake, or hiding behind someone else's confidence or talent. I was a fun-yet-snarky Russian translator. The key being the Russian-translator part, because my client was the reason for my newfound confidence and ability to blow the past away like the white seeds of a dead dandelion. The man who helped me recognize my confidence, strength, and worth. The man who still helped me believe it, even though we weren't in the same state. The man I should've never fallen in love with, but did.

No matter who'd been the original organizer, I was the front woman of Strange Attraction now. And it was time to take ownership and responsibility for our band, like I'd done with soccer and the Central Club. Picturing myself in a position of power was liberating and energizing. Greg and Aaron may have arranged the music and turned the words into songs, but those songs were my words. I was the one jotting all of the raw emotions swirling in my head onto whatever empty writing space I found, whether on receipts from the grocery store, or on the inside of a Pop-Tart box before it went into the recycling bin.

The guys fiddled behind me, strumming chords and waiting for me to turn some kind of corner on this whole rock-band-lead-singer thing. I couldn't keep the smile from my lips. I waved my hand toward the guys, and Josh's drumbeats pounded in response.

I'm ready. Bring it.

Chapter Twenty-Three

AUDEN

As I wait in the diner's parking lot for my car to heat up, I toss my head back and forth, properly rocking out to "Sex" by The 1975. A thunderous pounding against my window startles me out of rock-out mode.

When I lift my eyes, Jason Taylor stands on the other side of my door in full police uniform. Because of my traumatic childhood, the nervous buzz of hypervigilance always simmers under my skin. I don't like being snuck up on, don't like being touched, and I certainly don't like being surprised by cops banging on my window when I clearly haven't been breaking any laws.

As I roll down the window, my heart slams against my rib cage like kamikaze ninjas attempting to kick their way out. "Is everything all right, Officer Taylor?" I lean over to lower the stereo volume.

"Do you have a few minutes to talk?" he asks.

Well, that didn't answer my question.

"Is this an emergency?" I ask, tightening my grip on the steering wheel. Get to the point, Taylor.

"No! Geez, I'm sorry Auden. No, it's not an emergency."

I close my eyes and release my death grip on the steering wheel, letting out a deep breath. "Can it wait until later?" I glance at the clock on the dashboard. "I'm already late for class."

I'm not a big road rager, but I'm already running late for my three-thirty class, due to a last-minute table I'd taken. I'd felt guilty because Johnny was swamped, and she'd grabbed three tables at once to allow me to get going.

"Oh, sorry. Yeah. Yeah, I guess it can wait." Jason rubs his neck with a leather-gloved hand. "What time is your class over?"

This is a really weird situation. Jason is obviously nervous. The curiosity of what he needs to talk about that could make him so uncomfortable gets the best of me.

"You know what?" I kill the engine and unfasten my seat belt. "I'm already half an hour late. Class will be over by the time I get there."

"You sure?" Jason takes a step back, allowing me to open my door.

"Depends. Am I in trouble?" I need to know what the hell I'd done before I surrender myself without a fight.

"No, Auden, not at all." He kicks a mound of packed snow, sending brown ice balls flying. "I'm really sorry you're missing class. I just wanted to talk about your mom."

"Excuse me?"

"Let's go inside." He stuffs his hands in the pockets of his leather cop coat and nods toward the diner.

Jason's got my full attention, so I follow him back in to Johnny's. Now I'm the nervous one. Why would a police officer I barely know want to talk about my mom? Had something new about her death come to light? Maybe her killer had been found with DNA that couldn't be identified fourteen years ago?

And maybe I've watched a few too many Dateline marathons.

We slide into seats at Jason's favorite table. Johnny walks over with a pot of coffee. She glances up. "What can I get—" Her head snaps up again, eyes wide. "What are you doing back?" She flips over two mugs and starts filling the first.

I put my hand over Jason's mug. "Coke for him."

Johnny nods. "You would know." She has a teasing lilt to her voice. Which is super annoying.

Hell, yeah, because I'm a good server, I want to say, but with Jason fumbling nervously with the silverware rolled in a napkin, I'm not in my normal joking mood.

"Why would you want to talk about my mom?" I ask Jason after Johnny is out of earshot.

He continues flipping the silverware end over end. "After we met at the hockey game, I was talking to Aleksandr about you and he mentioned your last name. It sounded familiar, but I couldn't remember where I'd heard it before. Then I finally figured out where I knew the name Berezin from."

A loud, scratchy robotic voice fills the air, and I jump, almost knocking over the cup of coffee Johnny poured for me that I'm not going to drink.

Jason drops the silverware and reaches down to twist a knob on his radio, lowering the volume. It's still on, but faint. "Sorry about that."

Johnny comes back with a Coke for Jason and sets it in front of him. "Are you two eating?"

I shake my head. Johnny rushes off to get drinks for another table. The diner is still hopping, and Johnny is by herself. I should get up and help her, I think.

"Do you think we look alike, Auden?" Jason interrupts my thoughts.

It's such an odd question; I can't help but jerk my eyes up and search his face. He's handsome, with light blue eyes and dirty blond hair, like me. His face is long, whereas mine is round; his skin, olive toned; mine, alabaster.

I shrug. "I don't know. I guess our eyes and hair are similar."

"I definitely look like that older man you were talking to when I was in here last week."

"That was my grandfather." I cock my head. "Why are you trying to find similarities between you and my family?"

"Because I'm your brother."

"What?" I gag on my spit.

"Biologically."

"Dude, what are you talking about?"

"I told you I came from a big family, right? The Taylors adopted me. They've fostered a lot of kids and adopted three. They've always done open adoption, in case any of us wanted to find our biological families someday. Open means they list the biological mother's name on the paperwork." He pauses, but I don't speak, so he continues. "I called my mom and asked her if she could look up my real mom's name in my adoption papers. She did, and then I remembered why your name clicked. My biological mom's name is Valerie Berezin. That's your mom, right?"

"Yeah, except my mom never had any other kids." This guy is crazy. I'm relieved he made us come inside to a public area to have this conversation. Don't cops have to pass some kind of test to prove they aren't insane before they're provided a gun?

"How would you know? I'm four years older than you are."

"Wouldn't my family tell me?"

"I, well," he stammers, but I'm not listening because as soon as the question leaves my mouth, I knows he's telling the truth.

The answer is no. My repressed, secretive, we-don't-talk-about-unpleasant-things family probably wouldn't have told me.

I lean forward to inspect Jason's face again, from his eyebrows, across to his ears, and down the slope of his nose to his mouth and chin. He's right about the familial similarities. He looks exactly like pictures of Grandpa when he was young. Viktor Berezin and Jason Taylor have the same nose, which was also my mother's nose. Combine that with the blue eyes and blond hair we shared, and he's a Berezin for sure.

"Holy shit." I fall back against the chair and cover my mouth with my hands in a prayer-like formation. "So are we, like, half brother and sister? Same mom, different dad?"

Jason shrugs. "That I don't know. The only name on my paperwork is Valerie Berezin." He picks up the silverware and begins flipping it again. Must be a nervous habit.

"This is fucking crazy."

"I know." Jason's eyes meet mine. "I'm sorry I threw all this at you. I just"—he sighs—"I didn't know what to do. I still don't. I hope you don't hate me for telling you this way."

"Well, I don't think Hallmark makes a card for it, do they?" I ask, letting out a small laugh.

I'm not mad at Jason. I'm mad at my grandparents. How the hell could they keep my having a brother from me? Hey, just so you know, your mom gave a baby boy up for adoption before you were born. Thought we'd throw it out there, in case he looks you up someday since, you know, some adopted kids search for their biological families.

"You're taking this better than I thought you would." Jason cocks his head and leans back, as if I'm going to make like a lion and bite his head off.

"Well, I'm shocked. And confused. And angry. But not at you. I don't understand my family." I shake my head. "Whatever. I guess they figured me having a brother I could find out about someday wasn't my business."

"Should I, um—" Jason hesitates. "Should I stop eating here?"

"What? No." I put my hand on his, halting the annoying silverware gymnastics he has going. "I have to figure things out, but I don't hate you or anything."

"Thanks." He lets out a deep breath, sitting back in his chair.

"Plus, you make me look like a better server than I am. Did you see how impressed Johnny was that I knew exactly what you drink?" I joke. I don't want to take out any anger on him. He's just the messenger. And my brother, evidently.

"She thinks you have a crush on me."

"Ewwww. A big huge ewwww to that. You're my brother." I grin. "I don't know where we go from here. I mean, you have a family that you obviously love. Do you even want a relationship with me?"

"I do. Otherwise, I wouldn't have told you."

"Are your parents okay with it?" I'd probably be pissed if a kid I'd adopted and raised since birth wanted to find his biological family, wondering why I wasn't good enough.

"Yeah. I think Mom was upset at first, but she understands. She knew it might happen. It's one of the things you have to accept when you adopt a kid. Plus, I told her you and Aleksandr were dating. He's her favorite player."

"He is? Even when her son plays for the Aviators?" I ask.

He chuckles. "Other than Landon. Her own kid doesn't count."

I laugh.

"Was Landon adopted?" I ask. It's not my business, I'm just curious.

"No. He's a real Taylor. It's this totally weird scenario. Mom didn't think she could have kids, so they adopted me, and then she got pregnant with Landon. We have two younger brothers who are adopted, but I've seen more than twenty-five foster kids go in and out of our house. My parents are amazing people."

"Sounds like it," I say a bit too wistfully.

I should feel bad for Jason because our mom gave him up. Instead, shameful jealousy warms my cheeks. He'd been adopted by wonderful, open, loving people, while I got stuck with a repressed family who rarely broached the subject of the dead. Or the living, for that matter.

Just having those thoughts solidifies what a horrible person I am. When will I grow up and let go?

Jason scans the restaurant, his eyes darting from Angus, a local farmer with a weathered face hidden by his fuzzy white beard, to Johnny, who's refilling Angus's brown porcelain coffee mug.

"Sorry to drop all of this on you, Auden." Jason shove his seat back. "I better, um—I've got paperwork to do before my shift ends anyway."

"This was all on the taxpayers' dime?" I ask, glad for a subject change.

"I have my radio on. I heard the calls coming in."

"I'm teasing," I explain. "You're gonna have to get used to my humor, bro."

"Look forward to it." He stands up, getting a few bills out of his pocket.

"Oh, come on," I say, getting to my feet as well. "I think I can handle buying you a Coke."

"It's free, right?"

"Yep." I laugh. "See, you get me already."

"See you around, Auden." He starts walking to the door.

"Hey, Jay!" I call. He spins to face me. "I'm pretty lucky to have such a good guy as a brother."

He moves toward me. "Yeah, well, you're a rock star, dating a pro-hockey player, and you put together an after-school program for at-risk youth. I think I got pretty lucky in the sister department, too."

"Rock star. Ha!" I laugh. The rest made me sound pretty damn awesome. And it was all true.

"Landon is impressed with the program. He and a few guys on the team go every week." He puts his hand on the door. "If you start one here, let me know. I'd love to help."

"Cool." I nod. A program is already in the works for Bridgeland. I'm just waiting on approvals from my academic advisor and the grant money I need to rent a space.

I lift my hand in an awkward semi-wave before Jason disappears.

My brother.

The queasy feeling building in my stomach for the last ten minutes threatens its way to my throat. I grab the Cola on the table and take a gulp, before catching myself and slamming the glass back onto the table. Brown liquid and bubbles slosh out the sides. I don't know anything about this guy, he could have herpes or something.

What am I really worried about? Catching the honesty bug?

"Hot date tonight?" Johnny asks, whisking dirty plates off a table.

Gross.

I follow her to the kitchen carrying my coffee mug and Jason's glass. "That was my brother."

"Your brother? That boy's been eating here for a month, and you never told me he was your brother."

I set the dishes onto the back counter for the dishwasher. "I didn't know."

Chapter Twenty-Four
AUDEN

Ever made a snap decision that sounds great at the time, but once you act on it, you realize you've gone about it the wrong way?

Yeah. Story of my life.

I'd jumped in my car and driven for two hours, straight home from Johnny's parking lot. Never in my entire college career have I ever skipped multiple classes in one day, but confronting my grandparents about having a brother seemed like a good reason for it.

When I burst into my grandparents' house, they're both watching television in the living room.

"Auden!" Grandma exclaims when I barge through the door. "What are you doing here?"

"Some guy just told me he was my brother," I say. I've run through the conversation a hundred times in my head on the drive over, yet standing in front of my grandparents has me shackled with apprehension.

Technically, I don't know if Jason was telling the truth or not. But I do know that it wouldn't be the first time my grandparents didn't tell me something. I'm not sure if omission of the truth counts as lying, but all my pent-up frustration of never knowing anything is coming out right here, right now, as everything I thought I knew unravels around me.

"Jesus, Mary, and Joseph." Grandma clamps both hands together as if in prayer, holding them in front of her nose and mouth. Jason's account must be true, if Gram's calling on all three.

"Where were you?" Grandpa asks, snapping his recliner down and leaning forward, his usually calm face creased with angry lines.

"I was at work and the cop who always eats at the diner told me he was my brother." No turning back now. "Is it true?"

Grandpa shoots Grandma a glance, whose shoulders shake while tears trickle down her cheeks. He takes a deep breath, rubbing the back of his neck with the palm of his hand. I stay silent for as long as I can—which isn't long.

"Just tell me the truth!" Instead of avoiding the subject, I want to add.

"Don't you dare raise your voice to us," Grandpa snaps. "Why do you hate us so much, Auden? All we've ever done is try to give you the best life we could. Why are you so angry?"

I roll my eyes. "Here we go again, the famous guilt trip. It's always my fault. My attitude, my temper, my mood swings. You blame me for things I don't have control over. What did I do wrong? I just asked a question."

"You don't know what you're talking about. The past is the past. It is none of your business and there is no reason to bring it up again!" he shouts.

"There is a reason to bring it up when some guy says he's my brother because my mom gave him up for adoption!" I scream.

The blow is so sudden and unexpected, I feel the sting on my cheek before I even see Grandpa's hand. I've been yelled at, spanked across the thighs (which hurts more than the padded rear end)—hell, I've even been hit with a yard stick—but never slapped across the face.

I stare at him, breath heavy, shoulders heaving, my lips curling into a furious scowl, before spinning around and slamming my palms against the storm door. The wind catches it and stretches it all the way back on its hinges. I don't look back to see if it's broken, just load back into my car and back out of the driveway.

After the two-hour drive to figure out my approach, I thought I would've handled the situation better. But no.

I don't know how to handle anything.

Despite another two-hour drive back to school, I still haven't calmed down. I burst through the door to my apartment and rush to my bedroom, without checking to see if either Kristen or Lacy are home. I throw myself face down on my bed, shaking with convulsions.

Catching my breath is impossible with my face smothered by my pillow, so I turn my head to the side, choking up air in small gasps.

And analyze. In twenty years, I've analyzed events in my life to death. And now I have a reason to do it all again.

Why is Grandpa angry with me for what Jason told me? How is the situation my fault?

It's always the same, always my fault somehow. No matter what the incident, no matter how ridiculous. I get the blame.

Can I believe anything my grandparents have ever told me? Why would they keep so many parts of my mom's life secret? They've never been open to talking about her, but if they knew I had a brother for all these years, why hadn't they told me?

I rack my brain trying to figure out why our family has to repress everything. If we don't mention unpleasant things, do they go away? At what point does sheltering someone "for their own good" inflict more harm than good? I'm old enough to handle the truth.

I'll drive myself crazy trying to figure out my family, so I reach out to Aleksandr instead. The call goes straight to his voice mail, where I leave a shaky, rambling—possibly incoherent—message and hang up.

Then, I flip on the practically antique, thirteen-inch black-and-white TV on my dresser, hoping to find something mundane to take my mind off of the situation.

I settle on Grease, which I've seen fifty times. It's not one of my favorites, but it's like a car accident, you don't want to stop and look, but you do.

Musicals always crack me up. I can't remember ever breaking out into a song and perfectly choreographed dance. Unless you count the time at a high school athletics banquet when my teammates and I all busted out into the chorus to Biz Markie's "Just a Friend." The performance included swaying and clapping to the beat, but not a full-on dance routine.

Eventually, my mind hits its capacity for stimulation and I drift off to sleep.

Chapter Twenty-Five

AUDEN

"Hang around. We'll be back in twenty minutes," I shout to the audience. Then I spin around, holding one fist out, which Aaron bumps. "This is so freaking cool!"

Despite my anger with my grandparents, or maybe fueled by it, tonight has been my best performance as Strange Attraction's singer. There had only been two others before this one, but I'm improving and meshing well with the guys. We sound amazing, and we've drawn a large crowd who seem to like what they've heard based on the number of jumping and swaying bodies who'd littered the dance floor during our performance.

The makeshift DJ, who's known by the regular patrons of Wreckage as the head bouncer, pushes past me to get to the sound system, located to the left of Josh's drums. He presses some buttons and Wreckage's signature dance mix blasts through the speakers. According to the bouncers, a blend of old nineties hip-hop is the best way to keep people on the floor while bands take their breaks.

I bounce as I follow the guys to the bar. It's as if Wreckage's floor has been replaced with one of those huge inflatable things that little kids love to bounce in.

The guys drank during our set, but I hadn't for fear I might forget words or—god forbid—stage presence. I allow myself one drink before our final set, though. Maybe it'll help calm my nervous excitement.

Wreckage is a tiny, dingy bar whose claim to fame in its fifteen-year existence is that it's the only place in Bridgeland where you can hear live music every night of the week. Unlike the wannabe club-type bars in town, a typical Friday night at Wreckage usually draws a casual crowd.

Tonight, there seems to be more miniskirts and fuck-me boots than I've ever seen before, which means it's becoming the new "it" hangout for students. Bridgeland is small, so bars go through a popularity rotation. Anything new becomes the place to be, until it peaks with crowds and the newness fizzles, and then people return to their old favorites.

As I slide onto an empty bar stool next to Greg, I smooth down my blue-and-green mini-kilt. A black tank top and boots complete the outfit. "Singer" is my newest role to play, as "Soccer Girl" had been before this. The small stage at Wreckage replaces the field, and sexy clothes have become my new uniform.

"You know what I'm saying, Aud?" Aaron asks. "You went to Catholic school, right?"

"I did," I affirm, though I have no clue what he'd said before that. I hadn't been listening, busy contemplating my fashion status and all. I shift toward him, giving him my full attention.

"It's all bullshit, right? I mean, look at you. You're a straight-up product of that shit, and you're all about fucking and coveting stuff," he says.

"What am I coveting?" I'll let them think I live the rock and roll vixen lifestyle, because admitting I'm still a virgin isn't an option.

I nod my thanks to the bartender as he sets my trusty vodka club and a beer for Greg onto the bar.

"I bet you covet that dude standing over there staring at you." Aaron nods toward the door.

I roll my eyes but glance over my shoulder toward the door, half disbelieving, half curious. No one is there, just as I suspected. "You're completely mental. And for the record, I don't think you're using covet the right way."

"All the bullshit is fucking up my head." Aaron taps his temple. "That's what happens, man."

"I'd put my money on the drinks you just downed." I nod to the empty shot and pint glasses in front of him.

"Or the special brownies," Josh chimes in, curling his fingers into air quotes as he says it. Greg snorts. Aaron's alcohol—and edible—influenced rants are famous, even to a newcomer like me. I especially love it when he makes up words.

"Air quotes? Been watching I Love the Fucking Nineties on VH1 again, Joshua? Oh, shit!" Aaron jumps up, and his bar stool knocks against my knee. "Be right back."

"Ow." I rub my knee, then turn my attention to my drink, violently assaulting the three lime wedges with my straw. Lime pulp swirls around the fizzy whirlpool, making it as thick and murky as my thoughts.

I miss Aleksandr.

I haven't seen him since he'd been called up to Charlotte two months ago. I tried to tell myself the phone calls and Skype chats would be enough, but they aren't. Sometimes I just need to be wrapped in his arms, inhaling his sweet yet masculine scent. Even the pack of clove cigarettes I'd bought to sniff when I missed him just doesn't cut it.

I sigh and twirl my hair between my fingers.

"Nervous?" Greg asks, nodding to my twirling. I glance at my fingers and let my hair slide through them.

"No." I shake my head and straighten in my seat. The hair twirling has been a habit since I was a kid, not a sign of nerves.

"Something wrong?" he asks.

"I'm fine." It's a lie, but I don't want to talk about how much I miss Aleksandr—or any of the fucked-up tension in my family right now.

"You can talk to me. You know that, right?" Greg cups my shoulder, causing the hair on my arms to bristle at the unexpected touch. He sweeps the heavy bangs out of my eyes, only for them to fall right back into place. "Thinking about Varenkov?"

"Not having this discussion." I edge away from him as much as I can without sitting on my neighbor's lap.

"He's living his dream a thousand miles away. Without you. And he's wrecking it up there." Greg takes a long pull on his beer.

I silently will myself to keep my clenched fists at my sides. Greg knows exactly which wound to squeeze to promote bleeding. Even more than anyone else, since I'd given him poem after poem of my insecurities to pour through looking for song lyrics.

He sounds a lot like Pavel Gribov, which has my right-jab reflex on high alert.

But Greg is wrong. Charlotte is only 748 miles away.

"You're so blind, Auden," Greg mumbles.

"What?"

"I'm right here. I'll still be here when you realize he's not coming back."

Aleksandr had been right about me from the start; I really am clueless when it comes to guys. Greg spews trash because he's jealous. I try to recall a time when I'd given Greg the impression I had any interest in him.

"I can't do this right now." I pick up my drink and walk toward Josh. After just finding out I have a brother that my family never told me about, and my boyfriend being miles away when I need him most, I can't handle having a conversation about Greg's unrequited love for me.

Josh taps me on the shoulder, nodding to the door. "Celebrity sighting at Wreckage."

"Great. Fucking great." I hear Greg mumble.

Throwing a glance over my shoulder, I inhale sharp and quick when I see the man I only glimpse in my dreams these days. The left side of his mouth turns up in a smirk just like the first one he'd ever flashed me.

Aleksandr looks more god than ghost as he stands in the doorway of Wreckage. Though it's only been a couple of months, he seems taller, with unfamiliar muscles rippling through the tight black T-shirt he's modeling. Maybe it's the bar's lighting or the moonlight shining in from outside, but I swear his cobalt eyes are twinkling.

I elbow my way toward the door, throwing "Excuse me" and "Sorry" into the air. A dozen questions about his presence peppers my mind, but the smile on his full, inviting lips makes me forget them all.

I wrap my arms around his neck and twist my fingers in his crazy sexy hair before pulling him into the bathroom. Aleksandr's response is instant, encircling me in his arms and returning the intoxicating, dangerous, passionate kiss.

Once inside the bathroom, he shoves me against the door, freeing one of his hands to turn the lock. The muscles of his chest are rigid and unyielding as I slide my hands over them. His mouth is hot and wet as he parts my lips with his tongue. He holds my lower lip in his teeth, tugging before he releases me and pulls away.

As he holds me at arm's length, his swirling blue eyes pierce me with an intensity I recognize. Lust. Hunger. Want. I love when he looks at me that way, like he can't wait to devour me.

"You're absolutely delicious, my love," Aleksandr whispers in Russian. Hearing him speak his native language, the language we use to communicate knowing no one else understood us, sends flames through me.

"I missed you," I respond, my voice thick and raspy. My palms slide from his hair to the back of his head, prickled by soft stubble.

Aleksandr presses his mouth on mine again and places his palms against the door, boxing me in. I roll my head to the right, baring my neck for a barrage of fast, firm kisses. He kisses an invisible trail down my chest to the valley between my breasts. He whispers, "I love you," so softly, I'm not even sure if I heard it over our accelerated breathing and pumping hearts. Then he brings his face back up, crushing his lips on mine again.

Though every inch of his hard body still restrains me against the door, the intensity in his touch softens. Excitement pools in my core when his calloused fingers brush my cheeks.

Aleksandr is everything I need. Gentle and kind, yet hard and unyielding when necessary. His burning blue eyes implore mine for answers I can't give right now.

I look down, unable to meet the intensity. I want to bury my face in my hands, but his body has me immobilized. Though I'd planned on ignoring what Greg said, doubts about Aleksandr are always there.

I'll never know what happens when Aleksandr is in Charlotte or on a road trip. I'll never know who he's hanging out with or if he's flirting with other women, whether it's his personality or not. I have to push aside my doubts and insecurities about situations I can't control and focus on the ones I can.

Like this one.

I seize his lips again and jump up to wrap my legs around his waist. He adjusts his arms to cradle me easily, which makes me wish I hadn't worn fishnet stockings under my skirt. He pulls back from me, panting and smiling.

"I'm not going to fuck you in the bathroom of a bar, *Audushka*."

"Why not?" I ask, breathless and confused.

He leans in, his lips brushing my ear, and whispers, "When I fuck you, it'll be special. Like on the ice or the bar at my place."

"Those choices sure do sound romantic." I laugh and jump down. He releases his grip on my backside, but his hands stay on my hips. "What are you doing here?"

"You needed me. I came."

It's that simple for him.

"When do you have to go back?" I can't believe he'd hopped on a plane just to visit me. I must have sounded just as rough as I felt in the message I'd left him last night.

"Tomorrow morning."

I nod as my heart deflates. Puddles that have been accumulating in the rims of my eyes spill out.

"Please don't do that." He takes my face in his hands, pushing my hair back and wiping the skin under my eyes with his thumbs. "I thought you'd be happy, *Audushka*."

"I am." I nod again, lips quivering as I speak. "You didn't have to come here. You've got more important things to think about."

"When will you understand how much I love you?" He tilts my face until my eyes meet his. "Nothing is more important than you."

And just like that, Aleksandr Varenkov turns my world upside down again. He has a talent for cutting through my bullshit and calling me out when I'm acting like an idiot. He's the kind of person I need to keep me grounded.

"Can't wait to see your sexy ass on stage." He flips the lock on the bathroom door, biting his lower lip and throwing me a wink as he backs out.

I rush to the sink, taking a few deep breaths before turning the nozzle for the cold water and running the inside of my wrists under the stream. The frigid liquid does little to calm my excitement.

I needed Aleksandr, and he came. Someone dropping everything to rush to my side is as foreign a concept to me as asking for help. Maybe I don't realize what love really means.

When I hear one of the bathroom stalls behind me unlock, my shoulders stiffen and my knuckles turn white, gripping the sink. The reflection of one of Josh's many hook-ups appears in the mirror. I don't let on that I recognize her, ignoring her presence and grabbing a paper towel to dry my hands instead.

"Sorry, I didn't mean to listen. It's just, you locked the door and I didn't want to interrupt," she explains. She steps up to the sink next to me and begins washing her hands. "That was intense. Who was he?"

Without taking my eyes from my reflection, I wipe away the smeared eyeliner with my fingertips and coat my lips with red gloss before turning to face her.

"Who was who?" I answer, yanking the door open and exiting the room. Maybe it was rude, but unlike many girls I've come across in college town bathrooms, I don't discuss my love life with strangers in the bathroom.

The guys are probably getting antsy, so I hurry to the stage. I mull over a dozen excuses as I walk back. Though the other guys would want fist bumps, I doubt telling Greg, 'Sorry I'm running late. I almost fucked Aleksandr in the bathroom' would go over well.

"Social D!" Aaron yells as soon as I jump on stage and take my place behind the microphone stand. Thanks to my audition, the Social Distortion version of "Making Believe" has become one of our signature covers.

I close my eyes and take a deep breath. The song starts with a slow, heart-wrenching verse, just my voice against the backdrop of Aaron's guitar. The second verse is the same, but Greg's bass and Josh's drum beats kick in flawlessly. I put both hands on the microphone and look straight ahead, seeing only the tops of bobbing heads until I get into a groove. As I begin to loosen up, I release one hand to tap my upper thigh with the beat while I sing.

It's surprisingly easy to get into my groove despite knowing Aleksandr is somewhere in the audience watching. When I'm onstage, awkward, shy Auden leaves my body, and the unnamed, unrecognizable lead singer of Strange Attraction takes over. It's almost second nature for my alter ego to flirt with people in the crowd and writhe against the microphone stand.

I scan the crowd as I sing, making sure I pause to catch the eyes of men in the audience. I lock eyes with a guy right in front of the stage and throw him a seductive smirk before searching the crowd for another poor soul to tease. Being onstage always triggers Greg's earliest piece of advice.

The key to being a successful front woman is to be sultry and unforgettable. Bands with female singers are easy to ignore if their presence doesn't captivate the audience.

Aleksandr stands in the middle of the floor, eyes transfixed on me. I've never seen him look at me the way he's looking at me at this moment.

And I'm not talking about a lust-induced gaze like he had in the bathroom. I can only describe it as awe; maybe even admiration. As if he's suddenly aware of me in a manner he never has been before.

Do I catch a glint of pride? Whatever it is it makes me want to jump off the stage and run away with him.

Threads of self-doubt invade my thoughts, as I continue to analyze how Aleksandr views my performance. Lead singer Auden can sing Aaron's song choice with no emotional attachment, but Aleksandr's presence makes me feel like myself instead of my character.

Real Auden falters, forgetting the lyrics that come next.

Aaron catches my error and leans into his microphone to sing with me, leading me to the right words. Grabbing my own mike off the stand, I spin toward him and grin, then reach out and touch his shoulder in appreciation.

When I turn back to the crowd, my eyes instantly find Aleksandr. I don't want to focus on anyone else. Don't want to pretend I don't care that he'd dropped everything and came to see me because I was having a mental breakdown.

After six more songs, Aaron's voice booms, amplified by his microphone. "Thanks for coming out tonight."

He'd cut our set thirty minutes short by my estimation. I glance at him out of the corner of my eye, but face forward to thank the crowd and say good night myself.

"What the fuck was that?" Greg demands, stomping toward Aaron while violently pulling his guitar strap over his head. I almost laugh when it gets caught on his ear and jerks his head to the side. I chalk it up to karma for coming at Aaron like a madman.

Aaron ignores gregarious Greg and puts his hand on my shoulder. "Are you okay?"

"Rough night?" Josh asks, pulling the hem of his T-shirt up to wipe his sweaty face.

"Sorry, guys. Aleksandr's here and I haven't seen him since he left for Charlotte, and a bunch of family shit went down yesterday. I just couldn't concentrate." The words rush out because I don't want to spend one more moment with my bandmates when I could be with Aleksandr.

"Let her go. She's obviously in heat," Greg says, I flinch at his words though I know the ridiculous reaction came from jealousy.

"She's not a dog," Aaron snaps.

I ignore Greg. Lashing out at me because he's upset isn't right, but I don't want to deal with him right now.

"Great job tonight, guys." I bend down behind Josh's drum set and grab my messenger bag. "I'll see you at practice tomorrow."

It takes every ounce of self-control I have to not break out in a run when I see Aleksandr waiting for me at the door. When I reach him, I hurl myself at him, wrapping my arms around his neck and my legs around his hips. He laughs, a rich rumble that comes from deep in his stomach, as he easily cradles me and carries me out the door.

"Are you ready?" he whispers, lips brushing my ear, electricity pulsing through my veins.

"Yes," I say, firm and decisive.

And I am. This is it. The losing-my-virginity chapter of my life.

The bees-on-speed buzz around my stomach with excitement. I don't feel anxious around Aleksandr. When I'm with him, everything feels right.

Nothing could ruin this moment.

Chapter Twenty-Six

AUDEN

Except my best friend. My best friend could ruin this moment.

"There you are!" I hear Kristen's voice before I see her.

Aleksandr's surprise appearance makes me forget I promised Kristen we'd hang out after my show. The only thing I want right now is to summon Harry Potter's invisibility cloak, whip it over me and my boyfriend, and bolt.

After contemplating the friendship code for a situation like this, I know hoes before bros is the correct answer. Hoes being a term of endearment in this case, of course.

"Hey, KK," I greet her, releasing my leechlike grip on Aleksandr. He holds me tight as I dismount, and I shiver from the friction created by sliding down his hard body. "Hey, Lace." I nod to my other roommate, who pops up behind Kristen.

"Hey, Aud. Hey, Aleksandr," Lacy greets us with a cheerful smile.

"Josh told us you'd already left, so we were headed to Larry's to find you," Kristen says, eyeing Aleksandr and me. "You're still heading to Larry's, right?"

"Of course," Aleksandr answers, grabbing my hand.

I guess, in his mind, there's no need to rush. He's had sex before. I'm the overstimulated virgin, so ready to get it on with my hot hockey-god boyfriend I can barely walk due to the throbbing in my nether regions.

I catch his eyes, pleading for him to understand the release I need. His aggravating, yet sensual, trademark smirk splays across his lips. He leans down, using his cheek to push the hair away from my ears.

"Anticipation makes it so much better, my love," he whispers.

The man needs to think about carrying me if he keeps up that kind of talk. How does he expect me to walk on rubbery legs?

"After you." I sweep my hand in front of me, allowing Kristen to take the lead.

If Wreckage is small, Larry's is a storage closet inside of Wreckage. And it's a complete dump. But Larry's is the only place in town that never ID's us, so we've been drinking here since freshman year.

Kristen and I declared their gin and tonic the best in the world. Maybe it wasn't, but it's the only place we can order one, and the bartenders always give us extra limes, which makes the whole drink.

I turn my attention to the bar, filled with the usual—a few kids from the university, but mostly townies. Townies are people born and raised in Bridgeland and the surrounding small farm towns. I'm not insinuating townies stick out in any way. I've just frequented Larry's so often, that I know the locals from the students. Plus, the number of pickup trucks in the parking lot is a telltale sign of which group is represented at any given time.

Aleksandr nods to the three empty stools at the bar. Kristen and I both saddle up and order gin and tonics, while Lacy stands next to us and orders a beer.

"I saw Beth waiting in our booth. Come over when you guys are finished," Lacy tells us, grabbing her beer and making her way back to the front of the bar. There's a group of booths in the front corner, one of which we'd claimed as ours because we take it over every time we come to Larry's. I think Kristen might have even carved our names into the table during a very drunken evening.

"This is disgusting," Aleksandr announces, pulling the glass from his lips with a frown after I let him try my gin and tonic.

"You have to squeeze two or three lime wedges in it and mash them good with your straw. Then you get yummy lime pulp in every sip." I demonstrate by stabbing at my limes before taking another sip of mine. "Ummm. Perfection."

"I don't like fruit in my drinks," he says.

"Well, you deserve a gross gin and tonic then. The lime is what makes it. Otherwise, it just tastes like pine-flavored floor cleaner," I tell him.

Kristen bursts out laughing. "That's my girl." She turns to Aleksandr. "So, what are you doing in town?"

"Auden needed me," he responds, holding up a hand for the bartender. He'd waited to taste my gin and tonic before ordering something for himself, and judging by his reaction, he's sticking with his usual.

When Kristen's face lights up, I don't even have to ask to know why. She's beyond happy Aleksandr would drop everything for me. She'd been witness to the guys I'd fallen for during my early years at school, and she knows I deserve someone like Aleksandr.

"I wasn't sure about you at first, you know." Kristen waves her hand around Aleksandr's head. "With the crazy hair and all, but you're a good guy."

"Thank you." Aleksandr smiles, saluting her with his shot before downing it in one gulp.

Suddenly, Kristen's happy glow disappears. "Wait. Why do you need him? What happened?"

Instead of beating around the bush, I let the story gush. "Turns out I have a brother who my mom put up for adoption before I was born. And he lives here in Bridgeland." I turn to Aleksandr. "And it's Jason Taylor, Landon's brother."

"What?" they both ask in unison.

I just nod and tilt my gin and tonic back, sans straw. Wow. It really is disgusting.

"That's not even...I don't know what to...holy shit, Auden," Kristen stammers.

"Yeah, I know. It's fucked up." The television above the bar flashes various colors, sports highlights scrolling across the bottom, reminding me it's just a regular night for so many people.

Kristen wraps her arms around me, some of the contents of her drink splashing onto Aleksandr's leg in the bear-hug process.

"I feel left out of this hugging," Aleksandr jokes as he presses cocktail napkins he'd swiped from the bar against his jeans.

"I'm so glad you're here," I tell him when Kristen releases me. Then I grab his face with both hands and plant a quick, hard kiss on his mouth.

Aleksandr puts a hand up for the bartender. "Two gin and tonics and a shot of vodka."

"Make it two shots," Kristen calls.

"Make it three," I add.

Both Kristen's and Aleksandr's heads swivel toward me, eyes wide. I drop my shoulders and tilt my head to the side. Is wanting to drink myself into oblivion such a surprise after my story?

When the bartender brings our drinks, Aleksandr passes me and Kristen each a shot of vodka.

I scrunch my face. "I'm gonna need sugar and a lemon."

"Yeah, me too," Kristen agrees. "It's cold, right?"

"Americans." Aleksandr sighs. He scans the table behind us and plucks sugar packets out of the plastic holder. Then he grabs two slim lemon slices from the tray on the bar and hands one to Kristen.

We tear open our sugar packets and lick the inside of our wrists. Just as I'm about to summon my inner Def Leppard and pour some sugar on myself, Aleksandr places his hand over the wet spot I'd created. Jerking my head up in protest, I catch a mischievous glimmer in his eye as he runs his tongue over his wrist, douses it with sugar, and holds it out to me.

I love this man.

After licking the sweet granules off his warm skin, I down the shot and search the bar frantically for my lemon. Of course, it's wedged between Aleksandr's teeth. When I press my mouth to his, he releases the lemon. After I suck the juice out, I spit the rind into my empty shot glass and cough from both the vodka and the sour lemon.

Aleksandr takes my pursed lips as a green light, covering my mouth with his. He kisses me like he shouldn't kiss me while sitting at a bar with my best friend, but I don't care. I slide my hands into his hair and return it with fervor.

"I will lick this sugar off your stomach when you are naked in my bed," he whispers in English, lips softly scraping my ear.

My cheeks light up in flames, embarrassed that someone may have heard him.

"Damn. I need a Russian. You got any friends?" Kristen asks after watching our display.

Yep. Someone heard him.

Aleksandr laughs and I press my forehead into his chest.

"I'm gonna catch up with Lacy and Beth. Meet us in our booth whenever you're done with this," Kristen says.

"We'll be right over," I assure her.

"Slow it down or you're gonna be sick," she warns, nodding to our empty shot glasses and my half-full gin and tonic.

"Yes, ma'am." I salute her, already feeling the buzz from the liquor. She slides her shot glass onto the bar and grabs one of the gin and tonics before leaving.

I lower my voice for Aleksandr's ears only. "Thank you for coming."

"There was no other choice. I love you, *Audushka*." His voice is thick, heavy, heated.

"I love you, *Sasha*," I tell him, relaxing onto the bar stool. He holds up the shot he'd ordered for himself. I grab my gin and tonic.

"To us." He clinks his glass with mine.

"To us," I repeat, taking a small sip while he tilts back his shot. He orders a glass of vodka, pays our tab, and we stand up to join my friends.

As soon as we sit down, the girls bombard me with questions about my plans for Bridgeland's after-school program. I appreciate that only Kristen and Aleksandr had been around when I was talking about Jason. I don't want to explain my seething anger for my grandparents to Lacy and Beth.

"It'll be a replica of the one in Detroit," I explain.

I'd finally received approval for the program from my advisor and the Department Chair during my nine a.m. class. For the first time since I'd been cut from the soccer team, I was proud of myself. I don't pat myself on the back often, but I'm thrilled with the Central Club idea.

"I'll hold my fitness class three times a week at the new facility instead of at the student center. The theater is closer to the elementary and middle school, and I think more kids will hear about it and know it's free."

"That's a great idea," Kristen says. "You should offer singing lessons, too."

"Oh, geez, I don't even know proper singing technique. How am I supposed to teach kids?"

"Then we can have karaoke. That's easy and fun." Kristen's eyes light up.

"Can I teach a gymnastics class?" Lacy asks.

"Yeah." I nod, overwhelmed with gratitude by the outpouring of interest and volunteer ideas from my friends. I'll need a lot of help with the program, especially since I scheduled twenty-one credit hours this semester. Although, three of those hours are approved for independent study to work on setting up the program.

"We could totally host a talent show." Kristen downs the rest of her drink.

"I teach hockey," Aleksandr offers, his eyes bright with the excitement of contributing.

"You don't even live up here," Lacy points out.

He pauses, eyes on the waves of vodka gliding around the sides of his glass as he circles his wrist. "I teach in summer. Will be roller hockey. Same skills, different surface."

"They're poor. They don't have roller blades," Beth reminds him.

Oh my gosh, he's just trying to help! I want to scream.

But Aleksandr isn't deterred by the negativity. "I will donate this. Sticks, pucks, goals. All of this."

I squeeze his hand, excited for my friends to see his compassionate, generous side.

"All this talk has given me the singing bug." Kristen grabs my hand, tugging me from my seat. "Finish your drinks. We're going to the Thorne!"

I shake my head, though I know I'm in a losing battle.

"Dollar Beers!" Lacy cheers, referencing one of the Redthorne's famed specials. Besides karaoke, the Thorne is known for their dollar "big" beers—which is just an oversized Solo cup.

"You don't want to go to the Thorne, do you?" I ask Aleksandr. He could be my ticket out.

"Are you going to sing?" he asks.

"Yep. Looks like my Bitch Ass is roping me into a duet." I glance at Kristen for clarification.

"Yes, I am," she agrees, sliding out of the booth and throwing a few dollars on the table.

"Twice in one night. Lucky me." Aleksandr squeezes my thigh under the table.

I jump. For the second time that night I want to forget our plans and go to his hotel.

"Aleksandr is smoking hot," Beth whispers in my ear as we gather our coats and purses. I nod. What can I say? Yeah, he is. Or, He's mine. Stop looking at him.

"Should we get a cab?" Aleksandr asks when we stumble out to the street. Maybe I'm the only one stumbling.

"It's a block up and a block over," Kristen informs him.

Aleksandr doesn't let me get far before he has me pressed up against the wall of a building, kissing me senseless. His hands slide into my jacket and tug at the hem of my shirt until it pops from my waistband. His cold palms skim my warm stomach. I shiver clenching my fingers in his hair and snuggling closer to warm up.

"Get a room!" Kristen calls from in front of us.

"I have one," Aleksandr whispers into my ear before backing up.

"Do you want to go?" I ask him. Singing with Kristen at a bar takes a backseat to being naked with Aleksandr in his hotel room.

"No!" Kristen runs back to where we're standing and takes my hand. "I get it. You haven't seen each other in forever, but you owe me a night out, so I'm not letting you go yet. We're gonna sing. Then you can go have sex with him."

As my best friend pulls me toward Beth and Lacy, I glance back at Aleksandr. His shoulders shake in silent laughter, amused as he watches Kristen drag me toward the road.

"Come on, Crazy Hair! I don't know what the rules are where you're from, but we have to cross now," Kristen yells. The man-in-motion blinks white on the crosswalk.

"Seriously?"

"Aleksandr, whatever." She lowers her voice. "You know the first time hurts, right?"

I take a deep breath and nod, like I'm listening to instructions from my coach before checking in to an important soccer game. "Yes. Hence the drinking more tonight than I have in over a year."

"Auden. You don't want to puke on him, do you?"

I cringe at the thought. "No."

"Then slow it down." She squeezes my hand. "I'm happy for you. That boy loves you."

"Loves me or lusts me?"

"Both." She winks. "But mostly loves."

"Are you ladies talking about me?" Aleksandr splits us up by bumping our hips with his and throwing his arms across each of our shoulders.

Redthorne is more crowded than I expected for a random Wednesday night. Aleksandr waits in line for drinks, while I follow Kristen and Lacy to a table in the back near where karaoke is set up.

Kristen immediately puts our names down on a slip of paper and hands it to the guy running the show. Since she's a regular, I don't doubt that he'll move her up to the top of the list. Not next, because someone waiting might get angry, but very soon.

Minutes later, I notice the karaoke host waving a small scrap of paper at me. Reluctantly, I pull away from Aleksandr, waving my arm gallantly in front of Kristen. "After you, my dear."

"Nope. Just you," Kristen says with a sweet, yet sly smile. I respond with a mock scowl. What song had she picked for me?

Aleksandr pats my butt as I edge past him to the stage. When I look at the Teleprompter and see "I Want Your Sex" by George Michael, I shake my head and climb off the stage.

"Absolutely not!"

"Come on!" Kristen yells through a fit of giggles. She leans over and says something to Aleksandr. She must have told him the name of the song because he breaks into a huge grin.

"No one even knows that old-ass song!" I protest as I jump down from the stage. "That was lame, KK." I flip Kristen's hair with my fingers as I pass. "I'm gonna grab more drinks."

"I'll keep your man company so that vulture doesn't swoop in." She nods in the direction of a group of girls standing by our table. One of them keeps switching places with the others, casually trying to get closer to Aleksandr.

"Thanks." I give her a thumbs-up as I edge through the tables and chairs on my way to the bar. It's a sweet thought. Not necessary, but sweet.

I laugh at myself. Though puck bunnies were one of my biggest insecurities when I'd first met Aleksandr, I feel no jealousy toward the girl jockeying for position next to him now. I know he won't give her a glance.

I order drinks for Aleksandr and Kristen and get myself a water. As I weave through the crowd, I turn my hips to maneuver past two back-to-back, occupied chairs, bumping one of them with my behind.

"Sorry. Excuse me," I apologize without thinking.

"Aud," a familiar voice says.

I glance behind me to find Greg occupying the chair I'd bumped. I twist my neck, my focus on keeping the triangle of drinks upright. When Greg touches my thigh, I jump back, sloshing beer onto his shirt.

"Dude!" I exclaim. He has no right to touch me—ever.

Instinctively, I glance at Aleksandr, who's risen from his seat. His eyes unwavering, catching every movement, his arms crossed across his chest, but he has a slight smirk on his face. Since I can't tell if he's angry or amused, I try to scoot by quickly. I'm not about to ruin my relationship with Aleksandr for Greg.

"I'm sorry about—" Greg stands up and wavers, unsteady on his feet. "Sorry about earlier."

"Let's just not talk about it," I say, inching my way forward.

"No, really. I just—" Greg leans in, his face inches from mine. If I don't move quick, he'll be kissing me.

I lurch back and push my arms out to keep him away, sending more beer splashing over the sides of the huge plastic cups.

Great, just fucking great.

Aleksandr already hates Greg for talking to me the night we met in Canada. He hadn't been too happy when I joined Greg's band, either. Of course, Greg would try to kiss me while Aleksandr watches from a few tables away.

"It's not going to end well," he slurs before looking at Aleksandr.

I tighten my hold on the triangle of drinks and hurry to my table, setting the drinks down before maneuvering myself between Aleksandr's legs and sitting on one leg. I lean over to kiss him.

"What was that about?" Aleksandr asks me when I pull back.

"He's really drunk." I wrap my arms around his neck and nuzzle close.

"Is this like the Drew situation again?"

Aleksandr must assume my slight hesitation means yes.

"Wanna know something?" Aleksandr whispers, his breath warm against my ear.

I nod, making sure to slide my ear against his lips strictly for the pleasure it gives me.

"It gets me a little bit excited to see guys hit on you."

"It does?" I ask, puzzled. I lean in closer, tucking my face into the curve where his neck meets his collarbone and inhaling the scent of his sweat rather than the stench of stale alcohol.

"Yes, because I know you're going home with me." He runs his fingers over the curve of my butt and down the back of my thighs.

My lips drag against his throat as my mouth curls into a smile. I lift my head, throw my hair over my shoulder, and catch his eyes. "Yeah, about that. When is that happening?"

"I thought you wanted to hang out with your friends tonight."

"All I want is to hang on to you."

"Say the word, my love."

I lean over and whisper in Aleksandr's ear, "I'm ready now."

He hoists me up so I can wrap my legs around him. Much to my surprise, he doesn't put me down, barely letting me say goodbye to Kristen, Lacy, and Beth as he carries me to the door.

I wish we'd never even stopped at the Thorne. But it doesn't matter how long it takes, nothing will stop me from being with Aleksandr.

"We're never gonna make it," I murmur between kisses as we weave through the maze of hallways leading to Aleksandr's hotel room. The last petals of panic about losing my virginity fall away every time Aleksandr touches me.

"We're here." He removes his lips from mine long enough to slip the key card in the reader. He doesn't even fumble for the lights, just flicks his wrist, and I hear the plastic card bounce off something.

Aleksandr slides my coat off, letting it fall to the floor while I walk backward toward the bed. My calves hit the mattress, and all it takes is the slight push of his fingertips and I'm on my back. There are no words to explain the rapid anticipation surging through my veins as he situates himself between my legs and looks down at me. His eyes glaze over, a slight smile on his face.

The bed dips when he places his arms on either side of me like he's about to do some weird-ass push-ups. I reach up and grab the waistband of his jeans, but his lips curve into a sexy smile and he drops to his knees.

Then he moves his right hand to my shirt and gently tugs it up before he drops his head and licks the sensitive patch of skin below my belly button. My body arches and I reach up and grab his hair. When I hear him laugh, I quickly let go, hoping I hadn't hurt him. Once I come back down to the mattress, I dig around in my pocket, pulling out the sugar packets I'd swiped from Larry's.

"Didn't you want these?" I shake the packets back and forth.

"I fucking love you," he growls.

Chapter Twenty-Seven
AUDEN

I wake up in a foreign bed wondering where the hell I am. Pulling myself up onto an elbow and looking down, I recognize my usual pajamas—oversized T-shirt and underwear. I touch my hand to my throat, which is so dry it aches. My head pounds. Even my eyes feel raw. The glowing green numbers of an alarm clock on the table next to the bed tells me it's almost 3:00 a.m.

When I step out of bed, my left foot lands in a tiny garbage pail. I shake it off my foot, thankful it's empty. I get out of bed and navigate the room with caution, fumbling around for a kitchen or bathroom, somewhere to get a drink of water. When I bang my knee against a couch that appears out of nowhere, I realize I'm in a hotel room. The sharp pain coursing through my knee triggers my memory.

Aleksandr coming to town because he knew I needed him. Drinking more than I ever had in my life. And passing out on him just before we had sex.

Awesome.

Nothing says 'You excite the hell out of me' like passing out.

Out of the corner of my eye I see feet hanging over the edge of the couch against which I'd just nailed my knee. Abandoning my original mission, I creep over to it. A thin fleece blanket covers Aleksandr's lower body. He lays on his stomach, his back turned toward me, his face buried into one of the tiny pillows of the couch. The cut of each muscle in his back is evident, even in his relaxed state. He's a walking, talking fitness commercial.

I reach out and shake his shoulder gently, more from wanting to touch his bare skin than to wake him. Aleksandr bolts upright, as if there's an emergency. I must've recoiled five feet.

"*Audushka*, are you okay?" The twist of his torso reveals his bare chest, and I wonder if I'm sleepwalking. The chiseled muscles of Aleksandr's upper body, arms, and abdomen are straight out of my fantasies.

I pause to count the pack in his stomach. He jumps off the couch and places his hands on my shoulders before I can get higher than seven. "Do you feel sick again?"

"No, I—" I rub my eyes with my fingers.

"*Audushka*, you need some rest." Aleksandr's voice is gentle and soothing.

I crawl onto the couch and curl into a ball, resting my head on top of the arm. Aleksandr covers me up with the blanket he'd been using. Then he sits near my feet and rubs my back. As relaxation sets in, I have no choice but to close my eyes and drift into slumber.

The next time I wake, darkness still envelopes the room. It takes my eyes a few moments to adjust, enough where I can make out everything in the small living space. I didn't think I'd been asleep very long, but I'd changed position. Now, I'm facing the back of the couch, my head resting on Aleksandr's lap.

I tilt my neck to look up at him. His eyes are closed, his mouth slightly open. I flip onto my back and watch his chest expand and contract with the rhythm of his breathing. The visual defines perfection. I want to spend the rest of my existence this close to him.

I touch Aleksandr's chest with my fingertips, tracing velvet lines until I reached the top of his jeans. His eyes flicker under the lids, and his head rolls from left to right. I maneuver myself into a sitting position and brush his jawline with my fingers. He begins to breath heavier, his chest rising and falling rapidly until his eyes flutter open. I cover his mouth with mine before he has a chance to react. He responds by pulling me onto his lap and tangling his hands in my hair.

I straddle his torso, pressing myself against his chest, then settle my face in the warm gap where his neck meets his shoulder and inhale deep, filling my lungs with his familiar scent. My heart thumps; my head no longer clouded with sleep. Aleksandr kisses my temple and slides his large, strong hands to my hips. I press myself into his lap, circling my hips against him slowly, purposefully. His body immediately gives me the attention I crave.

Reaching around him, I dig in his back pocket and pull his wallet out. He cocks his head as I remove the small foil square I'm looking for.

"*Audushka*, I don't know how long that's been in there," he begins. I stop him with a kiss.

"Well, it's our only option, because I don't have any." I hold his eyes for a split second, before he nods. An old condom is better than no condom, in my opinion.

I unbutton his jeans, and he lifts his hips so I can pull them down. He doesn't have anything on underneath, so I tear open the packet, slowly rolling the condom over him, acting like I've done it before. I lift my face to meet his, tucking loose strands of hair behind my ear. I need to see his eyes. I need to know that this is right.

This is my Aleksandr. My dream. My love.

He doesn't disappoint, catching my gaze and holding it as he pushes away the fabric of my underwear and hoists me onto him. I clench my teeth, digging my fingernails into his shoulders as I slide onto him, releasing a soft cry from the jolt of pain.

"Fuck, *Audushka*!" Aleksandr swears. His eyes flash open, and his strong hands hold my hips still. I breathe in deeply and attempt to lift myself up and down. His halting the session is maddening and exhilarating at the same time.

"Easy," he says in Russian, his voice so husky I can barely translate the word. He flips me onto my back and pushes into me slowly. I squeeze his rib cage, tensing up as he pulls out a little before pushing in again. "Easy," he repeats.

Aleksandr holds himself up on his forearms, situated on either side of my shoulders. His hands tangle in my hair, his fingers clenching and pulling lightly. He's so gentle and controlled.

Sex is much different than I expected it to be. I never thought he'd hurt me on purpose, but I'd heard or read countless stories about people losing their virginity, I thought it would be fast and painful and miserable no matter how much I loved him. He buries his face into my neck, his breath hot and quick against my skin. Every time I feel a rush of warm air, his fingers squeeze my hair, and I tense up.

He lifts his head and brushes his lips on mine. "Relax, *Audushka*. I love you."

Normally, when someone tells me to relax, I tense up even more. But I feel comfortable with Aleksandr, and he's doing a damn good job of making this easy on me.

Once I loosen up, the discomfort subsides, and I focus on the sublime sensations his movements create. When he rolls his hips, it feels fantastic, rather than painful. Or maybe pain feels good when it's that kind of pain? I don't have any pleasurable painful experiences to compare it to, so I'm not sure.

"Is this okay, my love?" Aleksandr asks. He lifts his face to meet my eyes without stopping his slow rolls and soft thrusts into me.

I nod.

"Does it feel good for you?" he asks. His breath hitches and he squeezes my hair on the last word.

I nod again. "What about you?"

His lips perk up, and a gust of air leaves his nose. "It feels amazing for me."

"You can move more if you want. I think I'm fine," I tell him.

The current slow pulling up and thrusting in that he has going on has me worked up but isn't necessarily getting me anywhere.

Now, I'm not a complete idiot. I didn't think I would orgasm my first time having sex. I know that's the stuff of romance novels and porn movies, but I hope to get some kind of sensation like when he uses his tongue. I know the man has talent.

Aleksandr adjusts his arms and hands so he's holding my face. "You're sure?" he asks, without taking his gaze away from mine.

I love him. I love him for being so kind, and so slow, and so understanding.

"*Da.*" I hold on to his sides and take a deep breath.

"Don't tense up. I'm not gonna go hard on you," Aleksandr says. I catch the smile on his lips and gleam in his eye and relax. Though, it's difficult to calm my body when I'm freaked out, excited, and anticipating what's next simultaneously, but I do my best because I trust him.

He pulls himself up on his forearms again and continues his movements, with a little more vigor. He keeps his pace for a few minutes before holding my face in his hands and kissing my forehead, then laying his full body weight on me while staying completely still. I match his deep breathing, not because I'm exhausted, but because it helps when a two-hundred-pound man decides to lay on top of you.

"That's some way to wake a man up, *Audushka*." Aleksandr rolls off me, easing himself out slowly.

I laugh.

"Did I miss something?" He lifts an eyebrow.

"I thought it would be horrible, but it wasn't. It was awesome," I tell him, still trying to slow my breath. I'm not sure if I'll ever be able to. Just looking at him makes my pulse race again.

"Did I hurt you?" He holds my gaze until I shake my head. "I didn't know you—"

"I knew what I was doing," I say, then laugh again. "Well, not really, but I knew I wanted to do it—with you, that is. It's only ever been you. Obviously."

Aleksandr strokes my cheek with his palm and lowers his mouth onto mine, cutting off my nervous rambling.

"How did you know there was a condom in my wallet?"

"I took a stereotypical guess." I rub the buzzed sides of his head with my hands. Though it's grown out since I'd seen him last, it still has a soft peach-fuzz feeling.

"What am I going to do with you?" Aleksandr smiles, shaking his head.

"Anything you want," I tell him, closing my eyes as drowsiness pulls me into its grasp again.

Aleksandr gets up, removes the condom, and pulls his jeans up. He disappears from my sight for a moment. Then I feel him slide one arm under my knees and the other under my neck, and he carries me back to the bed. He sets me down and pulls the duvet over me.

"Don't leave me," I plead. Although I meant it in the context of the present situation, I want it to fit the future as well.

"Never, my love," he whispers, kissing my head. He climbs into bed next to me, draping an arm over me and snuggling into my back. His chest, thighs and knees mold against my body, perfectly interlocking.

I slow my breathing to match his, so our chests rise and fell together. I've never felt as safe as I do right now, wrapped in his strong arms.

Aleksandr kisses the back of my head, whispering something in Russian against my hair. I may misconstrue the translation in my sleepy haze, but I think he says, "You are my destiny, my sun. There is no happiness without you."

As I drift to sleep, sheltered underneath the warmth and strength of Aleksandr's body, I realize tonight was the first time I ever let myself lose control.

If that's what it takes to love and trust someone completely, I'm all in.

Chapter Twenty-Eight
AUDEN

A knock on the door wakes me for the third time that morning, but this time I'm in my own bed.

Aleksandr called a ride at the crack of dawn to drop me off at my apartment and take him to get his car. He had to be on the road early to make it to the airport in time for his game. I hadn't planned on jumping into bed when I got home, but I was exhausted from the little sleep I'd gotten in Aleksandr's hotel room.

Inspecting my ensemble as I shuffle to the door, I decide the T-shirt and boxer shorts I have on cover more than enough to be decent.

While stifling a yawn, I grab the handle and open the door to find Greg standing outside. I rub my fingers across my eyes and look behind him.

"Hey, Greg?" I ask in surprise. "What are you doing here?"

"I wanted to apologize for last night." He shoves his hands into his pockets and rocks back on his heels.

"Oh, well, thanks." Was a personal visit necessary?

"I'm sorry I tried to kiss you. I was confused. I mean, I read this poem again and I just thought," Greg begins, holding up a piece of paper. His shoulders drop as he lowers it. "Shit. I thought it was about me."

"What poem?" I ask as my head swirls with confusion. "And why would you ever think any of my poems were about you?"

Before Greg can answer, I notice a figure rushing toward him.

Aw, shit.

Now was not a good time for Aleksandr, who's supposed to be on his way out of town, to show up.

"What's going on?" Aleksandr demands. His face is stoic, but I can see the storm rolling in his eyes. The next Cold War could be brewing on the doorstep of my apartment.

Greg turns to look over his shoulder. Instead of a view of Aleksandr's face, he gets an eyeful of his fist.

Literally. Aleksandr punches him. The paper Greg holds falls to the ground.

"That's for hitting on my girlfriend," Aleksandr says as he bends over Greg, arm cocked and loaded.

Lunging at Aleksandr, I grab his arm so he can't swing again. "Stop, *Sasha*! Stop!"

"What the fuck?" Greg's doubled over, one hand on his knee, the other holding his eye. He clears his throat and spits. I'm thankful there's no blood.

"Don't 'What the fuck?' when you're the one at my girlfriend's door at eight in the morning." Aleksandr's breath is erratic, his body tense and ready to pounce. Again.

"Calm down." I hold him against my chest, and lock my arms around him.

"Why?" He wiggles out of my hold and spins around to face me. "What's going on here, *Audushka*?"

"Greg came over to apologize for being a jerk last night."

"Apologizing for being a jerk? Or for trying to kiss you?" Aleksandr asks. He stoops down to pick up the paper on the ground. At first, he scans the words quickly, his eyes darting across the page.

But when his eyelids droop and his brows inch closer, I realize which poem Greg had brought.

It's the poem I'd written after I first met Aleksandr. My creative way of purging the original feelings I had for him. A stupid reminder to not let myself get in too deep. Though I'd written it in frustration months ago, I still remember every wicked word by heart.

>Come inside
>You can sit or lay
>Just don't wait
>for me to say
>I love you
>because I won't lie
>and I know you
>won't say goodbye
>I'm the one thing
>you'll never have
>a chance with
>so as you take my hand
>remember
>I could never stand the thought of you
>on your knees
>begging
>for a way to please me
>that you wouldn't find
>not because
>I wasn't kind
>but because
>I couldn't handle
>your eyes burning into me
>like a candle
>a flame rising from the hell
>you're walking on the edge of
>and if you fell
>I'd catch you
>but I'll never say
>I love you

"Is this about him?" Aleksandr asks, thrusting the page toward Greg. His eyes swirl, an ocean before a storm.

"No. I wrote it a while ago."

"About who?"

Shit.

"Who did you write this about?"

"You." I lower my eyes. "But I wrote it right after I met you—before I knew you."

Aleksandr stares at the page, nodding as he rereads the words. The swirl of anger drains from his eyes. And that's what scares me the most.

Give me anger. Give me sorrow. But don't give me indifference.

"Yeah, well, thanks for last night, Auden. It's good to know where I really stand with you." He whirls around and bolts down the hallway.

"*Sasha*! *Sasha*, it's not like that. It was—" I stop explaining because he doesn't stop walking.

I slump against the door frame, listening to his heavy footsteps morph to a shuffle the farther down the hall he gets.

Abandoned again, only this time, it *is* all my fault.

Chapter Twenty-Nine

AUDEN

"Call him from my phone," Kristen offers. She grabs her phone off the end table next to the couch and holds it out to me.

"I can't do that. It's sneaky," I say as if I have any shame left. I've been calling Aleksandr tirelessly from the landline in our apartment for the last week.

"You need to talk to him so you can scrape your pathetic self off the couch and get on with your life. Have you even showered?"

"Yes." I throw a pillow at her. "I have." Once.

After a week of calling Aleksandr and leaving messages on his phone with no response, I'm only slightly against using Kristen's phone to call him. I want to apologize for the poem and explain that I'd written it after we'd first met. Back when I thought he was a douche bag, which—I know now—is one hundred eighty degrees from who he is as a person.

He's had plenty of time to cool off. He needs to pick up the phone and talk to me.

"Fine." I grab Kristen's phone from her outstretched hand, pressing the digits on the screen.

"Allo?" An unfamiliar male voice answers Aleksandr's phone. He has a Russian accent, but it's not the Russian accent I know and love.

"Who is this?" I ask, pulling the phone away from my ear and checking the screen to make sure I dialed the right number.

"*Pasha.*"

"Oh, hey, Pavel." I want to puke. I don't know Pavel Gribov well enough to call him *Pasha*, nor do I want to know him that well.

I miss Landon. Why couldn't Landon have gotten called up to Charlotte with Aleksandr rather than slimy Gribov?

"I need to speak with Aleksandr. Can you put him on?"

"He's unclothed." Pavel laughs. "Or indisposed, I get these English words confused. But you understand this, yes?"

"Auden?" Aleksandr calls out in the background.

"It's Angie, but whatever," a woman's voice responds.

"I am sorry you had to hear that," Pavel says, though his tone holds no hint of apology whatsoever. I want to crawl through the phone and kick his patronizing ass. "Actually, I'm not. You know he thinks you are a selfish, cheating whore, yes?"

"What?" My voice shakes on the verge of a meltdown.

"The only girl he's ever loved writes a horrible poem about him. You use him to cry about your mother, yet you don't even think about what losing his parents did to him? You are selfish. And you wonder why he hasn't called you back."

"Who the fuck is that, *Pasha?*" Aleksandr demands. I hear scraping in the earpiece, then Aleksandr's voice again, clear as ice. "Hold on, Angel."

"It's Angie," I whisper, pulling the phone away from my ear and staring at the screen.

Symbolically, a large red box with the word End lights up on the phone screen, waiting for my touch to seal the deal. When I press it, the phone slips out of my hand and crashes to the floor.

"Shit." I bend down to grab it. "Sorry, KK."

"We're good. I have an anti-destructo case." She assures me. "What happened?"

I cover my eyes with my hands and shake my head, my shoulders trembling.

"Oh, Aud." Kristen scoots closer and wraps her arms around me. I'm still shuddering when she brings my head into her lap and strokes my hair. She drops her voice to a soothing tone. "It's okay, sweetie. It's okay."

"It's not," I say between sniffles and gulps. "It's over."

"Don't say that."

"He was with another girl. I heard her."

Just then there's a knock on the door, and I suddenly remember asking my brother to hang out tonight.

"That's Jay." I wipe at my eyes again.

"I got it," Kristen says, unraveling herself from me.

"I brought popcorn and one of those sappy movies you girls seem to like." Jason greets us, holding out a huge bucket of popcorn straight from the movie theater. The gigantic grin on his face dissolves when he sees me. "What happened?"

"Chick flick is out. Did you bring the one about the jackass ex?" Kristen moves aside so Jason can slide by.

"Where they realize it was a misunderstanding, get back together, and live happily ever after?" Jason asks, a hopeful smile playing on his lips as he takes Kristen's seat next to me on the couch.

I shake my head and rub my temples, hoping to ease my mind and stop the tears. I don't want Jason to see me as a sobbing mess of a person.

"Who answered?" Kristen goes straight back to our conversation as she walks to the kitchen.

"Gribov." I grab the bucket from Jason's hands and inhale the buttery fragrance. "He said horrible things. True things."

"That ass-hat? He's been trying to break you and Aleksandr up since before you were together. You remember what he said at the arena, right?" Kristen comes back with a bowl and scoops up some of the popcorn. Then she sits on the floor at my feet. "He wouldn't know the truth if it bit him in the balls."

"I know." I nod. "I know Gribov is a fucking jerk, but he's right. I'm the one who wrote that stupid poem. I'm the selfish one. I'm the one who messed everything up."

"What poem?" Jason asks, pouring popcorn into the bowl Kristen had brought him.

Jason isn't totally up to speed on everything that had happened with Aleksandr. I'd asked him over for some brother and sister bonding time, since I hadn't seen him in a while, except for a few lunches at the diner.

"So, you know we met at the at bar in Canada, right? I thought he was a douchebag—a hot douchebag, but still."

Jason nods.

"After I found out I was his translator, I wrote this stupid poem back when we'd first met and were at each other's throats. It was an outlet for the feelings I was having about being attracted to him, but knowing nothing could come out of it because he was my client. He read it and I had to admit I'd written it about him."

"Damn. That sucks," Jason says. "But, I mean, he's got to understand it was old. You explained it to him, right?"

"I tried." I toss a kernel into my mouth. "But he walked away before I had the chance. He hasn't answered my calls in a week. So, I called him from Kristen's phone. It didn't go well."

"Because Pavel Gribov is acting as his personal answering machine," Kristen says.

"Gribov is a prick. He's so jealous of Aleksandr it's ridiculous." Jason shoves a handful of popcorn into his mouth.

"How so?" I ask.

Gribov had been one of the better players on the Aviators and had taken those skills into the NHL. He already has three goals and an assist. Aleksandr has yet to score, but he's gotten two assists and an amazing plus/minus rating.

"Beating Aleksandr is a personal challenge for him. Aleksandr was the better player when they were in Russia. When they were drafted, Aleksandr went in the second round, Gribov didn't go until the fifth. Aleksandr was the Aviators leading scorer and assistant captain. And Aleksandr always got more"—Jason stops midsentence—"attention."

"Female attention?" I ask. Jason's pause didn't fool me. I knew Aleksandr had plenty of that before we met.

"Enough with the stupid jealous crap, Aud," Kristen chastises. "You with the bunnies and him with the band. Both of you are so scared of being with someone, you both sabotaged it."

"Right, but he was with someone else, and I'll never go back to him. He knows how I feel about cheating."

"I haven't known him long, but he and Landon are really good friends, and I know that he is seriously in love with you." Jason rubs the back of his neck. "I just can't believe he would cheat on you."

"Technically, he wasn't even cheating since you guys broke up," Kristen says.

I hold up a hand and swallow back a sob. "I love you, KK, but I'm not in the mood for technicalities right now. If it's that easy to be with someone new a week after we broke up, I'm better off without him."

Kristen nods, but doesn't relent. "You're right. I mean, you don't want a relationship with a guy who leaves the bar to drive you home, and then climbs in your window to make sure you're alive. Someone who happily accepted a punishment from your mean-ass grandfather for hurting your feelings. Someone who loves you enough—not to replace the necklace you wear that belonged to your mom—but to add to it so you wouldn't have to take off something that means so much to you. And you, for sure, don't want to be with a guy who gets pissed because you originally thought of him as just a fuck and not relationship material. I would definitely throw away a guy like that. Especially over a stupid poem."

"It *was* stupid. And really badly written." I nod, ignoring all the excellent points she'd made.

Why am I the type of person who dwells on the negative? Four out of five dentists recommend Trident gum. Why do I believe the one who didn't?

"Auden." Kristen lowers her head, scrunches her eyebrows so they point down in the middle, and looks up so only the bottom of her irises show. I call it her evil face because it's so creepy. Killer Klowns from Outer Space creepy.

"I don't know how to fix things, KK. I just know how to run away."

"Well maybe this is the time to learn." She pretends she's getting up. "Want me to go get my Barbie tool kit?"

"'Barbie tool kit?'" Jason asks.

I laugh, thinking about the pink toolbox she'd busted out on the first day we met in our freshman dorm.

"Her toolbox and all the tools in it are pink. No joke."

"I believe that." Jason nods, taking in Kristen's outfit: a hot pink Under Armor jacket and black yoga pants with matching pink stripes down the sides.

"Aleksandr won't answer my calls. Gribov has him convinced I'm a selfish tramp who's sleeping with all my bandmates. So what do I do?"

"What do they say? If you love something, set it free. If it comes back it's meant to be?" Jason asks.

"Guess the poetry gene runs in the family," Kristen says.

"I didn't mean for it to rhyme. It just came out that way." Jason throws a handful of popcorn at her.

"Hey!" I wrap my arms around the bucket and hold it away from Jason. "Don't waste. This is the good stuff."

I never thought I'd be laughing after realizing I'd just lost the love of my life. Then again, I never thought I'd be sitting in my apartment eating popcorn and talking about relationships with a brother.

"Should I put this movie in now?" Jason holds up the chick flick he'd brought with him.

"No offense, but we need a man-hater movie. Let me check my stash." Kristen jumps up and runs to her room.

"Hey, Auden," Jason says quickly.

"Yeah?"

"I just—thank you." He chuckles. "It means a lot to me to hang out with you." He pauses and lifts his eyes to meet mine. "It's funny how life works out sometimes. I never had a desire to know my biological family, now I can't imagine life without you."

Tears fills my eyes. Just as I'm closing the door on the man who I thought would be my family, in walks my brother, who in just a few short weeks, already is family.

Funny how life works, indeed.

Chapter Thirty
AUDEN

"What'cha doing?" Kristen asks, sliding a lemonade across the table to me and setting down a drink and a small salad for herself. She just finished up her shift at Peak City. I'd come over straight from band practice to wait for her shift to end.

"Thanks." I shove my empty glass to the side and pull the new one closer. "I'm trying to write a letter to my grandparents." I look up with heavy eyes. "It's for an assignment, but instead of making up some bullshit thing, I wanted to use real life."

"You're the only person I know who puts real thought into their assignments."

"It's kind of a requirement for my major." Which is somewhat true. Most people can take themselves out of the equation. Though my ultimate goal is to help others, especially children affected by a traumatic event, I sometimes wonder if I chose to major in social work as a way to heal myself.

Probably should have picked psychology.

"What's got you stumped?"

"Can't think of the right thing to write."

"You're speaking to them now, aren't you?"

"Um." I sink my teeth into a roll, then point to my mouth and shrug. The old can't-talk-when-I'm-chewing excuse.

"Can I be honest with you without you pushing me away and never talking to me again?"

I nod, though my stomach lurches in preparation of what she'll say. So far, only Aleksandr and Kristen are the two people who can call me out without me blowing up. So far.

"Seriously?" She stabs a piece of lettuce with her fork. I feel bad for the poor iceberg leaf, but I'm glad it hadn't been my hand.

I nod again, the dry roll scraping my throat as I try to swallow the large chunk I'd bitten off.

"You should write an apology for being such a jerk to them about this Jason thing."

"What?"

"Look, I agree with you to an extent. How they handled it was shitty. I get that you're hurt and upset, but you can't push them away and pretend like you can live without them. Because you can't. They are your rock. Your tie to family. Your everything. And, not to be morbid, but they won't be around for much longer. So get over it." She shoves a forkful of salad into her mouth as if emphasizing her point.

"I don't know how."

"Don't know how to apologize?" She hasn't finished swallowing before spewing her irritated interjection, and bits of lettuce spray onto the table. She brushes her hand across it.

"Sorry."

"I don't know how to start. I've been a jerk since they first took me in," I admit before taking a sip of lemonade.

"Well, that's understandable, considering what happened, Aud," she tells me, her tone softening.

"Yeah, but I was totally two-faced. I was this good student who never got into trouble and would go out of my way to help everyone at school, and then turned into Medusa when I came home. I felt like my grandparents ignored everything I felt when I tried to talk about it. Everything they did ticked me off."

"I'm sure they were just trying to make life as normal for you as possible. I can't imagine it was easy to raise you when they were still grieving their daughter. There have been thousands of parenting books written, but I doubt there were any books on how to raise you." Kristen smiles, but it's hollow and sad. "I'm sure they were trying to do the best they could with the resources they had, you know?"

"How could I have never thought about that before?" I ask, rubbing my eyes with my fingers.

My heart aches for my grandparents in a way it never has before. I was selfish. So wrapped up in my anger about growing up without my mother that I never stopped to think about how it affected them.

As parents, it must haunt them every day that they hadn't been able to protect my mother. All the time and effort they'd spent worrying and sheltering their daughter when she was young didn't stop her from being murdered. It's suddenly easy to understand why they've always been excessively protective of me.

When would they learn? Worrying doesn't make a difference. They couldn't stop it. All their protective intentions couldn't save her. Or me.

"Because you were a child. Children are selfish. Teenagers are selfish. The world revolves around them, right?" Kristen smiles again at me, shaking her head. "We all thought that way, not just you. You're pretty mature, but you were still a child, Auden."

"I should have realized. Should have given them a break." I pull my glass back to my lips to divert attention from the tears welling up in my eyes. "I was such a complete jerk to them."

"Don't be so hard on yourself. You wouldn't have realized any of this at the time. You can't see the full picture until you've taken a step back and looked at it from the outside."

"It makes so much sense." I mark a huge X through the superficial words I'd written. I can't work on it now. I'll have to figure it out once I get a handle on the emotions flooding me.

"And just think, you still have time to make it right."

"Thanks," I tell her, closing my notebook and shoving it in my bag.

"What else can I solve for you? World peace? Global warming? I'm on a roll." Kristen holds up her drink, and I clink my glass with hers.

"I'll let you decide where we're going out tonight."

"How about tomorrow? Tonight, you're going to Detroit."

Chapter Thirty-One

AUDEN

Face-planting is not how I usually start my days. Evidently, I was so startled by the loud rapping on my door, and disoriented by my surroundings, that I'd rolled right off my bed.

I lift my head and wipe the drool off the side of my mouth, before realizing I'd fallen onto the familiar hardwood floor of my childhood bedroom.

When I'd arrived at my grandparents' house last night, they weren't home, which was odd, because they don't have a very active social life. I waited up until eleven p.m. before I wandered into my old room and collapsed.

Reluctantly, I get to my knees and lift myself up. When I open the door, Grandpa stands in front of me with a sandy brown shoe box in his hand. I step aside, and he sweeps past me. He looks around my room before taking a seat on my bed.

I can't remember the last time Grandpa was in my room. Standing in the doorway, a hundred times, but in my room? Not since I was a child.

He pats the bed next to him, and I sit down. He seems calm. At least I'm not getting yelled at—or smacked.

He removes the lid of the box and pulls out a picture. My mom stands behind a microphone on a stage at Our Lady of the Lakes High School, the place we'd both attended. The wall behind her is blurred out since she's the focal point of the picture, but I can make out a banner, balloons, and streamers.

"Your mom was in a band when she was in high school," Grandpa finally speaks. "This was her playing at a school dance. Probably one of her first times on stage."

Shock has me mute and immobile because I'm fairly certain my grandfather never had any intention of sharing this story with me.

"She loved music and had a beautiful voice. She and some friends from school got together to play. Just kids having fun. She fell in love with one of the boys in the band. His name was Vince. I thought he was a good kid." Grandpa rubs his mouth with the palm of his hand, before cupping his chin and taking a deep breath.

"Vince got your mother pregnant when she was fifteen. She shut us out at first, too scared to tell us. But she knew she couldn't raise a child at fifteen. Vince told her she should have an abortion. But your mother didn't want that. She wanted to give the child up for adoption. So your grandmother and I took her to a Catholic social services group. Together we interviewed and chose the family who would get the baby.

"And on the day the baby was born, she signed the papers and gave him up. It wasn't easy for her. But she made the decision because she couldn't give the boy a life."

Grandpa rummages in the box again, pulling out another picture of my mom. This time she's in a hospital bed with her pale lips pressed to the forehead of a tiny, red face peering out of the blanketed bundle in her arms.

"That's the only picture we have of Baby Boy Berezin. Valerie didn't name him, of course. A few minutes after that picture was taken he was given to his new parents, who were waiting in the hospital."

"So, this is Jason?"

"Jason? That's a strong name." Grandpa looks down, silent for a moment. "Was he the one in the diner when your grandmother and I were there?"

"The one you wouldn't stop staring at?" I ask.

Grandpa nods.

"Yeah, that was him. Did you know?"

"No. It never crossed my mind. But he looked familiar. I was trying to place him."

"He's a nice guy."

Grandpa ignores my comment and hands me the shoe box. "These were some pictures of your mom's. Maybe you'd like to keep them."

"Can I give this one to Jason?" I hold up the one of him and mom from his birth.

"It's yours now. You can do whatever you wish." Grandpa starts to get up.

"What about me?" I ask quickly. Since I'd already staged the big confrontation, I want all the skeletons out of the closet.

"What do you mean?"

"Well, that's Jason's story. What about mine? Did you know my dad? Was he an idiot like Vince?"

"He was." Grandpa sits back down. "In fact, it was the idiot Vince."

"What?" I almost snap my neck, as I instantly turn my attention from the contents of the shoe box in my lap to my grandpa's face.

"She was young and in love." He chuckles, but the laugh is distant and weary. "He said all the right things and she took him back. She was out of the house at that point, so your grandmother and I didn't know she was seeing him again. We didn't know they got married."

"What?" I ask. I can actually feel my eyes bulging from my head. I didn't know my mom and my sperm donor were married.

"Yes, well, it didn't last. As soon as he found out she was pregnant, he left and never came back. Your mom had taken on three jobs before she even told us about her pregnancy, just to prove that she could take care of you on her own." Grandpa takes my hand and looks into my eyes. His expression soft, but pained.

I can't imagine what he thinks when he looks at me. Probably that I ruined everyone's life: my mom's, my sperm donors', my grandparents'.

"She loved you, *Audushka*," he says, his eyes glassy, as if he'd read my mind. "She loved you so much."

The tension harbored in my shoulders for fourteen years releases in a massive slump. I didn't realize a simple sentence could be so powerful. My stoic, seemingly unaffectionate grandpa is the first person to tell me my mom loved me. I'm sure everyone assumed I knew how she felt, but since I can't even remember one minute with her, hearing him say it feels extraordinary.

"I'm sorry about the way your grandmother and I reacted when you told us about Jason, *Audushka*. We were startled and didn't know what to do. I'm sorry we never told you about him. We should have. In all these years, he'd never tried to find us, so we never thought you needed to know."

The newly confident part of me wants to ask why they would only tell me if my brother came looking for us. Why didn't they think having a brother was something I should be aware of no matter what the situation? Though Grandpa and I turned a corner in our relationship, I knew my questions would start a fight, and we'd come too far for me to take it there.

"It just doesn't seem right," I say, abandoning my questions and looking at the picture of my mom and Jason instead.

"She loved you, *Audushka*," Grandpa says again, squeezing me against his side. "She never once thought about giving you up. She said she could never do that again, which is why she worked her ass off. We helped, of course, if she needed it, but she rarely did. She was a strong, stubborn girl. That's where you get those qualities, in case you were wondering."

"Funny, I thought I got them from you."

Grandpa laughs, which makes me happy. I'm sick of fighting with my grandparents. Sick of being mad at them. Sick of anger and withdrawal always being my first reactions. I don't want to live that way anymore.

But how do I begin to change my mindset after being ingrained with ideas for twenty years? Maybe I already have changed—because even with Kristen's insistence—I never would have come here if I hadn't.

"Thank you for being honest with me. I'm sorry about how I brought it up and how I acted. It was childish and immature."

"Well, so were we. We should have been prepared. We knew it might come up someday. I promise to be better next time."

"Next time?" My shoulders stiffen as I wiggle out of Grandpa's half embrace. "More secrets?"

"No, *Audushka*, no more secrets. I meant next time we find ourselves in a highly emotional situation, I need to react better."

"Well, I hope we don't find ourselves in too many more." I scavenge through the shoe box, flipping through photos and concert ticket stubs with my index finger. "As long as we're being honest..."

"Yes?" Grandpa's tone lowers.

"I, um, I went through that envelope with articles about mom. The one in your locked cabinet upstairs. I'm really sorry for snooping. I was just curious."

He nods. "And?"

I shrug. "I don't know. I just wanted to know what happened."

"It's very hard for your grandmother and me to talk about." Grandpa clears his throat. "But you can ask us questions if you have any."

I open my mouth, then close it and shake my head.

"You're sure?"

I nod. "I just wanted to be honest."

"Thank you. You have grown up, *Audushka*. Your mother would be very proud of the woman that you are."

With that, I bury my face into Grandpa's shoulder, wrapping both arms around him in a massive bear hug. I almost feel bad soaking his navy Michigan University Language Department polo with tears. Almost.

Your mother would be very proud of the woman that you are.

Every kid wants to hear their parents say they love them and are proud of them, but it's especially crucial for those of us who don't have parents. Like forgotten fish, we race to the top of our bowl, desperately chomping the water for flakes of love and reassurance to fill us up.

Chapter Thirty-Two
AUDEN

"Here." I throw a candy necklace at Kristen. It's a prop we used in our younger days when we were on the prowl for men. What hot-blooded male wouldn't want to nuzzle up to a girl and bite a piece of candy off her neck?

"Auden, I don't think we should use these tonight," she warns, twirling the necklace around her index finger.

"Come on, KK. You're the one who said I needed to get back out there." Though I dread using the necklace myself, I knew Kristen would in order to help me get over Aleksandr. Even if I had to pull out the big guns to make it happen.

"This isn't what I meant."

I ignore her and run my straightener through the final section of my hair before sliding smoothing serum over the strands. I check my outfit in the mirror as I wipe the greasy hair product remains on a towel.

Once Kristen and I both finish getting ready, we grab our drinks and walk to the apartment next door where Scott, Lacy's boyfriend, lives with three other guys. I'd forgiven Scott for the bringing-a-friend-who-tried-to-drug-me fiasco, but I'm still leery of him. It's back to business-as-usual—which is keeping my guard up around him and his friends.

"Damn, ladies!" one of Scott's roommates calls out when we walk in the apartment. He hits a button on his CD player and the mellow hum at the beginning of Blackstreet's "No Diggity" fills the room. It's Kristen's favorite song. Yet another reason we'd become best friends—our shared love of nineties music.

Lacy and the guys are playing "I Never," a drinking game in which someone says they've never done something and everyone who has done it must drink. There are two ways to play. We could say something we thought was outlandish to see who had done it. Or we lie and say something everyone has done so the group got drunk quicker. The latter seems to be the case with tonight's game.

"I've never been drunk," Scott lies, and tips his beer back along with the rest of us.

"I've never been to a party." Kristen raises her beer so we could all toast before taking another long drink.

"I've never fucked an—" Bobby begins. I don't hear him finish because Brett, the guys' fourth roommate, pushes through the door.

"Hey, man! Pull up a seat." Scott slides Brett a chair from the kitchen table with his foot.

Brett is one of Central State's star rugby players. I've known him since freshman year because he lived on the floor below Kristen and me in the dorms.

"Drink, Auden. We all know you're fucking a hockey player," Chad teases me.

"I didn't even hear what Bobby said." I'd laughed at the previous responses in the game, but scowl when Chad mentions a hockey player.

"I said, I've never fucked an athlete," Bobby repeats.

Oh good, now everyone is listening.

"And I said drink because you're fucking Varenkov." Chad salutes me with his beer. I know the guys don't mean any harm. They don't know Aleksandr and I broke up.

"Was. I *was* fucking a hockey player," I mumble, and try to drop the subject by lifting my beer to my lips.

"What?" Bobby and Chad ask in unison.

"Lace, did you remember to get more milk?" Kristen asks, steering the conversation from Aleksandr to our grocery needs.

Worst diversion ever.

"I'm single and on the prowl." I pull the candy necklace away from my neck with my thumb and shimmy in my seat, feigning excitement about it.

"You should fuck Brett," Scott says with a wink. "I hear he's good."

So had I, but hearing Scott say it is just plain comical, since his current girlfriend is the one who'd told me all about how good Brett had been in bed.

Lacy slept with Brett before she started dating Scott, of course. It was all so soap-opera-incestual in our group of friends. Kristen dated Scott freshman year. Lacy hooked up with Brett around the same time. That was all before Scott and Brett joined the same fraternity and met each other, but still.

The guys we know are like a joint, everyone takes a turn and passes it on.

"Leave her alone," Brett says, snapping his Heineken bottle cap at Scott.

"Ow, dude!" Scott winces as the green cap bounces off his forehead.

There's no denying Brett is hot. Dark blond hair, bronze eyes, a square jaw, and a large, muscular rugby player's body—what's not to like? Instead of staring at his rock-hard thighs I'd previously been between, I down my beer and open another. The "I Never" game continues.

Did I forget to mention my being between Brett's rock-hard thighs before? Freshman year was my wild and crazy, I'm-away-from-my-overprotective-grandparents-for-the-first-time part of my life year. I'd been ecstatic when Brett invited me to his dorm to watch a movie.

Unbeknownst to me, "watching a movie" was eighteen-year-old boy slang for heavy making out on a lumpy futon.

It was the first time I'd ever made out with anyone. It was the first time I'd ever kissed anyone. Being nestled between Brett's hard—but not as hard as their current state—thighs, kissing and exploring, was pretty damn awesome. Until he wanted to go further, and I didn't. His palm groping my boob was further than I wanted to go, but I let it happen anyway.

I spilled every ounce of my guts to Kristen when I got back to our dorm. I couldn't stop talking about Brett. We made plans A and B for how I should act when I saw him next. We made plans C and D for what to say when he asked me over again. But Brett never invited me over again. In fact, he barely even spoke to me when I saw him in the elevator or at the dining hall.

Kristen said not to worry about it. He was a prick for expecting me to have sex with him on our first date. Except that it turned into a bit of a pattern with men. When I thought a guy liked me, I agreed to go out with him, and make out and not have sex, because I wasn't ready to have sex.

I'd even tried a no-kissing-on-the-first-date rule. Same result. The second date never came.

That's when I realized it was me. It had to be me, right?

After we finish pre-partying, we all head to a few house parties. Kristen and I both agree we don't want to stay with this crowd long, but we want to stop at a few places because I need to find guys to bite the candies off my necklace. After an hour or so, we planned on splitting from the group and heading over to a party at my bandmates' house.

It's almost two in the morning when Kristen and I stumble in the door of the house my bandmates share. We'd gotten slightly caught up in the parties, and may have taken a detour to have a drink at the Thorne before making our way here.

Aaron and Greg sit on the atrocious, light green couch littered with gaudy pink flowers. I can barely see the large, black beanbag that rests on the floor between the front door and the couch at the moment, since Josh and whoever he has pinned down, cover most of it.

"Better late than never, eh, Aud?" Aaron looks up from the guitar he's strumming. It's a relief to be in the company of guys I trust, rather than a guy who has friends who drugged me and a guy who stopped speaking to me because I wouldn't fuck him.

Though I know the beanbag is there, I still trip over it on my way to the couch. Thankfully, I hadn't interrupted Josh eating the face off what I assume is a girl, and not a shiny, brunette mop. Taking a huge step to clear the beanbag, I collapse onto the spot Aaron and Greg cleared between them.

"Jesus, Auden," Greg says, helping me straighten up. "I thought you didn't drink."

"I drink," I say as I wiggle into the couch cushion. "Just not much. Usually."

"Come on over, KK." Aaron sets his guitar on the floor, leaning it against the arm of the couch. He pats his thighs. "You know you want to sit on my lap."

"You know it, A-A-Ron." Kristen laughs but joins us on the couch, avoiding Josh's love bag by mere inches. She takes a seat on Aaron's lap, as a joke, I think. She's never mentioned any interest in Aaron.

My head falls back against the couch and I close my eyes. I could probably pass out if the room wasn't spinning.

I open my eyes to focus on Greg. "You don't look as drunk as the rest of us."

"I'm not. My mom's in town. We did the whole dinner-and-a-movie thing." Greg tips his beer back.

"Aww, date night with Mom." I smile.

"Looks like you did well tonight." Greg points his bottle at the few candy rings remaining on the necklace.

"Not gone yet," I tell him, pulling the elastic string away from my neck and holding it out to him. "Wanna help?"

Kristen leans over. "Don't do it, Greg."

I know she's looking out for me, and I appreciate it. But how do I expect to get over Aleksandr if I never get back into the singles scene?

"I'm all here, KK," I assure her, trying to tap my temple and poking myself in the eye instead. "Don't worry about me."

Greg ignores Kristen's warning and leans over to bite a piece of candy off, teeth grazing my neck as he nuzzles. It makes me tingle. He looks up at me, chewing slowly.

"Don't you want to finish me off?" I ask.

Greg nods, eyes glowing like a cat in the dark.

I groan when someone's full body weight crushes my stomach.

Kristen crawls across my lap and situates herself between me and Greg.

"No!" she says, her head swiveling between us. "You"—she pokes Greg in the chest—"don't touch her candies."

"She can do what she wants, Kristen." Greg pushes her hand away.

"She's fucking drunk, Greg. She wouldn't be all over you any other way."

Greg shoots up from the couch, his brown eyes narrowed at me.

"Aw, shit," Aaron hisses.

"Fucking drama. That's all you've been," Greg spits at me.

"What?" I ask as a giggle escapes my lips.

"You come here drunk and lead me on, but bring your friend as a fucking cock block. What's that all about?"

"It's just candy, Greg. Don't get your panties in a wad because I don't have feelings for you," I yawn.

"Your fucking boyfriend punched me."

"Dude, stop," Josh interrupts. He unwinds himself from his girl but they're still sprawled across the beanbag. The girl he'd been mauling stares at us with wide eyes, obviously bewildered a fight had started amid her ecstasy.

"You tried to kiss me right in front of him!" I stand up, meeting him eye-to-eye. "And you showed him that fucking poem that was none of your business."

"Oh, yeah, that was all my fault. The poem you wrote that you blamed me for."

"Calm the fuck down," Aaron says, trying to help Josh defuse the situation.

"This is fucking ridiculous." I shake my head. "Come on, KK."

"You know what, Auden?" Greg ignores his friends. "We don't need your drama."

"My drama? *My* drama?"

"I think we should take a break."

"What the fuck does that mean?" Josh yells, letting go of his girl this time.

"Exactly what I said. The band needs a break from Auden."

Stunned into silence, I can only stare at Greg. The usually unnoticeable crunch of the beans are deafening as Josh's girl shifts on the beanbag in the soundless room.

1. Dad
2. Mom
3. Soccer team
4. Aleksandr

And this would be major abandonment number five.
Not that I'm counting.

Chapter Thirty-Three

AUDEN

Incredible is the word that comes to mind as I survey the almost-finished transformation of a gutted, run-down movie theater in downtown Bridgeland to a beautiful open space that will house the Central Club's newest branch.

After two months of helping me work on the space in their free time, Jason, Kristen, Aaron, and Josh have given up one final Saturday night to help me complete the setup. Just in time for tomorrow's Open House fundraiser, where we'll unveil the Central Club to the community and, with any luck, get some donations to keep it running.

The ideas Kristen, Lacy, and I dreamed up and fleshed out while sprawled across our living room floor or in our booth at Larry's were finally coming to fruition. Together we'd created a schedule of free classes and workshops for the kids to participate in. The classes ranged from singing (me) and learning instruments (Aaron and Josh) to gymnastics (Lacy), crafting (Kristen, resident Queen of Creativity), and various others to be led by the more than thirty friends and classmates who'd volunteered to teach and tutor.

The support overwhelmed me. It thrills me to have the ability to see this project through instead of relying on someone else, like I do for the Detroit branch.

"Thanks, John," I tell the cop who'd just set down a second banquet table. I whisk a damp clump of hair off my sweaty forehead and begin unfolding the tables and chairs the Bridgeland police donated for the homework stations.

Kristen and Jason are creating a sports and games area, complete with a basketball hoop Jason installed yesterday. Though we posted a "No Hanging on the Rim" sign, I sure hope the stud in the wall could support the weight of the kids who were sure to ignore it.

Aaron and Josh set up instruments on a small raised stage Greg's dad donated. Greg himself isn't here. He's been avoiding me since our dramatic blow up.

At first, I thought being ignored wouldn't bother me, but it did. I missed his friendship and the camaraderie of being in the band. Though Aaron and Josh still hang out with me, I miss late-night, jam-and-songwriting sessions with all the guys. There aren't any romantic feelings, just the loneliness of being abandoned by something I love again.

"Testing, testing one, two, um, twelve," Aaron says into the microphone he's just plugged in.

"You aren't fucking Eminem, dude. Shut up," Josh says straight into the mike.

"Language! We're in a place for kids," Kristen yells from her corner.

"They aren't here yet," Aaron calls back, whipping a drumstick across the room. It bounces off the floor and lands on a mesh bag filled with basketballs.

"You are so lucky that didn't hit me," Kristen warns.

I chuckle at their exchange because it's the same kind of banter I have with the guys. It makes me think about my new-found brother—and the relationship we've started to form. Jason and I had missed the wedgie-attack and big-brother-helping-me-open-my-combination-lock-in-high-school stage, but he's all I have, and rather than push him away like I would have done in the past, I'll hold on to him and make future memories.

And he will be mine, and he will be my Squishy. I mean, Jason.

"Dude, we gotta get to Wreckage," I hear Josh say. I have a feeling it's supposed to be for Aaron's ears only, but he's standing next to the microphone, so his voice travels.

"Do you guys have a gig?" I ask as a mix of curiosity and jealousy swirl in my stomach.

"No." Aaron punches Josh's arm before he jumps off stage. "We're checking out a friend's gig."

"Oh." I nod. Aaron isn't a good liar. It's my fault I'm "on a break" from the band, so I don't have the right to be upset. Well, I do, but I can't show that I am.

I round the table, pushing the chairs I'd unfolded underneath, then unravel a maroon tablecloth and shake it out.

"It looks fucking sick in here," Aaron says, grabbing the free end of the fabric and pulling it toward the opposite end of the table.

"Yeah. It's pretty good compared to when we started." I set my hands on my hips and inspect the reformed room.

Jason helped me patch holes in the walls and paint the entire place. Lucky for us, the theater owners disposed of the seating years ago. All the tattered blue-and-gray-striped carpet needed was a vacuum and a deep cleaning. A friend of Uncle Rick's who owned a carpet cleaning business graciously donated his services.

Kristen and I scrubbed and bleached the bathrooms, which were in good working order otherwise. Since the theater closed fifteen years ago, the owners rented to various groups, and because of the constant activity, there wasn't as much to do as there could have been if the place had sat empty all that time.

Aaron sweeps me into a hug. "Great job, Aud."

When he lets me go, Josh does the same thing, except he lifts me off my feet and spins me around before letting me go. "I'm so proud of you."

It's impossible to keep the smile off my face because the transformation of the space—and the Central Club itself—fills me with pride.

"Thanks, guys," I say, lifting my eyes to the ceiling. Though I'm ecstatic to be filling up with happy tears, rather than thinking-about-Aleksandr tears, I still don't want everyone to see me cry.

"Don't make her cry, Dickweed!" Aaron chastises Josh. I laugh.

"We gotta get going, but we'll be here tomorrow," Josh tells me.

Aaron nods. "Bright and early to help eat the food."

"Help put out the food, you mean," I say.

"That's what I agreed to? Well, that blows." Aaron winks and throws me double finger-guns as he and Josh rush out. Wreckage is three doors down, so it's not like they'll be late for whatever they have going on.

"It looks great in here, Aud. This is going to be so awesome," Kristen says.

"What's left?" Jason asks, standing beside Kristen.

"I think that's it. I just have to take out the trash and—"

"Hey, Aud," a voice behind me interrupts my train of thought. When I turn around, Greg stands in the doorway, his hands stuffed into his skinny-jean pockets.

"Greg. Hey," I respond, trying to contain my surprise. I never expected to see him here.

"Can I?" He nods toward the threshold.

"Yeah, of course, come on in." I glance at Kristen as if she has answers, but she just shrugs.

"I came to apologize for being such a jerk." Greg's approach is slow, almost cautious, like he's trying not to wake a baby. Then he stumbles over a can of paint sitting on the floor, and I laugh.

"Sorry." I hold my fist in front of my mouth.

"I totally planned that," he says, nodding to the paint can, then chuckles before continuing. "I'm sorry for everything, Aud. I'm sorry I was such a dick about Aleksandr. I'm sorry I've been too stubborn to accept your apology. I'm sorry I kicked you out of the band."

Despite acting like a jealous jerk, Greg is a genuine, positive guy. Until his jealousy of Aleksandr reared its ugly head, he'd never said anything hurtful about anyone when I was around him, and he always wanted to help me get better. In that regard, I know his apologies are sincere, and I appreciate it, but hearing Aleksandr's name reminds me of the heartache I've been trying to suppress for almost two months.

He continues, "I've been a total dick, and I don't—"

"Everything About You" an old song by Ugly Kid Joe fills the air. I look around, creeped out by whatever weird-ass theater ghost would choose that particular one-hit wonder to spook us. I don't realize it's a ringtone until Greg reaches into his back pocket and pulls out his phone.

"Who has that song as their ringtone?" Kristen asks.

"Who even knows that song anymore?" Jason agrees.

"It's not," Greg starts to defend himself, and then shakes his head. "I gotta get this." He turns his back to me. "Yeah?"

I glance over my shoulder at Jason and Kristen, lifting my palms and shrugging my shoulders in total confusion. Kristen rolls her eyes, her disgust for Greg's disrespectful action apparent. Jason just watches everything unfold.

Suddenly Greg spins around and holds his phone out to me. "It's for you."

"Aaron?" I ask. What does he want to razz me about now?

Greg doesn't answer. He just thrusts the phone at me. When I look at the screen expecting to see the name or number of the caller, I realize it is a video call. A girl I've never seen in my life smiles brightly from Greg's smartphone screen.

"Hi, Auden!" she says. Then her head turns sideways for a split second and I realized she adjusted the phone. It looks as if she's standing among a large crowd of people. A guitar strums in the background.

"What's going on?" I ask the girl with an über-excited fake smile, before lifting my questioning eyes to Greg.

"Just watch. You might learn some stage presence." He winks before I have a chance to pout.

I've gotten better with stage presence over the last three months. He'd know I've been practicing if he'd let me back in the band earlier.

The video scans the crowd quickly before settling on a stage. While trying my hardest to get a glimpse of the band, the phone swings back around to the girl, and I huff.

"I'm Greg's sister, by the way." She still has the perma-grin on her face.

"Nice to meet you," I say, but I'm unsure if she caught it because she swings the focus back toward the stage.

Greg's sister's shaky camera skills have my stomach on edge. Puking is a possibility if she doesn't quit whipping the phone around.

"Hello, Charlotte!" the lead singer yells.

Though his head isn't in the camera's view, I can make out his outfit. A long-sleeved black shirt hugs every curve of his muscular upper body, and narrows into the waistband of classic rock and roll leather pants that fit him just right. His stature looks familiar, and I wonder if it's a band I've seen in concert before.

Why can't I figure out who it is? If only Greg's sister could fix the angle and zoom in on the singer's face a little.

"I fucked up with my girl. And I had to do something big to get her back because she is my sun, and I revolve around her," the singer tells the crowd.

I still can't see him, but I recognize the thick Slavic accent that makes my legs sway like palm trees in a hurricane.

Aleksandr appears larger and larger as he approaches the spot where Greg's sister is standing. He kneels down and grabs the phone. His gorgeous face fills the screen and he speaks directly to me, "I love you, *Audushka*. You're all I have."

He must have passed the phone back to Greg's sister because I hear a shrill shriek of, "Ohmygod! Ohmygod!"

The next image I catch is of my hot Russian hockey god's leather-clad backside retreating from the edge of the stage toward the microphone. Just then, the opening riffs and "Whooooo ooo ooo" of "You're All I Have" by Snow Patrol roar through the phone's speaker.

Unable to fully wrap my head around what's going on, I keep my eyes glued to the screen. Kristen and Jason have moved closer, pressing against my back as they peer over my shoulder to catch the show on the tiny screen.

When the first verse starts, Aleksandr is the one singing. And it isn't karaoke-style singing, either. He's standing on stage backed by a full band behind him.

And my man looks *damn sexy* behind that microphone. Though he told me he'd never sung karaoke before, his confident demeanor draws the same response as it does on the ice, a hoard of fans screaming and bouncing at his feet.

"That looks like Wreckage," Kristen says.

I shake my head. "He said 'Hello, Charlotte.' He must be at a bar there."

"Why would a bar in Charlotte have a Central State poster on their wall?" Kristen points to the screen.

She's right. The bold maroon text on the poster-sized Central State men's basketball schedule looms behind Aleksandr. How did I not notice that he's standing on the same stage I'd performed on for almost three months?

I lift my eyes, expecting to see Greg, but he's not there. I hadn't even noticed his exit.

Hiding behind a coward's mantra of nothing (and no one) is permanent, I've run away from countless important people in my twenty years on earth. Supportive friends who'd saved my sanity through elementary and high school, amazing teammates on Central State's soccer team, and even a few nice guys who may have wanted something more than I ever dared to give.

Though giving up on those relationships may have been a mistake, I never looked back with regret.

Only one relationship would haunt me for eternity if I ran away.

Instead, I sprint toward it, pushing through the front door of the Central Club and racing to Wreckage. I elbow my way from the back of the room to the stage, refusing to stop for anyone, even the bouncer. I know he won't mind, because he knows me, but I'll still buy him a couple of lottery tickets tomorrow as an apology gesture.

Greg's sister is at the front, still holding up the phone, mesmerized by Aleksandr's performance. I wonder if she even noticed the screen that's been filled with my face turned black as I clutch Greg's phone in my hand.

Aleksandr stands behind the microphone belting out the song as if he performs every night. Granted, he doesn't have the greatest vocals, but he's not bad, either. Behind him is my band; Josh on the drums, Aaron at the bass, and Greg on his guitar.

I'm completely dumbstruck. I can't believe my ex-boyfriend is on stage with my band singing a song about finally realizing I'm all he has.

How is it possible to feel my heart beating so ferociously, yet still wonder if I'm breathing? The two had to go hand in hand, right?

As Aleksandr sings, I feel the words seep into me like penetrating lotion on cracked and weathered skin.

After he finishes the last words of the song, he steps back from the microphone. I climb onto the stage quickly and launch myself into his arms. He catches me easily, squeezing my waist in his vise grip. When our mouths collide, the comforting taste of cloves mingles with the salty tears cascading down my cheeks and onto my lips.

"You're all I have. You're all I want. I love you," I say when we break from the kiss.

The words must have been picked up by the microphone because the crowd explodes.

Greg moves forward and grabs the mike. "Should we let these lovebirds go somewhere private?"

The audience responds with another thunderous cheer. I tap Greg's shoulder with his phone and hold it out to him, giving him a huge smile. He winks and returns the grin.

Aleksandr bends down and tucks one arm across my back and the other at the back of my knees. He lifts me up and jumps off the stage. His arms never waver as he jostles me through the crowd. Rather than have my head bonked by every shoulder we pass, I burrow into Aleksandr's neck.

"Where to?" he asks, setting me down once we arrive outside.

"This way." I grab his hand and lead him to the Central Club, which is private and close.

Aleksandr stops abruptly when we cross the threshold. "Is this—"

The way Aleksandr's head whips from side to side and up and down as he takes in every inch of the space, getting whiplash is a strong possibility.

"The newest branch of the Central Club," I finish.

"Wow. It's amazing, *Audushka*."

My cheeks burn at the compliment, excited that the person I care about most is proud of what I've done. But I don't want to make small talk right now. No beating around the bush. No running away until everything is out in the open. Whatever happens will be.

"I know the poem was horrible, but it was out of context," I explain. "It was a stupid outlet I use to get all my pent-up frustrations out. I was lusting after you, but I wouldn't let myself act on it. I never thought that way about you. I would never use you like that."

I continue without giving him a chance to speak because I need him to understand everything, to understand me. "That poem was fear. Fear of the unknown. Fear of getting too close. Fear of letting someone love me. Fear of ending up like my mom."

Without a word, Aleksandr grabs the hem of his shirt and lifts the left side, revealing one of the tattoos I've admired on numerous occasions but never asked about. Black Cyrillic script begins at his hip and drifts elegantly up his side.

"'To fear death is not to live,'" Aleksandr translates before I convert the words myself. Then he lifts the right side of his shirt and reveals the same beautiful script, only this time the words start under his arm and flow down his lean side. "No matter which way I turn, this is the message I must remember."

"You got those after your parents' accident."

"See? You know me better than anyone."

"Well, I'm sure anyone who knows your story could've guessed."

"Sorry I flipped out. Seeing you with Greg set me off. It's hard for me knowing you're with these guys all the time. I want it to be me you confide in, not them. But I should've trusted you like you trust me with the bunnies."

Suddenly my shoes are more important than anything else in the room. I don't trust him with the bunnies, I just push it out of my head and hope for the best.

"I don't confide in them, not really. I write stupid poems, and we try to use them for lyrics. I guess it's confiding in a way, but I'm not knocking on Greg's door at three a.m. looking for a shoulder to cry on. It's totally different."

"True. And I'm not answering the door when bunnies come knocking on it at three a.m."

"Bunnies come to your door? Not just the arena and bars?"

"Perspective, *Audushka*." He brings me back to the present. "I'm sorry I didn't answer your calls. I needed time to cool off, to think."

"To screw other women," I finish for him.

With the haze of admiration lifted, I remind myself that this isn't a fairy tale. I can't forget about his betrayals just because he made a (freakin' awesome) grand gesture. This is real, and the wounds of reality slice deep. Being with him again immerses my mind in melancholy thoughts, reminding me how difficult it is to modify deeply ingrained insecurities.

"I didn't touch another woman," he tells me. When I refuse to meet his eyes, he tilts my chin up with his fingers. "I haven't touched another woman since I've been with you. I swear."

"What about Angie?" I ask.

"Who's Angie?"

"The last time I called you Pavel answered. There was an Angie in the background. It sounded like you were—" I stop, shaking out of his hold. I can't bring myself to finish.

"Fucking *Pasha*." Aleksandr lets out a breath. "I didn't do anything with any woman. It may have sounded that way, but I didn't touch her. *Pasha* was, I don't know, trying to break us up or something."

"Why does he care?"

"He doesn't want me to be happy."

"What?"

Aleksandr drops his chin to his chest and clutches his hair with both hands, groaning as if in pain or anger.

"I didn't tell you the whole story of my parents' car accident, *Audushka*. It's not a secret, I just, I didn't want you to hate me like he does."

I reach up and grab his hands away from his hair, hoping that my touch gives him the strength to continue with what he wants to reveal. Though I don't know what it will be, I know we can handle it. Together.

"My father was driving the car. Pavel's father was in the passenger seat, and our mothers were in back. They were all killed." Aleksandr's voice is almost a whisper. He clears his throat and looks into my eyes. "My father didn't do anything wrong. He wasn't speeding, wasn't going the wrong way. It was the wrong place, at the wrong time against a bus making a fast, wide turn. But Pavel blamed my father. And ever since then—" I squeeze his hands for him to continue.

"He's made my life hell ever since then. Said I don't deserve happiness because my father killed his parents."

"But it wasn't your fault. Even if your dad was driving. It wasn't your fault. You lost the same thing Pavel did."

"He doesn't see it that way."

"He's grieving and looking for someone to blame. We've both been there." I keep my eyes glued to Aleksandr's until he squeezes his shut and nods. "Gribov was right about me, though. I am selfish."

"He's not right, Auden. You are the most wonderful, loving person I've ever met. Look at this place." He gestures around the Central Club. "You have this ridiculous idea that talking about your own tragedy is selfish, but it's not. I want you to trust me enough to talk to me. I want everything from you. Your pain, your insecurity, your trust, and your heart. And I want to give all of mine to you. You're the only person who knows how I got this." He takes my hand and lifts my fingers to the scar on his cheek. "You are the only person who knows me at all."

"I want to trust you. I do, but I don't know if I can get over some of the issues we have."

"Like what?"

"You left me."

"*Audushka*, you know I have to leave for—"

"No." I cut him off. "After you read the poem you left without even looking back. Without answering my phone calls to talk about it. You left even when you knew that was my biggest fear."

"I ran from the situation, not from you." He rubs his face in his hands. "It's what I do, *Audushka*. I run. I drink. I smoke. That's how I deal with things. You shut down and let people go. I run. Being a hockey player suits me. I escape to a different city every other day, and I get my aggression out on the ice. Slap shots, skating hard, checking hard."

"How do I know you won't do it again?" I ask, my voice shaky, on the verge of tears.

"Because deep down you know that everything we feel for each other is real," Aleksandr pleads, passion radiating in his voice. "I love you, Auden. I know we're young, and it happened fast, but I had other girls before you, and none of them came close to making me feel the way I feel with you. I want to be with someone who sparks something inside me. Someone I can't stop thinking about. That's you."

Our eyes lock for a split second, before Aleksandr spins around and yanks his shirt off. Without thinking, I reach out and brush the words scrawled across his shoulders with my fingertips. At my touch, his head jerks to the side, and a ripple courses through his muscles.

"'How well you live makes a difference, not how long,'" he translates, and drops his shirt to the floor before turning to face me.

I ignore the desire to spin him around and trace the words with my tongue and speak instead. "Your parents would be proud of you. You're living pretty well right now."

"I didn't get that for my parents. I got it two weeks ago, when I started planning this with Greg. There is no living well without you, *Audushka*. I couldn't do it. I didn't care that I made it to the NHL. I didn't care about scoring, about winning, about hockey. Being without you was like my parents' death all over again. Life sucks when there's no one you care about to share it with. You're all that I have."

The hem of my maroon Central State football T-shirt is sweaty and dirty, but I pull it up and dab at the tears building in my eyes anyway. They're probably already racooned-out from crying off my eyeliner while he sang.

"Not true. You have your family in Russia. You have your friends and teammates and coaches. You even have my grandparents," I add.

"But you are the only one who matters. I need to know if I have the most important person."

As someone whose identity was created around a father who never wanted to know her, and a mother who was killed before she was seven years old, it would be an impossible task for me to let go of everything in a minute, or a month, or even six months.

But I have to get over my trust issues, or let Aleksandr go for good. If I can't trust him what kind of life could we have together?

Aleksandr is the one person I can't hide from or filter myself around. The person who calls me out on my bullshit and persuades me to open up to get to the bottom of my feelings. He's the person who taught me that not everyone will abandon me, and I don't have to abandon others.

Despite the insecurities muddling my brain like a three-year-old's finger painting, there's no hesitation in my answer.

"Yes."

EPILOGUE

Auden

"Show me your school, *Audushka*." Aleksandr opens the passenger door of his Jeep and steps back so I have room to exit.

"Really?" I glance at him to make sure he isn't teasing me before I jump out.

He nods. "I've never been to college."

"I'll take you to my favorite place." After he helps me climb out of the Jeep, I lace my fingers with his and lead him up the path toward Wagner Hall, my favorite building on campus. It feels surreal to have him walking around campus with me, as if we're in a parallel universe. A perfect universe.

"It's beautiful here," Aleksandr says as we follow the concrete trail among the perfectly manicured grass.

"It is, yeah. I love it." I love every inch of Central State's campus. The charming brick buildings, the massive, mature trees, the meticulous maroon and gold flowers outside every building.

I'm lost in thought of the understated beauty I take for granted every day, when Aleksandr suddenly yanks me toward a tree in front of Wagner. Squeezing my hand, he drops to one knee and digs in his pocket with his free hand. I glance around, then back at him.

He isn't.

No.

He couldn't.

"Auden Catherine Berezin, will you marry me?" The cool, confident man formerly known as "Douche Bag, King of All Douches," shakes as he thrusts an open black box at me.

When I peer into it, I see not one, but two, rings: one is silver with a single diamond twinkling up at me and the other, a thin, gold band.

Everything stops. People stop walking, birds stop singing, cars stop whizzing by on the road. The world stops turning with Aleksandr on his knee, holding his life out to me.

"I, no, I still have a year of school and I'm already planning my master's degree...and...and you're in Charlotte," I stammer, wiping sweat off an eyebrow, though the temperature had barely reached sixty-five degrees.

Aleksandr squeezes my hand, a jolt of electricity zapping through my veins from his simple touch. "I'm not rushing you, love. You can finish school here and find a master's program in Charlotte. Or stay here for your program. It doesn't matter. We'll make it work. You and me forever. I want this. No excuses. No pushing me away. No more walls."

No excuses. No walls? That I can't guarantee. We've only known each other for six months. That's barely out of the honeymoon stage. But I guess we never had a honeymoon stage with both of us laying all our cards on the table from day one.

When I was a little girl, I never yearned for the fairy tale love of the Cinderellas and Snow Whites. I craved the flawed, consuming, passionate, obsessive, can't-live-without-you, eternal love of poets and playwrights. I wanted the Karenina and Vronsky kind of love. Because life isn't glass slippers and balls. It's jealousy and imperfection and forgiveness. Despite everything in my past, or maybe because of everything, I truly believe Aleksandr loves me.

"I think Charlotte needs a Central Club branch, don't you?" Aleksandr's voice fills the air, and I meet his eyes. He always knows exactly what to say.

The world starts again as I push negative thoughts away with a shake of my head.

"Yeah. Yes. Of course, I will," I tell him, pulling him to his feet.

I brush my lips against his, but he deepens the kiss. Then he wraps his arms around me, and I nuzzle into his chest. After a few minutes locked in an embrace, he pulls back. His eyes are glassy. Or maybe they only look that way because I'm seeing him through the tears in my own eyes. His hands shake as he pushes the diamond ring up my left ring finger.

Aleksandr and I are engaged.

"What's that one for?" I point to the thin gold band in the box. "Not trying to be greedy, just wondering."

"We don't give engagement rings in Russia. We wear bands on our right hands. This one was Mama's. I, um, I wanted you to have it." Tears slip down Aleksandr's cheeks, and my eyes widen. I burrow myself into his chest again.

"*Sasha*," I whisper. "Thank you."

"It sucks not to share this with them. I wish they could've known you." He pulls away, wiping at the wetness on his cheeks with his fingers.

"I know."

He doesn't need to explain. I don't need to explain. Because this is Aleksandr and me—and we already understand each other.

His parents and my mom will miss every monumental occasion in our lives. Both of us have already figured that out, but it doesn't mean it hurts any less. Every time a huge event comes up, Aleksandr and I will both grieve for our parents again. Only now we won't be grieving alone, trying to hide it from others who don't understand. We have each other.

I hold out my right hand, and he slides his mother's ring onto my finger, rubbing the gold band with his thumb.

"I don't want you to think we should do it like in Russia. I know traditions are different here. I just wanted you to have it." He sniffs and wipes his face again. Has he ever looked so handsome as he does right now, baring himself to me with watery eyes?

"What is it like there?"

"Go to the registry office, say yes to a couple of questions, and walk out married."

"Well, I think we do that here, too." I laugh. "At the courthouse. But we'd have to get a marriage license first." I catch his eyes.

Did I just ask him to go to the courthouse with me?

"How do we do that?"

"Wanna run by the county clerk's office and find out?"

Yep, definitely just asked him to go to the courthouse.

* * * * *

"Do you have your birth certificate?" I ask Aleksandr when the woman at the clerk's desk tells us the documents we need.

"Back at the hotel."

"Translated?"

"I have been playing hockey outside of Russia for years, *Audushka*. I've needed it many times."

Maybe it's the thrill of the moment, or maybe it's the realization that I'll be with Aleksandr for the rest of my life, but requesting a marriage application feels as normal as walking up to the counter at a fast food restaurant and ordering a burger.

The clerk tells us there's a three-day waiting period after handing it in before we can get married. We thank her, and take an application with us.

"Three days to change your mind," I tell Aleksandr as we walk back to the car.

What if we get into a huge fight and he gets mad and wants to run away? What if I freak out about him leaving for a road trip?

"I knew I would marry you when you checked out my package in a bar in Canada six months ago. What's three more days?" He pulls me in for a kiss.

I can't help the laugh that escapes my lips, because my fiancé always knows what to say to calm my fears. And that's how I know this is real.

No more walls.

No more walking dead through another twenty years of life.

Just accepting people for who they are and what they have to give. And being grateful for the family and friends who finally got me to realize I don't have to go through it alone.

THE END

Need more Aviators Hockey?
Start reading UNSPORTSMANLIKE CONDUCT now!

USA Today Bestselling Author Sophia Henry returns with the story of a free spirit who believes she's found forever with a playboy on a singles cruise. Discover why Kelly Jamieson calls the Aviators Hockey series "fun and flirty."

Life is too short not to embrace each day to the fullest. And that's exactly what I intended to do. My parents paid for me to take part in a post-grad singles cruise to the Caribbean in hopes I would find a fine, Greek husband.

Instead, I hooked up with the hottest guy I've ever met.

Pavel might not be Greek, but he's got fun written all over his rock-hard abs. We agreed we would walk away with no regrets when the ship docks. Yet as that day nears, we both realize there is something far deeper than lust brewing between us.

Will the real world destroy the fantasy of our vacation fling? Or can romance forged under swaying palm trees withstand the icy chill of reality?

"Unsportsmanlike Conduct is definitely an entertaining read, delightful and dreamy. I mean, hunky hockey player with a stunning Greek girl? Sign. Me. Up!"—Sweetheart Reads

Turn the page for a taste of UNSPORTSMANLIKE CONDUCT

UNSPORTSMANLIKE CONDUCT EXCERPT

CHAPTER 1

KRISTEN

Day 1 - Cruising in the Caribbean

Is there anything more perfect than breathing in the salty scent of the ocean while jogging around the top deck of a cruise ship in ninety-degree weather?

Well, sure, seventy-five degrees would have been a better temperature for running, but I'm not complaining.

Sweat glistens on my arms and a gentle wind blows the flyaway strands of hair away from my face as my feet pound the track.

Mental fist bump to my parents. They'd succeeded in their quest to find me the perfect college graduation gift, even if I hadn't realized it at first. When they presented me with a printout of an itinerary for a cruise a few months ago, my first reaction was complete and utter terror, because the mere thought of being on a large body of water with no land in sight gave me hives. But I didn't want my amazing parents to think I didn't appreciate their generous gift, so I kept it inside and went along with the planning.

And so here I am. Sea breeze in my hair, a cardio remix of Lil Wayne's "How to Love" blasting through my earbuds, and a tropical destination. Nothing could ruin this moment.

Except the familiar face of the person running toward me. Which sends my version of personal paradise plummeting to the ocean floor. Because in this case, "familiar" and "welcome" are not synonymous.

Maybe Spiros hadn't recognized me. Maybe I can pretend I didn't see him.

"Kristen!" he calls.

Not even paradise can deter Murphy's Law.

So I do what any smart girl who wants to avoid her friendly stalker would do: I spin around, and run the opposite way, putting more distance between us.

Note: When the self-proclaimed "smart girl" is unfamiliar with the territory where she's running, glancing over her shoulder to see if Spiros is still there is not the best idea. Because within three strides, I smack into another runner.

Not a light, whoops-sorry-I-bumped-you collision. A head-on, semi-to-semi crash, where both bodies lay crumpled in a pile of twisted, burning limbs.

Burning, not only because the scorching Caribbean sun pounds on us from above, but also because the other semi has the body of a Greek god.

No joke.

As a good Greek girl on a singles cruise set up by my Greek Orthodox church and paid for by my straight-off-the-boat Greek parents, I know Greek gods. And the hunk of muscle I'd knocked into is Adonis in the flesh.

Instead of scrambling to my feet, I find my gaze frozen on his face. Particularly on the sexy scruff dusting his upper lip and jawline. His twelve o'clock shadow is a distinct contrast to the absence of hair on his chiseled chest. Even the sweat rolling off the tip of his nose doesn't detract from his perfection, nor does the red undertone on his sun-kissed skin, flushed from running in the heat.

"Dude!" I exclaim, yanking the earbuds from my ears. Then I break into a cough and can't stop.

Adonis picks up his sunglasses, which must've fallen when we crashed, and replaces them over his eyes. He waits until I finish my coughing fit before speaking. "Maybe you need to pay attention, since you were running the wrong way on this track, yes?"

"I didn't—" I can't finish my thought. I'm still trying to catch my breath as I consider the situation: Adonis knocked me down, and he has the audacity to blame me?

"Well, if you were going the right way, why didn't you run around me?" I ask breathlessly.

"I was playing chicken."

"Excuse me?" Who says something like that?

He jumps to his feet. "I waited to see if you would back off first. You call this game chicken, yes?" He bends down and holds out his hand.

At least he has some manners. I clasp his hand and allow him to pull me up, impressed at the lack of effort it took him to lift me.

"Common courtesy dictates that people don't usually play chicken while running." I brush a palm over my butt, even though the track seems fairly debris-free.

He draws the back of his hand across his hairline, wiping away a film of moisture. "I think this same common courtesy say that people don't look over their shoulder when they run."

True. Technically, my poorly planned attempt to escape Spiros's approach caused the collision.

"I'm sorry I ran into you," I say.

"Are you also sorry because you were running the wrong way?"

"Who are you, the track police?" I ask, resting my hands on my hips and leaning away from him, my breath finally under control.

"This track has rules. Today we run this way." He points in the direction I'd originally started running. Then I follow his finger as it travels in another direction, stopping at a red sign with the heading track rules in thick white letters.

Who pays attention to what day it is or obnoxiously large signs about rules when they're on a cruise?

"Well, I'm really sorry. I got flustered. I'm trying to avoid that guy running toward us." I nod slightly toward Spiros, who had caught up to us.

Yep. Spiros Loukas, my annoying admirer, who'd also been running the wrong way on the track, stands at my heels. Just like at home.

Paradise lost.

BE KIND. LOVE HARD.

At the beginning of my career, I vowed to give a portion of royalties from each of my books to charity. I choose charities that are close to my heart and that are involved in my books in some way. You can learn more about each charity on my website.
- A heartfelt *Thank You* to each one of you -
Sophia x

A portion of the royalties from the sale of DELAYED PENALTY will be donated to the St. John Providence Open Arms program.

For information on the Open Arms Program: http://www.stjohn-providence.org/OpenArms

#BeKindLoveHard

DON'T MISS OUT!

Sophia Henry's mailing list is the place to be if you like steamy romance novels that tug at your heart strings. Stay notified of new releases, sales, exclusive content with newsletters twice a month. Get a FREE book when you sign up at sophiahenry.com.

Join Sophia's Reader Group

When you join Sophia's Patreon Community you get exclusive access to AUDIO of her books, get sneak peeks, exclusive posts, and extra surprises just for members. You even get to name characters! (Seriously, it happens. Sophia's readers named Zayne, the hero of CRAZY FOR YOU).
Join the Fun: patreon.com/sophiahenry313

Merch Store

Choose kindness and love with everything you've got. It's not just a motto. It's a way of life. Grab some motivational or bookish merch today! www.bekindlovehard.com

REVIEWS ROCK!

THANK YOU so much for taking the time to read DELAYED PENALTY. I truly appreciate every single one of you. If you enjoyed reading DELAYED PENALTY as much as I enjoyed writing it, it would mean the world to me if you would consider leaving a review on Amazon.

(If you really loved the book, copy and paste the same review to Bookbub & Goodreads!)

Sophia x

PLAYLIST

Complete Playlist on YouTube: SophiaHenryOfficial

Your Winter – Sister Hazel
No Diggity - Blackstreet
Mulder and Scully - Catatonia
The More You Ignore Me, The Closer I Get - Morrissey
Making Believe – Social Distortion
On Fire - Sebadoh
Best I'll Ever Be – Sister Hazel
Good Feeling – Violent Femmes
Wild - Poe
Wobble – V.I.C.
Hey Jealousy – Gin Blossom
Halfway to Crazy – The Jesus and Mary Chain
Sit Down - James
If I Can't Change Your Mind - Sugar
Everything – Alanis Morissette
Trust – The Cure
You're All I Have – Snow Patrol
Motownphilly – Boyz II Men
Boys Don't Cry – The Cure
A Question of Lust – Depeche Mode

PLAYLIST

Are You Ready For Me – Tom Sartori
Me and Bobby McGee – Janis Joplin
I'll Stand by You – The Pretenders
Sex – The 1975
Everybody Lost Somebody - Bleachers

ALSO BY SOPHIA HENRY

SAINTS AND SINNERS SERIES

Ebook and Paperback Available on Amazon

SAINTS

SINNERS

AVIATORS HOCKEY SERIES

Ebook and Paperback Available on Amazon

DELAYED PENALTY

UNSPORTSMANLIKE CONDUCT

POWER PLAY

JINGLE BALL BENDER: An Aviators Hockey Short Story

BLUE LINES

STANDALONE CROSSOVER NOVELS

EVEN STRENGTH

Saints & Sinners/Aviators Hockey Crossover Novel

MATERIAL GIRLS SERIES

Ebook and Paperback Available on Amazon

OPEN YOUR HEART

LIVE TO TELL

CRAZY FOR YOU

DEVIL IN DISGUISE

Material Girls/Saints & Sinners Crossover Novel

FOREIGN EDITIONS

FRENCH

SAGA MATERIAL GIRLS

OPEN YOUR HEART

LIVE TO TELL

CRAZY FOR YOU

DEVIL IN DISGUISE

DUO SAINTS AND SINNERS

SAINTS

SINNERS

ROMANS AUTONOMES LIÉS AUX SAGAS

EVEN STRENGTH

Saints & Sinners/Aviators Hockey Crossover Novel

SAGA AVIATORS HOCKEY

JINGLE BALL BENDER

BLUE LINES

GERMAN

MATERIAL GIRLS SERIES

OPEN YOUR HEART

LIVE TO TELL

CRAZY FOR YOU

RUSSIAN

SAINTS AND SINNERS SERIES

SAINTS

SINNERS

ABOUT THE AUTHOR

USA Today Bestselling Author Sophia Henry is a proud Detroit native who fell in love with reading, writing, and hockey all before she became a teenager. After graduating with a Creative Writing degree from Central Michigan University, she moved to warm and sunny North Carolina where she spent twenty glorious years before heading back to her roots and settling in Michigan.

She spends her days writing steamy, heartfelt contemporary romance and posting personal stories in her Patreon community hoping they resonate with and encourage others. When Sophia's not writing, she's hanging out with her two high-energy sons, an equally high-energy Plott Hound, and two cats who want nothing to do with any of them. She can also be found watching her beloved Detroit Red Wings and rocking out at as many concerts as she can possibly attend.

Receive a FREE ebook and get all the latest releases and updates exclusively for readers! Subscribe to Sophia's newsletter today. https://bit.ly/FreeSHBookNL

Made in the USA
Columbia, SC
26 January 2023